THE RESTORATION ARTIST

The
Restoration Artist

A NOVEL

LEWIS DeSoto

HarperCollinsPublishersLtd
A PHYLLIS BRUCE BOOK

A Phyllis Bruce Book, published by HarperCollins Publishers Ltd

First edition

HarperCollins books may be purchased for educational, business,
or sales promotional use through our Special Markets Department.

HarperCollins Publishers Ltd
2 Bloor Street East, 20th Floor
Toronto, Ontario, Canada
M4W 1A8

www.harpercollins.ca

Library and Archives Canada Cataloguing in Publication
information is available upon request.

ISBN 978-0-00-200583-8

Printed and bound in the United States of America
RRD 9 8 7 6 5 4 3 2 1

I once saw a very beautiful picture. It was a landscape at evening. Through the landscape a road leads to a high mountain far far away. On the road walks a pilgrim. He has been walking for a good long while already and he is very tired. And now he meets a woman, or a figure in black.

And the pilgrim asks her: Does the road go on then uphill all the way?
And the answer is: Yes, to the very end.
And he asks again: And will the journey take all day long?
And the answer is: From morn till night, my friend.
—FROM A LETTER BY VINCENT VAN GOGH

CHAPTER 1

THIS WAS THE END OF THE WORLD, THE LAST PLACE.

I stood on the stone pier of the island's small harbour as the rumble of the departing boat's engine receded into the muffling fog. The dim silhouette of the masts disappeared first, then the green starboard light slowly shrank to a pinpoint of colour. The beat of the engine dwindled to a faint pulse, and after a while that too died away, leaving only the waves lapping at the pier, and finally, silence. I ran a hand across my face to wipe away the dampness, tasting the salty moisture on my lips, as salty as tears.

Behind me was Paris, France, the whole continent—what used to be my home. What used to be my life. I turned away.

Looking at my watch, I saw that it was almost evening. I unfastened the strap from my wrist and put the watch in my pants pocket. I would have no need of it any more. As I bent to pick up my bag I thought I heard a voice from a distance, someone calling a name. Cocking my head I listened, then started up the damp cobblestones towards a yellow lamp shimmering like a solitary candle in the gloom. At the lamppost, the path diverged in two directions. An arrow pointed to Notre-Dame de la Victoire on the right—a church, I assumed—and in the other direction to the Hôtel des Îles. Neither the hotel nor the church were visible in the fog. Turning left, I made my way towards the hotel. They were expecting me there.

The mist thinned slightly as the path rose and I soon caught sight of the glow of lighted windows, followed a minute later by the white facade of the hotel. I could see that it had two floors, the upper windows all shuttered except for one, where a light was on. The place reminded me of those modest family hotels that were found up and down the coast, vaguely Mediterranean in appearance.

Passing through the opening in the thick hedge that enclosed the garden, I made my way around the wet wrought-iron chairs upended on tables and opened the front door. The foyer was a white-painted room decorated with a nautical theme, pictures of Normandy schooners, netting and scallop shells artfully draped, a big iron anchor next to the door. Through another doorway I could see a small bar, wooden stools and a couple of shelves containing liquor bottles. A plump tabby cat lay asleep on the counter.

A young couple came forward to greet me. The man was tall and thin with a dark beard. His wife wore her long hair in a braid over one shoulder and her blue eyes lit up in a smile as she extended her hand.

"Monsieur Millar? We weren't sure if we'd heard a boat in this fog. I'm Linda Guillaume and this is my husband, Victor."

Victor Guillaume said, "Was the trip over all right? Would you like a drink, something to warm you up? It's miserable weather tonight."

"Thank you, I'll just wash up first."

"Give the man a moment, Victor," Linda said, reaching for my bag. "Let me show you up. You're the only guest right now, so I've given you a room with a fireplace and a view, although with this fog you might as well be looking at a white wall."

"Is it often like this?"

"The weather on the island is what you might call 'variable,'" Victor answered. "The fog stays for days sometimes. We accept what comes." He shrugged. "When it clears up you'll be amazed at the beauty of our island. Will you be staying long?"

"I'm not sure. A few days." When I'd called from Saint-Alban on the radio-telephone and reserved a room, I'd told them that I was a painter, interested in the island landscape.

"There is a lighthouse at the north end and a pretty little village called LeBec on the opposite side. The views from the cliffs to the west are quite dramatic."

My room was simply furnished: a fireplace already laid with logs, a double bed covered in a fluffy white quilt, a small table near the window, a chest of drawers, all of dark wood in the traditional Normandy style that I remembered so well from Claudine's family home in Montmartin-sur-Mer.

"Should I light the fire for you?" Linda asked.

"No thanks, that's fine."

"Come down when you're ready and I will make you a bite to eat."

"I'm not very hungry."

She drew the lace curtains against the fog. "It's a long ride from the mainland. Some food will revive you. I'll make you an omelette."

I sensed that she was curious about me, but politeness prevented her from asking me anything further.

{3}

After washing my face and hands in the adjoining bathroom, I unpacked the few things I'd brought with me. On the mantelpiece above the fireplace I arranged the silver whistle, the paintbox with the boy's name carved onto the lid, and a simple gold wedding band matching my own, but too small for any of my fingers.

I didn't want to go downstairs and talk to anybody, but I did want a drink, and when I reached the landing and smelled food cooking I realized that I was hungry after all. An omelette and a salad of chopped endive were on the table. A *pichet* of red wine sat next to the bread basket. Perhaps sensing my frame of mind, my hosts served the food and then let me be. I ate half the omelette and drank all the wine.

A copy of the newspaper *L'Humanité* had been placed on the table next to me. The headlines were about the bombing of Hanoi in the ongoing Vietnam war and de Gaulle's planned trip to the USSR. I pushed it away.

From the kitchen came the murmur of voices, the muted clatter of dishes, a radio playing "In a Sentimental Mood" by Duke Ellington. The cat lying on the bar counter regarded me languidly. The atmosphere was domestic, harmonious, but such things no longer touched me.

Linda Guillaume glanced in through the doorway every so often and when she saw I was no longer eating she came in to collect my plate.

"If you would like a dessert there is an apple Charlotte." I shook my head and she said, "Some cheese?"

"No, thank you. I'm not very hungry tonight. The omelette was very good, though."

"I'll bring you a coffee."

"And a bit more wine, please."

"A glass?"

"Another *pichet*, please."

A fire was crackling in the grate when I returned to my room. I opened the window a couple of inches but left the shutters closed against the clammy darkness. There was a bottle of Jameson whiskey in my bag and I sipped from it while I got ready for bed.

When I'd undressed I crouched naked in front of the fire a minute, holding the whistle in my hand, warming it, then I raised it to my lips, tasting the silver on my tongue. With the softest of breaths I blew two notes, the boy's name, as familiar as my own voice, *Pier-o, Pier-o*.

Then, clutching the whistle in my fist, I climbed between the sheets for what would be the last time, and shut off the light.

CHAPTER 2

IN THE MORNING WHEN I OPENED THE SHUTTERS, A wall of fog still obscured the island. Not bothering to shave, I went downstairs, where a pot of fresh coffee and newly baked bread with apricot preserves were set out at a table. My hosts were not in sight, although I could hear the radio in the kitchen playing The Beatles' "Michelle." Claudine had liked that tune, maybe because some of the words were in French and we could sing them together.

I drank a half cup of coffee and then went out into the white mist. A cobweb glittered with dewdrops between the gateposts and I brushed through it, turning onto a narrow path that meandered upwards, away from where I'd disembarked last night. The mist enveloped me, damp and cloying and tasting of the sea, but the path was visible for a couple of metres ahead and I followed it slowly.

The silence as I walked was broken only by the sound of my own breathing and the regular thud of my footsteps on the path. Curtains of mist drifted in folds around me, revealing here and there patches of yellow-flowered gorse bushes. When stone buildings with blue window shutters loomed up on my left I veered away, avoiding the possibility of human contact. The silhouettes of dark yew trees appeared then vanished as I trudged on. The fog grew thicker, pressing in, obscuring the vague shapes around me until I moved only in a featureless grey light.

I slowed my pace. Here and there on the path clumps of goat droppings lay scattered like black marbles, the only sign that life existed in this void. It was as if the world had disappeared.

Beyond the veil of fog to my left I could just hear the ocean. Soon I entered a forest of pines, their black branches crowding in, the light dimming even further, and my footsteps were now soft on the carpet of leaves underfoot. I turned up the collar of my jacket against the dampness and fastened the buttons all the way up to my neck, continuing with my head down and my hands thrust into my pockets, one palm enclosing the silver whistle.

The path suddenly ended at a battered wooden sign reading, DANGER! PRÉCIPICE. Beyond lay a patch of meadow. I could hear the murmurs of the invisible sea again.

Behind me, from within the mist came a faint metallic clanking. When I turned and cocked my head to listen, the sound stopped immediately. A strange sensation made the back of my neck tingle and I had the acute feeling that someone else was near, standing in the fog and listening, just as I was. Then, it seemed as if another presence moved very close to me, creating a subtle disturbance of the atmosphere. There was a pause, then a ripple in the fog, and I knew myself alone once more.

I walked on, crossing the narrow meadow, and arrived at the cliff edge. Somewhere below, unseen waves broke with muffled booms against the rocks. Through a break in the fog I glimpsed the grey Atlantic. Shuffling forward to the edge of the cliff, I stood swaying with the tips of my shoes resting on the very limit of the precipice. The land ended here.

I didn't need to look down. I knew what waited below.

I reached into my pocket, my fingers touching Claudine's ring, and brought out the whistle I had bought for Piero so long ago, in another lifetime, when the world seemed a brighter place. I weighed it in my palm, then put it to my lips. I inhaled and blew, and a high shrill blast pierced the stillness.

There was no echo, nor any answer.

Now I allowed myself to look down into the emptiness. A wave of dizziness swayed my body. I took a deep breath and looked up into the white mist. I could feel the tears on my face and yet a great calm was settling over me.

Just at that moment, from behind me came that metallic sound again. I looked back over my shoulder and saw a goat emerging from the shrouded trees, a large ram with long fleece the same off-white as the fog. Around its neck a copper bell clanked. The ram came towards me, stopped and raised its head, displaying a pair of heavy curved horns. And then, beyond the ram, a figure moved in the trees.

I didn't call out. The mist parted, and in that brief instant of revelation, I saw a boy, standing motionless, like a statue, one arm raised towards me.

I knew that shape, I knew that gesture, that face. Slowly I raised my own hand, his name on my lips. Then the ram charged. I staggered back. The soil at the edge of the cliff crumbled beneath my shoes and gave way and I was suddenly falling, spinning backwards into the void.

THE SEA STOPPED MOVING, the waves froze in place. The land and the sea and the sky were a desolate plain, vast in a pale haze. A single heart pulsed with an irregular beat, loud at first then fading. There was no time but now, there was no place but here. There was no life but my own.

My face was damp. I raised a hand to wipe my mouth and my fingers came away moist and red with blood. I stared at the red stains and knew neither the blood nor the hand as mine. I tried to lift my head but fell back, weighted with an immense fatigue, listening to the beating of a faraway heart.

A dark shape swooped overhead, darker than darkness, with the leathery sound of immense flapping wings.

A terrible sense of despair and abandonment washed over me. Where was I? Then I remembered. I remembered the end of hope.

CHAPTER 3

THE BLUE FIAT RENTAL CAR CRESTED THE HILL.
Claudine was in the back seat with the maps and guidebook
on her lap while Piero sat next to me in the front, scanning the
valley through a pair of binoculars. I could see the road ahead
twisting and turning in the dry, ochre-coloured hills before it
emerged onto the plain where a distant village lay under the
brilliant blue sky.

I steered onto the side of the road and applied the hand-
brake. "I'm not sure we're heading in the right direction," I
said, glancing at Claudine. "That last turnoff could have been
the one we were supposed to take. Can you see it on the map?"
We were on the island of Cyprus, heading towards the north
coast from Salamis, where we had been visiting the Roman
ruins. Our destination was Agios Lazaros, an eleventh-century
Byzantine chapel near the town of Pagratis.

A few years ago I had come across an old book on the art of
perspective in one of the *bouquiniste* stalls that line the Quai de
Montebello in the shadow of Notre Dame cathedral. One of the

illustrations caught my eye, a black and white photograph of a small chapel. The building's proportions and its placement in the landscape struck me as an image of absolute perfection and harmony. A second photograph showed the interior of the chapel, where a fresco covered one wall. This had a majesty and serenity reminiscent of the work of Piero della Francesca.

I had cut out the two photographs and pinned them to the section of the studio wall where I kept various images that stimulated my eye and imagination—postcards, photos, pictures torn from magazines. I would often stand in front of the pictures lost in reverie, gazing at the church in its landscape, longing to be there, to experience that harmony and perfection.

That wish had finally been realized. The details were arranged through a travel agent on boulevard Beaumarchais, and we flew from Paris to Nicosia, where we picked up a rental car the following day and drove to our hotel in Famagusta on the east coast.

Now, Claudine set the guidebook aside and spread out the map. "I think we should go on a bit and see if there is a signpost."

I put the car in motion again. "We can't be that far away."

At the next curve, as we motored down the incline, I noticed a white van parked on the side of the road. A man leaned against the door smoking a cigarette. I pulled alongside and rolled down the window.

"Pagratis?" I pointed to the road ahead.

The man answered in Greek. He was tall with a reddish beard, dressed in a uniform of light blue shirt and darker trousers. I couldn't quite make out the insignia on his van.

"*Parlez-vous français?*" I asked. Then, "English?"

"English is better. You are going to Pagratis?"

"Are we headed in the right direction?"

The man bent and looked through the window at Piero then at Claudine in the back seat. "May I ask where you are coming from?"

"Famagusta," I said.

"Are you Americans?"

"We're from Paris." I at first took the man to be a local policeman, but his accent sounded German.

He extended his hand. "Koos Vandermey. From Rotterdam. I'm here with the United Nations observer team."

I shook the proffered hand. "This is my wife Claudine, and my son, Piero."

"Right now is not the best time to visit Pagratis," Koos Vandermey said. "There has been some trouble in that area."

"What kind of trouble?" Claudine asked anxiously, leaning forward over the seat.

Vandermey gestured to the plain below. "Are you aware that there has been conflict around here between Greek and Turkish Cypriots?"

"I did read in the papers about it a while ago. But I thought the problems were being resolved," I answered.

"Exactly what kind of trouble?" Claudine asked.

"A farm was burned nearby a week ago. We've had reports of arms being smuggled in—mortars and other explosives. It's a tense situation at the moment."

"Maybe we should go back, Leo," Claudine said.

"Just a minute." I addressed Vandermey again. "We want to visit the Agios Lazaros church. To look at the fresco."

Vandermey nodded. "You shouldn't have any problems there. But don't stop in the town. And for God's sake don't drive too fast and run down anybody's donkey or goat or you'll never get out of here. Let me see your map." He explained the route. "You have plenty of gasoline?"

"Almost a full tank. Thanks for your advice."

As I drove off I glanced in the rear-view mirror and saw the man writing something down in a notebook, perhaps our licence number.

"I don't think we should go on," Claudine said, leaning again over the front seat.

"He said we wouldn't have any trouble. We've come all this way—it would be a pity to go back now just because somebody's farm got burned."

"Isn't that serious enough? Or does nothing else matter except that you want to make a painting?"

I shook my head.

"We always come second to your painting. I thought this was supposed to be a holiday. For all of us. Isn't that why we came? Or was that just an excuse?" She sat back and folded her arms, glaring at me. When she was angry her grey eyes burned with a cold light. "In that case, you should have come alone."

"It is a holiday," I said. "For all of us. Don't worry about the local politics. People have been arguing over this island for centuries."

"What about the terrorists?"

"There aren't any. This isn't Algeria."

Piero, who was scanning the landscape with his binoculars, said, "I like it here. I want to go to the church." Lowering the glasses, he turned to his mother. "I want to paint too. Like Papa."

I glanced at Claudine in the mirror and raised my eyebrows. I knew her judgment wouldn't allow her to start an argument in which she sided against both of us.

"Fine," Claudine said, raising her shoulders in a shrug. "Fine. But I want to be at the hotel in Famagusta in time to go for a swim this afternoon. And I want to eat in a good restaurant tonight, not at some kebab stand."

"We can eat calamari!" Piero exclaimed.

"Not me. I want a first-class restaurant that serves lobster." In a softer tone she added, "And champagne. Not that terrible retsina we had last night."

I smiled at her in the mirror, glad at the change in her voice. "It's a deal. Lobster and champagne."

"And octopus," Piero said. "It means eight arms. *Octo.*"

"And an eight-legged octopus," I said.

Soon, Pagratis appeared, a poor town consisting of a few two-storey houses and a concrete building with a flag hanging over the entrance. The speed limit sign read "25." I slowed the car, keeping an eye on the speedometer.

"There's nobody here," Piero said. The town seemed to be deserted.

Then, a group of men came into view, standing outside a café. They all turned to stare at the car as it passed. Their faces were unsmiling.

"Drive faster," Claudine urged, shrinking away from the window, but I resisted the temptation to speed up. Piero twisted in his seat and watched the silent men through the back window until they were out of sight. Claudine kept her eyes straight ahead.

I let out a sigh of relief as we reached the edge of the town and accelerated on the next stretch of pavement. The road ascended into the hills, now wooded with pine and cedar. I felt my mood lighten.

"The turn should be coming soon," Claudine said after a while, her fingers marking the place on the map. "On the right."

At the signpost I turned off onto an unpaved road that soon dwindled into a steep rutted track. The car bounced over the furrows, jostling us from side to side, making Piero giggle. I slowed and put the car into first gear as the engine strained up the incline.

Just as we reached the top of the ridge a herd of goats came scrambling over the crest, halting abruptly at the sight of the car. I braked quickly. The goats surveyed the car, waiting, then the front of the group parted to allow a large ram to come forward. As it approached, Piero rolled down his window, letting in the smell of dry dust and the clanking of the copper bell around the ram's neck. No shepherd was in sight.

The ram came closer and raised its head to the window, regarding us with yellow eyes under long lashes. Piero extended a hand and touched one of the curved horns. The animal twisted its head and licked his fingers with a long pink tongue. With a laugh Piero jerked his hand back. At the sound of his voice the rest of the herd sauntered forward, their thick barnyard odour filling the interior of the car.

"Close your window, Piero," Claudine said, wrinkling her nose.

She took off her sunhat and fanned her face. Her hair, which she wore cut short these days, stuck up from her head, giving her a gamine look. Glancing at her in the rear-view mirror, I felt a surge of tenderness.

I put the car in gear again, drove on to the crest of the ridge and stopped. And there below us, in a hollow next to a grove of trees, stood Agios Lazaros. A thrill quivered through me. This was the place I had longed for.

Piero jumped from the car and ran down the slope, Claudine close behind him. His blue and white striped T-shirt and her pink dress were splashes of colour against the landscape. I got out and breathed in the clean smell of grass and a faint pine scent. Below me, the chapel nestled between the rolling hills and the olive trees, their outlines like black flames, and the building white against ochre and sienna.

I strolled down towards the church. The voices of Piero and Claudine drifted from the shade of the olive grove. The heavy wooden doors creaked and scraped across the stone floor as I entered. The dark interior had that particular cool mustiness of ancient stone, of time itself.

As my eyes adjusted, the door opened wider behind me and the elongated shadow of Piero fell across the floor. In the sudden increase of light, I saw the fresco covering the entire side wall.

I was unprepared for the splendour—the rich depths of the blues, the clarity of the whites, the intense reds, the lustre of the gold. But the theme I knew well.

The whole painting measured about ten feet high by twenty feet long and seemed remarkably well preserved for something so old, with only one high patch where the colour had flaked off to reveal bare plaster beneath. A haloed figure, obviously Christ, stood just to the left of centre, one hand raised towards an open grave at the lower right corner. I walked closer, and because the scene had been painted to life size, it was as if I stepped right into the painting, coming to rest on the edge of the open grave in the foreground.

"Who are those people, Papa?" Piero asked, tugging at my sleeve. "What are they doing?"

"It's called *The Raising of Lazarus*, from a story in the Bible."

"Why is that man covered in bandages?" Piero pointed to where two men were lifting the stone lid from the tomb, revealing a figure swathed in a burial cloth, an expression of profound astonishment on his features as daylight penetrated the shadows and fell upon his face.

"That is Lazarus," I explained. "Jesus came to visit him but when he arrived he found that Lazarus had died. Lazarus's family begged Jesus to bring him back from death, so Jesus told the men to uncover the tomb, and then he called Lazarus's name. When Lazarus heard his name he woke up and came out of his grave into the world again."

"And then what did he do?" Piero asked, his voice lowered to a whisper.

I pondered the question. One I'd never asked myself. "I don't know. Nobody knows." Realizing I had whispered too, I said in a normal tone, "It's just a story."

Piero moved nearer to the fresco and stood with his face close to that of Lazarus, peering at it intently. He stood with such silent concentration, almost as if he were listening, that I reached out gently and put a hand on his shoulder.

He took a few steps backward, looking at the figures, then turned and hurried out again into the daylight, leaving me alone with the painting. Tiny motes of dust hung in the shafts of light emanating from the window openings, and from outside came the murmur of doves cooing. The sounds, which should have been soothing, gave me a feeling of disquiet.

Moments later two piercing blasts from a whistle outside

broke the silence. I raised my head and listened. The whistle called again, summoning me. I left the painting and made my way to the door.

Halfway up the slope, Piero stood looking up to where Claudine waited just near the summit of the ridge. She was turned away, observing something out of sight. For a moment I felt I was still looking at a painting—two figures isolated in an elemental stillness, a mother and child in a landscape, looking or listening to something only they could perceive, that I would never see.

Piero blew the whistle again. Two notes, one rising, the second descending.

The whistle had been a gift from me. A couple of weeks earlier, on a visit to Jardin des Plantes, which was crowded with tourists and groups of school children, I had become separated from him. I'd been gazing at one of the statues along the walkway, and when I turned, the boy was gone. I rushed around in a panic, shouting his name, my heart gone cold with terror. It was probably only seconds later that a smiling Piero emerged from behind the plinth on which the statue stood. It was a game to him, but I had fallen to my knees and grabbed the boy into my embrace with such ferocity that Piero had patted me on the back, saying, "I'm here, Papa. I'm here."

A few days later I had stopped to look into the window of one of the antiques stores along rue Saint-Paul. On a lower shelf I noticed a silver whistle of the kind that referees use in sporting events, but smaller and engraved with an intricate floral design. As coincidence would have it, the name of the manufacturer was also engraved on the surface—*Piero.*

"If you get lost again and can't find me," I told Piero when I presented it to him, "just blow on the whistle and I will come to you."

He ran his finger over the engraving with a look of pleased amazement. But when he tested it and filled the apartment with piercing blasts, I covered my ears and retreated to the studio to escape the noise. A little later I become aware that the whistle was sounding two repeated notes, softly, the first a bit higher and briefer in pitch than the second, like a bird call. I realized that the sounds mimicked the syllables of my name—*Lee-oooh, Leee-oooh.* When I opened the studio door, Piero was standing at the other end of the hall with the whistle to his lips.

"It works, Papa. You came," Piero had said to me.

Now, the whistle sounded a third time. The scene came to life. Claudine beckoned to me, waving her sun hat. Piero raised both arms in a salute. I walked up to join them.

Claudine had spread a blanket on the dry grass and unpacked the lunch we'd purchased in Famagusta before setting out: goat cheese wrapped in sage leaves; a sort of pancake filled with herb-seasoned meat; a baklava of honey and nuts; and a flask of Commandaria, a local sweet wine. I fetched a bottle of water from the back seat and sat down in the shade of the car.

"This is a wonderful spot, Leo," Claudine said, leaning against me and placing a cup of wine in my hand. "I'm glad we came."

I kissed her and ran my fingers through her hair. "And I'm glad you're here to see this with me. You should go and have a look at the fresco afterwards. It's really fantastic."

When lunch was over, I helped Claudine tidy up, then collected my paintbox from the car and sauntered along the ridge, a little sleepy from the wine but eager to set to work.

"We're not going to stay long, are we?" Claudine called. She was stretched out on the blanket in the sun. "I want to get back in time for that swim."

"Just a quick sketch. Piero, are you going to come and paint?" I was disappointed when the boy shook his head. I'd hoped that we could paint the scene together.

I found a vantage point where the church and the olive grove formed a pleasing composition. I sat down and opened the paintbox. At my feet, blue cornflowers grew among the blades of yellowed grass. In the distant sky swallows chirped their high-pitched cries. I reached for my palette and paints and set out dabs of titanium white, lamp black, yellow ochre and cobalt blue. The purity of the landscape required no other colours.

With the tip of my brush on the board I focused on the scene below. I waited. I waited for the place to reveal itself, to speak to me. All sounds gradually fell away, the faint rustle of the breeze over the grass, the birdcalls, Piero's footsteps as he chased up and down the slope in pursuit of grasshoppers. A radiance gradually emanated from the scene below me; the church filled my vision, growing larger, its colours more intense.

My hand hovered in a moment of indecision, then stroked the canvas lightly, making a mark, then another. Working quickly, I drew outlines for the building, laying on washes of pale blue for the sky and blocking in the darker greens of the olive trees. I forgot myself as I worked and the vision that I had held inside myself began to flow from my brush. I was only dimly aware of Claudine and Piero moving about in the olive grove. I barely registered the door of the chapel scraping open, their faint voices as they entered, the door thudding shut.

It may have been only a second later, or minutes, when I heard a boom, like thunder. The doves in the olive grove took flight in all directions. Startled in mid-brushstroke, I looked up at the cloudless sky, and then across towards the nearby hillside where a puff of white smoke blossomed. Then the air above me rippled and tore as something unseen hurtled past, and with a deafening bang, the tower of the church collapsed inward. A second explosion sent a blast of hot, grit-filled smoke towards me. Everything went black.

And then I was running into the darkness, screaming their names.

CHAPTER 4

AN EYE, DARK AND ROUND AS A SHINY BLACK MAR-
ble, studied me with a steady, curious gaze. I lifted my head
and tried to focus on it. A gull, which had been hovering on a
current of air just near my face, wheeled away with a screech.

Raising myself on my elbows, I grimaced as a pain shot
through my right side. All around me there was only a featureless pale blue haze. As I struggled to sit up, my legs swung
free in the air. Between my knees and my dangling shoes I
glimpsed, far below, a silent ragged line of white foam breaking against black rocks.

A glance to the left and right revealed that I was perched
on a narrow shelf fifteen feet below the cliff edge. Sheer stone
extended on both sides, and the rock-studded ocean lay a hundred feet below. Above was the cliff. A swarm of tiny spots
swam across my vision and the vertigo almost made me vomit.

By shifting myself sideways, I was able to stretch out full
length on the ledge, and then position my body so that my
back was to the sea and the sky. With my arm folded under my

cheek, I lay with my face a few inches from the wall of rock and closed my eyes. My whole body shivered.

Slowly, I began to remember—leaving the hotel and walking through a landscape of mist, then finding the cliff, and my resolution as I stood there. After that, all was confused in my mind. A ram charging out of the mist, driving me to the edge. I had no memory of falling. Had I jumped after all? Was I dreaming? But the hard surface of the stone beneath my cheek was real, the pain in my side was real. I kept my eyes shut. I didn't want to see again what was around me. My throat was dry. I was thirsty. And tired. Very tired.

When I opened my eyes again the fog was gone, the blue above me was the sky, and gulls were sailing over the sea below. How much time had passed? Had I slept?

Then it came back to me—something in the mist. Someone. A boy. I had seen a boy, I knew it.

I listened. Nothing.

Of course, nothing. Piero was dead.

It had been more than a year since I watched the coffins containing Piero and Claudine sink into the black Normandy earth, had watched as the wet soil covered the burnished wood and brass fittings, had watched until the hole was filled and the strip of sod was placed over the grave where son and mother were buried. I turned my face to the rock wall again.

I could still end it. All I had to do was roll over a few inches and let myself fall and all of this would disappear, real or not. Isn't that what I had wanted?

Time passed, if such a thing as time existed in this place. I remained with my face to the rock and my back to the emptiness that used to be the world, not moving. As I lay there, I became

aware of a small caterpillar inching its way across the rough surface of the ledge, just in front of my eyes. It measured no more
than the length of my little finger and was yellow-orange, with
a brighter stripe of yellow down the centre. The entire body was
covered with bristly hair, and if it weren't for the forward movement of the creature's expansions and contractions, I wouldn't
have been able to tell the front from the rear.

As I watched its awkward progress across the ledge into a
crevice in the cliff face, I wondered how the creature had got
to this inaccessible spot in the first place, or where it would go
from here.

Slowly I sat up. Bracing my legs with care and keeping my
face against the cliff, hands grasping where they could, I gently
levered myself upright and took stock of my surroundings.

To my right, just where the ledge ended, a vinelike plant
with white flowers wound its way up a narrow fissure in the
rock. By stretching out my arm, I was able to grasp and tug
at the thick stem of the vine. It appeared to be firmly attached
to the cliff. I edged closer and found a secure handhold in the
rock. I searched for a foothold, but realized that the toes of my
shoes were too wide to fit into the narrow niches and cracks.
With one hand I eased off my shoes and socks and then, grasping the vine tightly, began to make my way up.

The vine trembled under my weight, but seemed strong
enough, and I reached higher. A sudden pain bit into my palm
and I inhaled sharply, but hung on. Sharp green thorns hid
among the leaves and clusters of white flowers.

Gradually, I moved closer to the top. My legs were rub-
bery, the muscles in my arms taut with the strain. In another
minute gravity would do its work on my weak body and I

would have to let go. It would be so easy to let go, to just let go and fall free. But I didn't want to die. Even if I didn't really want to live either. But whatever I'd thought previously, whatever I'd intended as I stood on the precipice earlier, something now felt different.

The vine ended. The cliff edge was just above me. Not quite within reach. Stretching my arm up, I searched for a handhold, anything, the smallest fissure. My toes settled into a crack, my fingers closed on an outcrop. I took a deep breath, and with a great groan I launched myself upwards in a tremendous push. The side of my face scraped against the rock, my fingernails scrabbled and tore, my legs kicked free in the air. For a moment I was suspended in space, untethered from the earth.

Then, in a desperate scramble, I was on solid ground, rolling onto all fours and crawling as far as possible from the edge before I collapsed face-down on the sweet grass of the meadow, my whole body convulsing with sobs of relief. Every muscle ached, the ribs on my right side throbbed, my hands were scraped raw, my fingernails were broken, and I had lost my shoes. But I was alive.

The ground around me was scuffed and trodden with the hoofprints of goats and a scattering of dung pellets. There had been goats here, I hadn't imagined that part at least. Then I saw it—the clear imprint of a small bare foot. Human. Just one. A child's footprint. A boy had stood here. I placed my hand next to the print, measuring it, tracing my fingertip around the outline of the sole and the five toes.

In front of me were the woods, thick oaks and the outlines of dark yew trees. But everything was so still, so strange. The light was brilliant, hurting my eyes. Glancing back at the cliff edge only a few feet away, I began to tremble with the realization of what had happened, of what I had almost done. I rolled over onto my back and looked up at the empty sky, and when I shut my eyes I could still see it, all white and brilliant. I heard a voice calling, faintly, or thought I did.

I opened my eyes. A woman stood looking down at me. Her black hair fell around her shoulders and the golden sunlight behind her head radiated outwards in a halo of light. In her arms she held a bouquet of wildflowers and grasses.

I felt at peace, calmed by this beautiful apparition that was like an angelic figure from a painting—like Aurora in that picture by Naudé in the Louvre, *The Gates of Dawn*. She shifted the bouquet and leaned closer, stretching out a hand to me. The faintest scent of perfume hung in the air—lily of the valley.

"Are you all right?" she asked.

Then I remembered. I sat up. A pain arced down my right side and I grimaced. The woman stepped back quickly.

I struggled to my feet, brushing the dirt from my hands, wincing from the burning cuts and abrasions on my palms.

"You've had an accident?" she said.

"I was lost." I looked around, making a vague gesture towards the woods. "I fell."

Now I noticed the espadrilles on her feet, the pale green capri pants and white shirt, the watch with a metal band on her wrist. Neither a dream nor an apparition from a painting, but a flesh-and-blood woman. She looked to be about ten years older than me, maybe forty. Her clothes were stylish and seemed expensive. She didn't look like an islander.

Then I saw the bruise on her cheek, a purple blotch, as if from a blow. I stared at it.

She took a step away from me and brought a pair of sunglasses out of her pocket, slipping them over her eyes. "Where are you going?" she asked. "Can I help you?"

"Did you . . . did you see a boy?" I said.

"A boy? Where? No."

"I just wanted to talk to him."

She looked back along the path.

"Are you from around here?" I asked. She shrugged. She seemed uneasy. I realized that I wasn't making much sense, and might even be scaring her. "My name is Leo Millar. I'm staying at the hotel."

"I think you might need a doctor."

I glanced down at myself, at my scuffed clothes, a smear of dried blood on one bare foot, conscious of how much my whole body ached. "I'll be fine. Are you sure you didn't see a boy? He was here earlier."

She gave a noncommittal shake of her head. "You're injured. Do you need help getting back to the hotel?"

"I have to find him." I scanned the unfamiliar landscape and limped back along the path, peering down at the ground for footprints.

A minute later I halted and looked back. The woman was gone.

CHAPTER 5

WHAT HAD HAPPENED? WHO HAD I SEEN IN THE mist? Piero was dead, I knew that. But I had known that figure standing in the trees, and I had felt the recognition as something physical, with my body. Was I going mad? I shook my head and tried to clear my thoughts. The first thing to do was get back to the hotel and clean myself up. And a drink. God, I needed a drink. And shoes.

I felt unsteady, confused, still reeling with disbelief over what I had almost done. Which way was the hotel? I should have asked that woman. I stopped and looked back. I couldn't really recall what she looked like. Dark-haired. A bouquet of wildflowers. A bruise on one cheek. The faint scent of lily of the valley.

I walked on, flinching every now and then when my bare feet trod on a sharp stone. Farther down the path I could see a row of poplars and the roof of a house where a thin wisp of smoke drifted up from a chimney. I'd only been walking a few minutes when I saw someone coming towards me, a short man wearing a dark jacket and white shirt and a large floppy beret. He was in his late fifties, with a broad chest and a very thick moustache peppered with grey. In his hand he carried a stout walking stick, which he raised in greeting at the sight of me.

"*Bonjour.* You must be Leo Millar." He stopped abruptly, frowning. "But what has happened to you?"

"Do you know me?" I asked, further confused.

"I ate breakfast this morning at the hotel and Linda mentioned that a painter had come to stay. I assumed that would be you. I am the priest here on La Mouche. Père Caron. Or just plain André Caron, if you prefer." He extended his hand and I shook it, flinching at the pressure. He looked down at the cuts and the dried blood on my fingers. "You've had an accident! Can I help you?"

"There was fog. I couldn't see. I . . . I fell. Off the cliff and onto a ledge." I hid my hands in my pockets. "I managed to climb up."

"You were walking on the cliff in that fog? It's very dangerous. Didn't you see the warning sign?"

I shook my head.

"If you don't mind me stating the obvious," the priest said, "you don't look at all well."

"I'm okay."

He pointed at my feet. "Where are your shoes?"

"I guess I lost them, back there."

"Look, I think you'd better come with me to my house. It's nearby. I can give you a pair of boots."

I looked back up the path, searching.

"Is someone with you?" the priest asked.

"No. There's nobody. I just need to get back to the hotel. If you could point out the direction."

"This way then. Come." He took me by the arm.

In a few minutes we reached a house built on a rise overlooking the ocean, stone walls painted white, a slate roof. Mauve hollyhocks grew along the sunward walls and the blue wooden shutters were fastened open. A small enclosed orchard of apple trees stood behind the house.

"Come in a minute," the priest urged. "You can't walk all the way to the hotel in bare feet. I'll lend you a pair of boots."

We went round to the side and I followed him in through a low doorway. He tossed his beret onto a table in the hall under a crucifix and led the way into a snug kitchen, where he opened a cupboard and took down a bottle of liquor, pouring out two glasses.

"Sit down. Drink this."

I swallowed and the silky liquid slid over my tongue and down my throat, spreading warmth through my chest. The apple flavour that filled my mouth transported me instantly back to those first lonely months in Paris, just after I'd arrived from Canada, when I'd had a room at the Hôtel Mistral on rue Cels, and my one acquaintance in the whole city had been a writer from Vancouver, David McCullough, three doors down the corridor from me. One evening after he'd sold a short story to Esquire magazine he took me to dinner at La Coupole, where, he said, he intended to make up for all the months of bean soup and mutton stew. We dined on oysters, and then magret de canard with a bottle of Saint-Julien that cost as much as the food combined, and after dessert we each smoked a cigar on the terrace with snifters of eighteen-year-old Calvados.

Everything had seemed possible. Paris awaited us. David was going to be the next Hemingway and I was going to give Picasso a run for his money.

Now I shook my head ruefully and took another sip.

Perhaps mistaking my expression, the priest said, "It's locally made. From some of my own apples."

He drank his own measure down in a quick swallow and fetched a porcelain basin, which he filled with water and set on the table. "Soak your hands in this. I'll get the disinfectant." He returned with a brown glass bottle and a towel, which I used to wipe the dirt and dried blood from my hands.

"This will sting a bit," the priest said, uncorking the disinfectant, "but it will do you good. You'd better wash your feet as well." Watching me dab at my hands with the disinfectant, he said, "Let me see if I can find you some shoes. Our size might be roughly the same."

A minute later, he reappeared with a pair of worn boots and some socks. "These will do, I think. They're a bit old but still in good condition."

While I tried on the boots, the priest poured two more glasses of Calvados. Then he reached into his pocket for a package of Caporal tobacco and sprinkled the flakes into a sheaf of paper, which he rolled into a cigarette. He lit it with a match from a box on the table.

"So, you were out walking and had a fall?"

"Yes. Stupid of me. In all that fog I didn't really pay attention to where I was going. Luckily I landed on a kind of ledge and managed to climb up."

"I know the place. You're extremely lucky that you didn't tumble straight into the sea." He tapped the ash from his cigarette into a large scallop shell that served as an ashtray. "So you're a painter? I can't recall any artists visiting our island before. They tend to prefer the more dramatic vistas in Brittany."

"I'm always on the lookout for new landscapes, and when I saw La Mouche on the map I thought it might be worth a visit." I was amazed that I could lie so easily, and to a priest.

Père Caron regarded the tip of his cigarette and blew on it while giving me a long, searching look. "Are you . . . in any sort of trouble?"

"No," I answered quickly. "I'm just a tourist."

The priest held up his hands in a placating gesture. "I didn't mean to offend you. But you must admit that your appearance is, how should I say, a little unusual."

"I told you, I fell."

"You're not French, are you."

"I'm Canadian. But I've lived in Paris for the last ten years. I came to study art and I stayed. It's my home now."

"Canada. It's a long way to come. Do you still have family there?"

"There isn't anyone. Not any more."

But there never had been. I'd grown up in the Guild Home for Boys in Vancouver. A home for those without homes. The closest to family I'd ever had was a dormitory of other boys: the lost, the forgotten, the unwanted and the abandoned. At the Guild, we didn't ask questions about parents. We'd all learned that there were no answers.

I stood up and put my hands in my pockets, then took them out and rubbed the ache in my left arm. I wanted to leave, but I also wanted to know more about the island. "Are there many people living here?"

"Alas no," he said. "Most were sent away during the war years when the Germans occupied the island. Not many returned. And now, with the decline in the fishing industry, few of us are left. Some fishermen and their families in LeBec, the village on the other side of the island. The hotel and the shop on this side. Ester Chauvin's farm. One or two others. That's about it."

I wanted to frame my next question carefully. "What about the children?"

"Since the war there has been no school here. Twenty years now. At first those families with children used to board them in Saint-Alban because we didn't have enough pupils to warrant a school. But that wasn't really suitable in the long run. People ended up moving to the mainland. A few tourists come in the summer." He shook his head sadly. "Perhaps soon only the birds and the goats will live here."

"I thought I saw a child in the fog earlier."

"What did the child look like? I know everybody on the island."

"It was a boy. About ten years old, with dark curly hair."

"Really?" He paused. "And why are you interested in this boy?"

Was it my imagination or did he seem evasive? "Perhaps I was seeing things." I looked away and stared out the window for a minute, then turned back to the priest. "Let me ask you a question, Père. In your capacity as a priest."

"Of course."

"Do you think the dead ever communicate with us?"

He glanced sharply at me, then took a moment to roll another cigarette, studying me with curiosity as he lit it.

"Is there another life after this one?" I pressed.

"Well, I can tell you, as a priest, what the Church says. I can tell you what Science says. Or I can speculate as a man, ignorant as the rest."

There had been a time at the Guild when I'd made a sincere effort at praying, wanting to believe during those long dreary Sunday mornings, nauseated by the smell of incense and furniture polish, longing for breakfast, staring up at the carved wooden figure on the crucifix behind the altar in the chapel, wanting it to move, to blink, to do something. But whatever God listened to prayers had not stirred on my behalf. By the time I'd entered my teens I'd realized that you got through this life with your guile, your fists and whatever measure of talent you could scrape together.

The priest was regarding me thoughtfully. "Why do you ask?"

"I saw . . . I thought I saw . . . Nothing."

He leaned forward. "What have you seen?"

Shaking my head I turned away and got to my feet. "I've taken enough of your time. Thank you for your help, Père. And for the boots. I'll return them as soon as I can."

"No matter. Anytime." He was still frowning as he accompanied me out to the garden. "Will you be staying long?"

I looked past him, up to the woods. "No, not long."

He placed a hand on my shoulder. "I might not have the right answers to your questions, but it helps to confide in someone when we are troubled. Come and talk to me again. Will you do that, Leo Millar?"

"Yes, I will. Thank you."

He remained standing at the gate as I turned and made my way in the direction of the hotel.

CHAPTER 6

WHEN I GOT BACK TO MY ROOM AND I SAW MY FACE in the mirror—haggard, pale, desperate looking—I was shocked. I looked older than my thirty years. Like a man on the run, like someone being hunted.

As I studied the cuts and scrapes on my palms, remembering, my hands began to tremble. Then suddenly my whole body was shivering and my heart started thudding against my ribs. A cold clammy sweat broke out on my skin. A terrible feeling of shame came over me. I staggered over to the bed and collapsed across the cover. How close I'd come. Even though I'd thought I wanted it, I hadn't.

But what *did* I want? I had no purpose. Except to find that boy. And why? Did I think it was some sort of miracle? My son come back to life? It was absurd to have such thoughts. The fact that I was even here was pure chance. This island, La Mouche, was just a speck on the map off the coast of France.

I'd woken one morning in the apartment on rue du Figuier in Paris after drinking myself into a stupor the night before, the only way I could fall asleep, with a dry mouth, clammy sweaty sheets tangled around my body, overwhelmed by sudden terror. All that I stopped myself from thinking about during the day I dreamed of in the night. I did not remember my dreams, but I knew I had dreamed because I woke, trembling, my hands searching out the bottle of wine on the bedside table.

When I walked through the apartment I was overcome by a sense of strangeness—all the furniture, all their belongings, everything that had physically defined our lives together, even the contents of the studio when I glanced in quickly seemed unfamiliar, as if they belonged to other people, people I had never known. I was a stranger here.

In less than half an hour I'd showered and dressed and thrown a few things into a bag. I left the apartment without a backward glance towards all those years of happiness, and the months of solitary grief and misery and hopelessness that had followed.

Before driving onto the autoroute and quitting Paris for good—I had no destination except to leave the past behind—I headed up to the heights of Montmartre. All over the city, posters adorned the news kiosks, advertising Brigitte Bardot's new film, À Coeur Joie. I parked on the side of the basilica and walked round to Place du Parvis du Sacré-Coeur. Claudine had liked to come up here, especially on Sunday mornings to have coffee in the Café Jongkind on Place du Tertre. Paris looked like a village from up here, she had once said. Along the skyline a haze was touching the rooftops and chimneys while south of Gare du Nord the buildings faded into ragged edges where they met the sky. Everything was shades of grey and muted whites.

"What do you think of, when you look down on the city?" she had asked me.

"The colours. How I would paint it," I replied immediately. "And how impossible it is to really paint Paris without making it look like kitsch." I'd thrown up my hands in a mock gesture of defeat. "And you, what do you think of?"

"I think of all the apartments, all the bedrooms. I think of all the people who made love last night, all the people who are making love at this very moment in their warm beds. All the promises kept."

I'd kissed her then, in the damp hazy air, overcome by a flood of happiness, slipping my hands under her raincoat to feel the living warmth of her body and knowing myself blessed. If it had been possible I would have made love to her right then.

But as I stood there remembering, with my hands on the stone balustrade, I felt only sorrow. I looked down at the place that had been the only real home I had ever known: the grey and black rooftops, the familiar landmarks of the Eiffel Tower, the dome of the Pantheon, Notre-Dame, and just barely discernible, the slender column in Place de la Bastille not far from my own neighbourhood.

All those lives, all the struggles and hopes and fears. The desperate illusions. The futility of all the promises. Now I could see the darkness that was around everybody all the time, even those who loved.

I left Paris and drove out on the highway.

The motion of the car and the constancy of the unfolding road were soothing, numbing my mind, and as the name of each town flashed by, I left the past further behind. It didn't matter where I was going as long as I kept moving. The spinning of the wheels, the roar of the engine, the wind rushing in through the window.

All through the day I drove. I found myself reluctant to leave the car, as if the mass of metal hurtling down the auto-route was my only home now. I travelled through the alien landscape, nothing more than a shadow flitting across the fields and through the towns. I drove onward as evening fell, and I felt myself almost invisible, leaving no trace or impression, a wraith that passed on the periphery of people's awareness, already a ghost.

At some point I registered that I was steering southwest, taking the known turnings, following the signs down into La Manche. The familiar names flashed by the windshield: Caen, Bayeux, Saint-Lô. I was travelling through the patchwork of the bocage—lush green fields bordered by tight hedgerows, stone houses with slate roofs, pink and blue hydrangeas alongside the walls of farmhouses, sturdy white cattle sometimes raising their heads to watch the car passing.

Only when I saw the sign for Coutances did I realize that I was driving towards Montmartin-sur-Mer. Where we'd been married. Where they were buried. The realization shocked me out of my dazed state. At the very next exit I turned around and headed towards Villedieu-les-Poêles and the Avranches road instead. Perhaps it was cowardly not to go to Montmartin, at least to put flowers in the graveyard. But I could not bear the thought.

On the seat next to me was the little paintbox, the one I'd bought for Piero at André Jocelyn on boulevard Edgar Quinet. I often rested my hand on it as I drove, running my fingers across the name inscribed on the lid. But I never opened the box. I had not painted since that day.

Hours later, I saw lights from a town and a sign that read St. Alban. The road ended at a harbour. Fishing boats were moored under the darkening sky where one patch of blood-red light from the sinking sun smeared across the water. To my left stood rows of orderly houses, a church on the heights, the lamps of evening glowing on the streets and in the windows. I drove up into the town until I saw a hotel.

I ate in the dining room. At the bar nearby sat a young couple, stools drawn together, their heads closely inclined to each other. The blonde woman had her back to me, but the way she moved made me think of Claudine. I ordered a glass of fiery Calvados when my wine was finished, and another after that, continuing to sit and watch the woman, wanting to see her face, but she never turned around. Later, in my room, dizzy from the alcohol, I conjured up sensual memories of Claudine from the darkness and in a desperate attempt to make my body remember her, I tried to masturbate, but my imagination failed me. I searched for the half bottle of whiskey in my bag, and I drank all of it, then lay down on the bed again, waiting for oblivion.

At some dark hour I woke to a cry in the night, a sound so full of anguish that I jerked awake and reached for the bedside lamp immediately. I was surprised to find myself lying on the bedcovers fully dressed, in a room I didn't recognize. The window between the open curtains framed darkness. I looked at the watch on my wrist, dismayed to see that daylight remained a long way off. In was that dead time of the night, when the past seems a failure and the future an impossibility.

The cry came again. I hurried to the window. The parking lot, lit by a single harsh sodium lamp, was empty except for my car. The surrounding buildings were in darkness, shutters drawn. Then I saw it. Just below my window an animal moved, a dog I thought at first, but as the long bushy tail swished from side to side and the sleek head with its pointed snout came up I saw a fox.

It pricked its black-tipped ears forward, lifted its snout and looked directly up at me. I stared down at the fox in the hard white light, then I let the curtain fall, located my shoes under the bed and pulled them on before fetching my jacket from the closet.

Damp salt air washed over my face as I stepped outside. The fox was nowhere in sight, but I crossed the parking lot and down a sloping alley, my feet ringing out on the cobblestones and echoing back at me from the high ancient walls of the sleeping town. As I passed through an archway the air changed, a sudden freshness, and there below me lay the dark slow-moving sea. Far out, where the horizon must be, the sky lit up with a white glow. A storm at sea, I thought. In the flashes of distant blue light I could make out, with unusual clarity, the shape of an island, the black silhouette of buildings, wooded cliffs, a church steeple.

It seemed to me a place that I recognized, that I knew, a long-lost landscape echoing in my mind. One of those places I used to create in my paintings. The sky fell to darkness again. The island vanished.

In the morning I retraced my steps along the ramparts. I peered out to sea, searching for the island I'd seen, but the ocean was unbroken by any landforms all the way to the horizon. I made my way to the tourist office. Yes, they told me, there was an island offshore, La Mouche, but it was impossible to see from the mainland. It had a hotel and I could radio to them from the harbourmaster's office if I wanted to go there. They could send a boat or I could hire one of the locals to ferry me over.

It wasn't much later that I was standing on the deck of a fishing boat, watching Saint-Alban recede. And when it finally slipped from sight I turned towards the wide empty sea ahead, and the island somewhere beyond my vision.

CHAPTER 7

WHEN I WOKE IN THE MORNINGS, THERE WAS AN instant, less than a minute, when I would forget, when memory was kind to me and I was without the burden of grief I carried, even in my dreams. In that brief suspension between the blank state of sleep and full consciousness, I was free, just a normal man wakening on an ordinary day. And I would feel hope, the eternally renewed hope with which human beings rise each morning to engage life. But then I would hear a distant cry from the darkness and smell the smoke, and memory would come. And like a condemned man I would rise to face my prison and the eternity of my sentence.

At first today was no different. Then I remembered the boy. I opened the shutters of my room onto the sky and the green landscape and the blue ocean.

At breakfast, as I was drinking my bowl of café au lait, I noticed a hand-painted map of the island hanging on the wall of the dining room. I placed my finger on the Hôtel des Îles, then moved it to the priest's house, and then traced the route back to the woods and the cliffs where I'd fallen. The trees on the map had been painted in daintily with a dark green, and the word *Précipice* marked in red where the woods met the cliff. West of the presbytery, near the centre of the island, was a farm called Manoir de Soulles. Here and there, other dwellings were indicated, mostly along the shore. The island seemed to have no actual roads, just paths of varying lengths, most of them with unusual names, criss-crossing and leading in all directions.

At the farthest end from the hotel, where the land came to a crooked point, was a lighthouse, Phare du Monde, and just past it a cluster of cottages in a curve of harbour indicated the village of LeBec. If I took the lane marked Route des Matelots, which bisected the island, I estimated that I could reach the village in about an hour, depending on the terrain. It would be the logical place to start my search.

But what was I searching for? A ghost?

I drained my coffee and placed the bowl on the table, tucked Piero's paintbox under my arm, and left the hotel. Of course I wasn't going to paint, but since I'd explained to Père Caron as well as to Linda and Victor that I'd come to the island to sketch, the paintbox would forestall any further questions.

I headed first straight back to the meadow on the cliff edge, where I examined the ground. It was well trampled with the indentations of goat hooves, but there was no longer any sign of a child's footprints. Closer to the edge, I saw my own footprints, and a little farther off, those of the rope-soled espadrilles the woman had been wearing. But no others.

Cautiously, I approached the precipice and peered over. The ledge was below me, it hardly seemed so far away now, but my shoes were nowhere in sight. Blown off by wind, I assumed. As I stood there in the sunlight, the events of yesterday seemed unreal, a dream, and although I knew they were not, I was still unsure of exactly what I had seen. I told myself not to be ridiculous, but a part of me hoped for the impossible. I had to see the boy again.

From the meadow I headed back along the path, following a track that led down into a wide flat heath of coarse grass bordered by dunes. The regular boom and hiss of waves breaking on the shoreline sounded beyond. Making my way up the ridge, through grass thick with purple bindweed flowers, I reached the crest that sloped down to a long beach. The wind was stronger here, whipping fine particles of sand through the air.

Shorebirds took flight at my appearance, flashing silver above the waves that crashed down on the sand in spumes of white foam, bringing a memory of a summer on the beach at Montmartin-sur-Mer. There, hundreds of sandpipers had flocked on the coast that year, darting along the shoreline on their dainty legs, their high piping calls mingling with the voices of Claudine and Piero as they ran after the birds, which took to the air in great curved arabesques.

Piero was five that summer and it was the first time the three of us had the house to ourselves for the whole holiday. Claudine's mother had passed away the year before. I'd never met her father, who died when she was a teenager. In my mind's eye I pictured the beach that year, a summer of perfect sun. How brown Claudine had become. And she'd let Piero's hair grow, so that his black curls and his tanned skin had given him the appearance of a little faun. Like that boy I'd seen.

Now, just as I was about to slide down the slope to the beach, I stopped. I heard a voice calling. But when I looked up and down the sand, in both directions, there was no one. I was alone. It must have been the wind, or the sandpipers. I walked on.

The village appeared as I rounded one of the curves in the shoreline: a handful of cottages facing the harbour, which was tiny, just two stone piers like the arms of a crab sheltering a narrow entrance. A couple of boats were anchored in the harbour with ropes attached to the piers. Heaps of netting and lobster pots lined the quay and the fecund smells of the seaweed and mud were rich in my nostrils as I followed a lane up from the shore between the houses. An unseen dog barked nearby. I recalled the woman I'd met near the cliff yesterday. Did she live here?

The village seemed to be deserted, most of the cottages fastened shut. Disappointed, I continued along the path, which cut inland now. Soon I was beneath the dappled shade of widely spaced oaks. In a hollow where the ground underfoot was thick with brown acorns, I came upon the black pellets of goat droppings. At the same instant, I heard a flat clinking, like the rattle of pebbles in a tin can, and in a gully to my left, among the rocks and grass, I saw the goats. I positioned myself next to the trunk of an oak, keeping very still, my eyes scanning the surrounding area.

Was the boy with them?

The goats hadn't noticed me. They cropped at the grass and shrubs, clambering among the rocks that edged the gully, the bells at their throats clanking. There was no sign of the big ram that had confronted me on the cliff. Just then, from beyond the trees, three long low notes resonated over the landscape—the tolling of a church bell. The goats lifted their heads to stare across the gully at me, as if the sound were of my making.

I waited, half expecting some answering sound. The bells pealed again, three deep notes that echoed into one another. As the sounds died away, the goats scampered out of sight. Once again, I was disappointed. I had expected something. But what? After waiting a couple of minutes longer, I walked on, soon coming to the sea again.

Below me, just off shore, stood a small stone church, unusually situated on its own little islet of rock, separated from the main island by about fifty metres of sand. The building wasn't really substantial enough to be called a church—chapel was more appropriate—but it was sturdily built of the local granite, with a black slate roof. In the tower, silhouetted against the sea and sky, sunlight gleamed on the bronze of the bell that I had heard minutes earlier.

I made my way down to the beach and across the damp, spongy sand to the islet of rock. The chapel doors were substantial slabs of oak with black iron hinges and a knocker in the shape of a braid of rope. One door was partially open.

I hesitated. A tremor shivered through me. Ever since that day in Cyprus, at the chapel of Agios Lazaros, I'd avoided every sort of religious building. I associated them with darkness, with death. Was that other chapel still standing? Had it been repaired, or was it just a bombed-out ruin? As for who was responsible—Turks, or Greeks, or both—that had never been established. Another small war in another small place.

The shepherds who had seen the explosion that day and pulled me unconscious from the rubble had turned me over to the United Nations Peacekeeping force. After a few days in hospital, where my shock at what had happened was worse than any injuries, the French consulate arranged for my return to Paris. Our return, I should say. Claudine and Piero's bodies were on the same flight, enclosed in their coffins in the cargo hold.

My desire for justice, for revenge, had burned out in the long months afterwards, until only despair remained. In the end, I was responsible. No one else.

I looked back across to the main island, which was so silent and still that it might as well have been completely uninhabited. But if I did not go forward, where else was there to go?

Fighting off the memories, I grasped the handle and pushed open the door. I was surprised to find not darkness but light, not emptiness but life. About a dozen or so people were gathered in the pews in front of Père Caron, who stood before a simple altar with his hands raised in a blessing.

Hearing the door, most of the congregation turned to observe me. With an embarrassed nod I slipped into the nearest seat as the priest inclined his head in a greeting and resumed the service. Was it Sunday? I had long ago stopped keeping track of the days, but I must have wandered into a Mass.

The interior of the chapel was very plain, just a few rows of wooden benches and an altar covered with a white embroidered cloth. A wooden model of a schooner, about six feet long, hung from the ceiling against the wall where a crucifix would normally be. I guessed that this was a mariner's chapel, for I'd seen similar wooden boats in country churches along the Normandy coast.

While the priest continued with the service, my eyes searched among the people seated in front of me. The only children were two youths in their teens and a small girl of about two sucking her thumb. But no boy.

I'd been sitting there for only a few minutes when the door behind me creaked and a thin shaft of daylight fell across the pew where I sat. I looked back over my shoulder. A figure was framed in the doorway. The woman from the cliff. She slipped into a seat across the aisle. The light from a high window fell on her face but her eyes were dark as ink as she looked at me. It was one of those looks that can sometimes pass between two strangers, on a street or bus, of recognition, not in the sense of knowing each other, but of possibility. I remembered her leaning over me on the path, like an apparition. I stared at her, thinking how striking she was. She wore a thin transparent scarf over her hair, tied under her chin, and she had pulled it forward a bit over one cheek. As she turned to face forward, I remembered the bruise.

At the altar, Père Caron made a final benediction and exited through a low doorway into the vestry. Mumbles of *Amen* sounded from the congregation and the shuffle of people rising to their feet signalled that the service was over. A murmur of conversation started up. Somebody opened the doors wide to admit daylight and the flood of brightness dazzled my eyes.

I remained in my seat, subject to the curious glances of the congregation as they filed out. Victor and Linda from the hotel passed and nodded with smiles. I dropped my eyes, avoiding curious glances. What did they know about me? Père Caron had probably guessed what had happened on the cliff, but I doubt he would have gossiped. On the other hand I knew nothing about him, and it was a small island after all. My presence had undoubtedly been noted and remarked upon.

When I looked around moments later, I was alone in the church. I got up from the pew and walked towards the doorway. For the first time I noticed the painting hanging over the entrance. Curious, I drew nearer and studied it. Although the surface was not in good condition and obviously needed a cleaning, I could make out the subject.

The scene showed two figures dressed in classical clothes of an indeterminate period, moving across a landscape. A woman walked first, with a lyre in one hand, the other reaching back to the man behind, her fingers almost touching his outstretched hand. Behind him, an obscure dark patch could be a thicket of thorn bushes, or the entrance to a cave, or just a patch of the painting that had weathered badly.

What caught my attention was a building in the background—this very chapel in which I now stood. I realized that the landscape in the picture was that of the island itself. The work was very accomplished; the style reminded me vaguely of Poussin, but mistier, more atmospheric.

"It's by Davide Asmodeus." Père Caron was coming down the nave, dressed again as I had first seen him, in a navy blue jacket, white shirt and his floppy beret. He was holding his tobacco and rolling papers in his hand.

"Asmodeus. Really?" I stepped closer still to study it.

The priest pointed at a blurry signature on the bottom right. "You are familiar with his work?"

"I've seen the famous one in the Louvre, *The Rites of Spring*. He died young, I understand. He didn't leave many paintings behind." I moved back to get a better view. "How did this one come to be here?"

"Asmodeus was exiled from France by Louis Napoleon in

1858 for so-called 'seditious activities' and was on his way to Spain by sea. A storm brought the ship here to La Mouche. He stayed for three months, painting. Some say he fell in love with the island landscape, others that it was a woman he loved here. Whatever the truth, the painting remains."

"It's very compelling. Could it actually be an original Asmodeus?"

"A scholar was here before the war to examine the painting and he made no conclusion, although he was inclined to doubt the authenticity of the signature. I like to think it is genuine."

"And the subject?"

"The expert said it should be titled 'Love and the Pilgrim.' Something about the figures being similar to another painting on that subject."

"It's a pity about the bloom," I said, pointing to where the varnish had discoloured. "And that bit on the man's face where the pigment has flaked off from the gesso. The sea air, I suppose. The church isn't heated, is it? That would explain the damage. Humidity must have got in with the varnish. And maybe there wasn't enough binder in that section around the face. The artist probably never imagined this painting hanging in an unheated building so close to the ocean."

"Of course, you know about these things, you're a painter yourself." He pointed to the paintbox under my arm.

"Not really. Not any more."

"Oh. Aren't you here to paint?"

"I'm not . . . feeling inspired at the moment."

The priest was silent as he rolled himself a cigarette. "How are you today?" he asked when he'd flared a match to the tobacco and inhaled.

"Much better, thank you. I'm afraid I haven't been able to find my shoes."

"No problem. Keep those." He studied me while he drew on his cigarette. "When we first met, you asked some questions about a boy."

"I was confused," I answered quickly. "Forget about my questions."

He seemed to be about to ask more, then he gave a small shrug and said, "And the damage, is it irreversible?"

I looked at him sharply.

"To the painting."

"No, probably not. But the decay will continue. It really ought to be restored."

"Why don't you do it?"

"Me?"

"You apparently know what the problem is, and the solution."

I smiled and shook my head. "You need a professional restorer."

"I don't think the bishop will agree to that. This is a very poor parish."

I tilted my head and squinted at the painting.

"You could try," the priest said.

Something in his tone brought back a memory.

Brother Adams, at the Guild. I used to draw cartoons as a kid, usually obscene ones, which was a way to be popular with the other boys. One day I was called in to Brother Adams's office. On his desk lay one of my drawings, this one of Brother Adams himself. I'd drawn him as a baboon, exaggerating his brush-cut and large ears. Adams watched me as I looked at the drawing. He picked up a thin bamboo cane from the sill and tapped it in his palm. Brother Rod. I was well acquainted with Brother Rod, having felt his painful bite on my backside many times. I resigned myself to getting a beating. But Adams surprised me.

He told me to pick up the sketch. Underneath was a book. *Understanding Drawing* by Geoffrey Smedley. Adams told me that he was going to take a chance on me, that he was going to put his faith and his hope in me. The talent for drawing was a powerful force, he said, a gift that should not be squandered in amusing buffoons. That book became a bible to me. I still had it. But I no longer deserved Brother Adams's faith and hope.

It was true what I'd said about not being inspired. How could I be? I hadn't lifted a brush since that day in Cyprus. The door to my studio in Paris had remained shut for a long time. I looked up at the painting on the chapel wall and shook my head. "No."

"Do you have somewhere else to be, other things to do at the moment?" the priest asked.

I shrugged. He was right, but that didn't mean I wanted to paint.

"It would mean a lot to the people here, to have that painting restored, to have something beautiful in the church. Who knows, it might even bring in a few tourists if word got around that we had an original Asmodeus."

The way he looked at me, with a meaning behind his words, made me realize that he was trying to offer me something.

"I don't have the materials for any restoration."

"They can be ordered and sent over from the mainland."

"It could be expensive."

"Then I will take up a collection from the congregation. They are poor but they would give if it was for the painting."

"You have a solution to my every objection, Père. I'll think about it. I don't promise anything."

"Thank you." He patted me on the arm. "If you're going to be spending any time over here I should warn you about the tides. As you see, our *chapelle* is not actually part of the island. At low tide, as it is now, you can come and go as freely as you like across the sand. But at high tide the chapel is cut off. You can cross by boat, or even swim, although the current is very strong and I would not advise it."

"There are worse things than being stuck here, I suppose," I said. "One could at least work in peace."

"I will make sure to give you an almanac listing the tides and help you obtain whatever materials you need."

I nodded, but it wasn't the painting I was considering. I was thinking again of the boy.

CHAPTER 8

BALANCED ON A SCAFFOLD ASSEMBLED FROM A LONG board supported between two tables, I was within easy reach of the painting on the chapel wall. Next to me, an empty Mère Poulard cookie tin held a quarter *boule* of white bread, a Thermos of tap water, a bar of soap, and a handful of clean white rags. These had all been provided by Victor at the Hôtel des Îles. My paintbox, or rather Piero's, containing brushes, a handful of colours and a small jar of turpentine, was arranged beside the tin.

I had no intention of agreeing to the restoration, but something had drawn me back here. A couple of days had passed since I wandered in on the Mass and despite my explorations of the island, I had not seen the boy again. If he existed. Perhaps he had been part of my delirium that day.

I had spent a couple of hours examining Asmodeus's "Love and the Pilgrim," even lifting it off the wall and carrying it out into the sunlight. While the painting could never be restored to its original state, or certainly not by me, I could see it would not be difficult to at least clean off some of the grime and do a bit of retouching. This wouldn't bring back the former brilliance of the colours, but it would make the features of the scene more visible.

Back inside, I rubbed my hand lightly across the face of the painting, as if it were a misted window that I could wipe clear and peer through. The feel of the small ridges and bumps of dried paint under my fingertips, the sensation of touch, unexpectedly transported me back to the past, to another painting, where I had once done the same thing.

When I was a boy at the Guild, we were sometimes taken on visits into the city. I never really liked being outside the walls of the Guild. If people looked at us in our blazers and grey flannel trousers and asked what school we came from and we had to say the Guild Home for Boys, I always felt ashamed at the way they looked at us. As if there were something wrong with us.

One day I was part of a small group that Brother Adams took to the Vancouver Art Gallery. And there I saw a picture that changed everything.

It was a painting of a riverbank, with some trees on the left and a man in a rowboat just off shore. A woman stood under the trees. The painting was all silvery blue and hazy grey tones, misty and mysterious like an autumn evening, with just a thin sliver of pink light showing on the horizon. Everything was very still. I felt a strange longing, like homesickness, for a place like this one. It was like that feeling that comes in the evening in October, when the lights go on in windows and there is the sound of voices in the dusk and the scent of burning leaves in the air and you're standing somewhere all alone, there but not there, like one of the shadows. And you're strangely happy.

I reached out a hand and touched the painting.

And I was there, under the slender pale birch trees on the shore. The slight coolness from the river mist caressed my skin and I could smell the damp earthy forest scents. Who was the woman standing under the trees? I wondered. Was the man in the boat leaving or arriving? Everything was so real. At the same time, it was just a picture. I could see the brush marks, the smears and ridges of paint, and in the right hand corner the name of the painter scrawled in an untidy hand, Corot.

A realization hit me. Someone had made this. Someone took a brush and dipped it in paint and touched it to the canvas, making these marks and shapes and colours. And he made the world in the picture appear. It was a kind of magic. A hand had made this. A hand like any other, even mine. I looked down at my own fingers, almost expecting to see a trace of paint on my knuckle.

Afterwards, I used to dream about that place at night as I lay in the darkened dormitory, listening to the snufflings and whimpers and snores of the other boys. That place existed, and I wanted to find a way there. Could I learn the magic? I wondered. I was determined to become a painter. Even though I didn't know exactly how a painter lived, or how to do it, I knew one thing. I wanted to be someone who creates his own worlds.

THE SOUND OF CURLEWS on the sand outside the chapel brought me back to the present, to this island, this shore. I set to work.

Breaking off a piece of the soft interior of the loaf, I rolled it into a little ball and rubbed at a section of the painting near the bottom right hand corner. The bread came away black with grime. I discarded the soiled part and repeated the process until the square inch of canvas I was working on showed up as lighter and brighter than the surrounding area.

Next I tipped water into the cup of the Thermos and wet a corner of linen rag, which I lathered on the bar of soap. Carefully I rubbed at the painting, cleaning away years of accumulated ocean salt and soot from candles and lamps. What had been an area of blackish green now gradually became visible as a light olive foliage with a yellowish tint.

This task demanded absolute concentration—the last thing I wanted was to ruin the picture—but at the same time it stilled my thoughts. How long had it been since I was able to forget, unless my mind was numbed by alcohol?

The biscuit tin was propped open, the inner lid reflecting the daylight from the open door behind me, and I shifted it slightly so that the glare wouldn't be in my eyes. I leaned closer to the painting, carefully working away the grime. The next step in the process was to dip a soft sable brush into the turpentine. With light, feathery motions, I stroked the painting, wiping the brush frequently on a rag. I wanted to soften and dislodge the yellowed varnish and reveal the true colour of the pigments underneath.

The danger in any restoration was always the possibility of disturbing the original paint layer itself and removing it along with the dirt. Such an error would be irrevocable. Without any real knowledge of restoration, I was relying instead on my own understanding of the science of painting.

I worked on, feeling a sense of kinship with Asmodeus, the original painter, as my brush followed his dabs and strokes.

The smell of oil paint and the piney turpentine, pungent and familiar, prompted a faint stirring of the old excitement that painting used to bring. It was like rediscovering the taste of a long unavailable fruit. I wasn't exactly painting, but at the same time I was creating an image, or at least revealing one.

The tide was out and the chapel was silent—I was astonished at how silent. My movements—of the brush tapping against the glass jar of turpentine, the creak of the board I was sitting on, or the rattle of something in my paintbox when I reached for it—sounded amplified. From outside came the high piping sounds of the curlews I'd seen on the sand earlier.

Just as I was rubbing cautiously at what was slowly becoming a patch of bright green, I became aware that the birds had fallen silent. In the reflected image of the room behind me, visible in the lid of the biscuit tin, a stealthy flicker of movement caught my attention as a shape darkened the doorway. A different kind of picture showed on the bright metal, like a mirror, but clouded as if seen through a mist. Framed in the light was a human figure. A boy.

My heart started racing, but I pretended to carry on working, dabbing at the painting, reaching for the bread and rolling a pellet, all the while watching the reflected image and trying to contain my excitement. More than anything, I wanted to turn around. But I was afraid—not that the figure might disappear, but of what I might see.

At last, slowly, I turned my head and looked back over my shoulder. I saw only a silhouette because of the bright sunshine around the child. Then, as my eyes adjusted, another pair of eyes met mine, round and serious and unblinking.

"Hello?" I whispered.

At the sound of my voice, the boy flinched and sprang backwards through the doorway like a shadow and was gone. The door banged shut, and the interior of the chapel was plunged into darkness.

By the time I had climbed down from the scaffold and hurried outside there was nobody in sight. I was about to re-enter the chapel, when, on the steps just in front of the doors I saw an extraordinary thing—two things, rather—my shoes, the ones I'd lost on the cliff. I picked them up.

Here was proof of the boy in the mist. He had been there. He'd seen me. Strange, though, that he had not gone for help when I fell. Maybe he'd been frightened and had run away. But at some point he obviously went back and climbed down to the ledge and retrieved my shoes. It wouldn't have been difficult for someone young and agile. But whatever his reasons, I now knew that he was as real as the shoes in my hand.

I unlaced the boots the priest had lent me and slipped my feet into my own shoes. They had been wiped clean, I saw. I stood up and turned once more to scan the landscape. Was a pair of eyes watching me from the trees?

Lifting a hand, I waved a thank-you.

CHAPTER 9

"Well?"

"It can be done."

"And you will do it?" Père Caron asked.

I shrugged. "I don't think I have the skills. Not for a proper restoration."

"But you said it could be cleaned. You showed me."

"That much, yes."

"You obviously have the skills for that."

"It's a long job. And I don't know if I'm staying."

"No?" He studied me for a minute. "Do you have somewhere else to be?"

It was the second time he'd asked me that, and I had the impression he knew the answer already. I shrugged again.

We were sitting in the last light of the day at a table in the garden of the hotel with a bottle of Ricard pastis between us, our glasses filled with the pale milky yellow liquid. The air carried the licorice aroma of the anise liqueur. On the grass next to the wrought-iron legs of my chair sat the brown paper bag I had brought down from my room.

Earlier, the priest had come by the chapel and I'd shown him the area I'd cleaned on the painting. "Remarkable," he'd said. "I would never have thought it was so bright underneath. All these years I've thought of it as a dark painting. And it's gotten darker gradually, without me even noticing. Life can be like that, *n'est-ce pas?*" He'd then invited me to join him for dinner later in the garden of the hotel.

The door to the kitchen swung open and Linda appeared with a tray. She set down a plate containing small black olives and slices of dried sausage. "Since you are drinking pastis I thought you should have it the way they do in the south, where I come from, with salty olives and dried sausage. This one is flavoured with thyme."

"Why don't you and Victor come and join us?" I said. "There aren't any other guests for you to look after, are there?"

"No. But we're cooking. Père Caron ordered the specialty of the house tonight. We'll sit down and eat with you later."

The priest smiled and rubbed his hands together. "*L'agneau pré-salé.* You've tasted it?"

"I don't think so."

Linda said, "*Pré-salé* lamb is fed on the salt marshes, where the grasses are often covered by the high tides. The marshes are on the other side of the island, near the lighthouse. You might have noticed them?"

I shook my head.

"You are in for a treat, young man," the priest said. "There is nothing better than our own island lamb."

As Linda left, her foot knocked over the paper bag next to my chair. "Sorry." She bent to set it upright before continuing to the kitchen.

I picked up the bag and handed it to Père Caron. "These are the boots you lent me. Thank you."

He leaned over and looked at my legs.

"I found my own shoes," I said.

"You found them?"

"Yes, on the cliff. I don't know how I could have missed them before."

There was a disbelieving expression on his face, and I was on the verge of telling him about the boy, but I decided not to.

He lit one of his Caporal cigarettes and dropped the extinguished match on the lawn, lifting his face to the last rays of the sun. Just beyond him a honeysuckle bush was lush with blooms on the verge of opening, the closed flowers like thin red flames in the fading light.

Without looking at me, he said, "I think you should tell me why you are here, Leo."

"I told you, to look at the landscape. To paint it."

"Yet you said to me that you are not really a painter. 'Not any more' were your words."

"I'm not a desperado, Père, if that's what you're thinking. The police aren't after me. Nobody is, for that matter."

Something about his silent scrutiny made me nervous and I blurted out, "Let's just say I am running from the past."

"And your 'accident' on the cliff?" He accented the word, but without irony.

I put an olive in my mouth and chewed it before dropping the pit into the saucer. I took a sip of pastis. "It was misty. I lost my footing."

"Those things you said earlier," the priest continued, "the questions you asked, about the dead communicating with us. What was behind them?"

"I would rather not talk about my personal life."

"Of course, I understand. As you wish." He smiled kindly. "But if you ever want to talk, I am here."

Emptying his glass, he peered towards the kitchen. "Where has our dinner gotten to? Let me go and see if they have opened the wine." He stood up and brushed cigarette ashes from his trousers. He was wearing his habitual blue linen jacket but had put on a clean white shirt for the occasion. His floppy beret sat on the table.

I was left alone in the gathering dusk. The moon had come up behind the trees, almost full, white and gleaming. Of course I could talk to Père Caron, I knew that, sensing his kindness and genuine desire to help, and perhaps I should confide in him, or at least tell him about Piero and Claudine. On the other hand, better not to open up old wounds. As for the boy, well, I would find him myself.

A glow of light threw itself across the grass as Linda appeared bearing two candelabra, followed by Père Caron cradling a wine bottle.

"A few more minutes," Linda said. "I'm just waiting for the haricots to finish cooking. Victor is carving the lamb now."

The priest resumed his seat and poured wine into our glasses. As I reached for mine, he held up a halting finger. "Not just yet. Give it five minutes of the night air." Pushing the bread basket across the table he said, "Eat a piece of this and clear your palate of the anise taste."

I waited. Finally, he took a swallow of his wine and leaned back with his eyes closed, pursing his lips. When he opened his eyes he said, "Délicieux. Truly. What do you think?"

I tasted from my glass. The scent of black currant wafted up to my nostrils. I was no wine connoisseur, but after all these years in France I knew a very good wine when I tasted it.

I thought of Serge Bruneau, my friend, who ran the gallery where I used to show my paintings. He often used to take me out for lunches to restaurants he'd discovered, and he always had his little rituals with wine. He would have enjoyed an evening like this. I missed him suddenly. But if I thought of Serge then I thought of my old life in Paris, and I didn't want to remember it, I didn't want to know it continued to exist. Better to be here on this island, where I knew no one and nobody knew me.

"I have a proposal for you, Leo. If you agree to clean the painting, I will provide a cottage for you, rent free, over in LeBec, and any materials you need. You can take your meals here at the hotel if you don't cook. It won't cost you anything."

"I have money. More than I need." Serge had been selling my work steadily over the past couple of years, and without Claudine and Piero there was nothing to spend the money on.

"Well then?"

"Why is it so important to you that the painting is cleaned, Père?"

"Perhaps it is more important for you, Leo." He looked down to the darkening harbour, holding his wineglass to his nose, swirling the liquid back and forth.

I thought about this statement as I watched the white moon slowly rising over the sea. Below it on the calm dark water a long carpet of shimmering reflection stretched towards me. The night was warm, the air was pleasant. What reason did I have to leave this place?

"All right," I said. "I'll do it."

"You'll stay on, here on the island, until it is finished?"

I shrugged. "I have nowhere else to be."

"*Très bien.* Very good. I am glad, for both of us." He leaned across the table and squeezed my arm. "I'll make the arrangements first thing in the morning. And I have just the cottage in mind. Sheltered from the wind but with a view of the sea. Perfect for a painter."

I was going to ask him about the woman I'd seen in the chapel, if he knew who she was. But I'd already made him suspicious with my questions, and anyway, just then the kitchen door opened and Victor and Linda emerged bearing platters of food.

"*Voilà!*" said the priest. "Now to the pleasure of food and wine and good company."

CHAPTER 10

AT EIGHT O'CLOCK IN THE MORNING, AFTER A
breakfast of goat's milk yogourt, and fresh crusty bread, along
with the usual cup of strong café au lait, I was walking along the
path from the hotel with an oversized brass key in my pocket,
on my way to the village of LeBec. I intended to take a look at
the cottage that Père Caron had offered me.

He had described it as having two large rooms, suitable for
a studio, and although I didn't plan on doing any painting, just
the thought of having a place of my own, a new place without
memories, appealed to me. I wanted routines, habits, a job to
go to—like cleaning the painting in the chapel—and a place to
which I could come home at the end of the day. Inspecting the
cottage was really just a formality. I already knew I would take
it, whatever its condition.

I hadn't walked for very long before I came upon a lane
marked LE CHEMIN DES SIRÈNES. Earlier, before leaving
the hotel, I'd made a quick copy of the island map, and I consulted it now, then followed the lane. This took me through a

wooded area that soon opened onto a view of a small house. The windows on the upper floors were closed with blue wooden shutters but the lower shutters had been fastened back. A blue clematis grew up the facade and hydrangeas thick with pink flowers clustered beneath the windows. A low stone wall with an iron gate enclosed the front garden. On the gate was a sign, LA MAISON DU PARADIS. It was a pretty place, and romantic, situated with the sea behind it and the sunlight on its walls.

A figure moved through the interior of the house; it was only a glimpse, a shape, but something about that shape made me think of the woman I had seen in the chapel. I hadn't mentioned her to anyone, nor did I know if she was still on the island. Did she live here alone? And what about that bruised eye? I was curious. More than curious, but I didn't want to be seen snooping, so I cut back inland.

I climbed a low hill on the slopes of which brown cows grazed, their flanks glowing in the yellow morning light. On the other side of the hill the sea was visible across the fields, pale cerulean blue under a sky thick with puffy banks of cumulus clouds. Once I had descended the hill and crossed a narrow stone bridge below which sheep paused in their cropping of the grass to watch me pass, I arrived at the dunes. I clambered up the shifting sands and slid down to the beach on the other side.

The sun had been up for a couple of hours already but it still sat low in the sky, and my shadow stretched down to the pale morning blue of the sea where the waves were lapping on the sand. The village was not yet in sight, but far down the beach I could make out a stationary white shape, perhaps a small boat beached on the shore. The usual flocks of seabirds were not around today and I was quite alone.

As I walked, my attention was caught by the oyster shells littering the sand, bright and bleached white in the raking morning light, their shapes like abstract sculptures. When I was an art student I'd been fascinated for a period by the challenges of painting all-white objects and I'd done countless still-lifes of jugs and cups and white flowers, even snow, learning to see colour where others saw only its absence. Looking at the shells now I could make out violets and greens in the shaded sides and pinks and yellows in the illuminated parts. For a painter, the task was always to convince the viewers it was a white object, even though the only touches of pure white pigment were the highlights.

When we used to go to Montmartin in the summers, Piero always collected shells, often deciding to look for only one type at a time, generally something hard to find like razor clams or the very small pink ones that resemble a baby's fingernails. He'd surprised me once, back in Paris, by using some white modelling clay to make a copy of an oyster shell, which I'd mistaken for the genuine article. What had become of that little sculpture? He'd been so proud of it.

I picked up a couple of the shells and put them in my pocket. By now I was closer to what I'd thought was a white rowboat on the shoreline, but it struck me that the shape was wrong, and it was too small to be a boat. A person, I thought. But, coming closer, I could see it was a large dog, a Labrador breed, its colour somewhere between the beige of the sand and the white of the oyster shells. It was standing immobile, staring straight ahead.

I veered away up the beach, keeping a cautious eye on the dog until I was on the other side of it. I'm not afraid of dogs, but a past experience had made me wary of them.

As a boy of ten, I'd once been riding down a quiet street lined with houses behind leafy gardens—I can't recollect the circumstances or who the bike had belonged to, maybe it was one of those unsuccessful occasions when the Guild had tried to place me in a foster home—when a large Doberman had come streaking out from an open gate and charged at me. There had been no time to react or register anything other than the bared teeth and the low rumbling growl in the dog's throat as it leaped up and fastened its jaws on my thigh, pulling me from the bike. Before I knew it the bike was skidding across the sidewalk, I was on my back and the dog was standing over me. I could smell its foul breath and in its eyes I saw a kind of insane rage that terrified me.

In the next instant a man was there, swinging a garden rake down across the dog's back. With a howl the dog raced off down the street. I was basically unhurt, but so shaken that I couldn't speak. The man took me into the house and gave me a glass of milk and calmed me down. I don't remember anything else from that day. Just the dog and the man and the glass of milk.

Now I stopped some distance away and looked back at the dog, intrigued by its behaviour. It hadn't even looked at me. The waves were washing around its legs yet it seemed planted in the sand, not even lifting its chin when a crest of foam surged up around its chest, all its attention focused out to sea.

I followed the direction of the dog's fixed stare, but saw nothing, no bird nor boat nor swimmer, not even a piece of driftwood. Just the ocean and the sky and clouds. What had caught the dog's attention? I clapped my hands together and whistled. The dog ignored me. Its peculiar intensity and still-ness was unsettling, eerie.

It barked, once, like a shout of recognition. And there, from behind a break in the clouds, the moon was suddenly visible in the blueness of the sky, almost full, low and white and crisp as the bleached oyster shells on the beach. The dog and the moon brought back a memory, of a Corot painting in the Musée Dubourg. *La Bête* it was called. A white bull standing on a riverbank in the morning light with its head raised to the dawning day. I remembered how the painting had touched me, as if it showed some spark of self-consciousness in the animal, some yearning after the mystery that is in all things.

The day I'd first seen that painting was also the day I met Claudine. Ironically, it was also two days before I was scheduled to leave Paris.

Paris had been a failure, I'd realized by then. I had no gallery, no friends—even my neighbour from the Hôtel Mistral had gone on to better things—no prospects, and if I was honest with myself, the paintings I was doing were not very good. So I'd bought my ticket back to New York on the SS *Volendam*. From there I would take a train across the country to Vancouver and try to start over. Maybe look for a real job.

The visit to see the Corot was a farewell of sorts. After all, it was through his paintings that I'd come to Paris in the first place. A light drizzle had filled the September air as I made my way from La Muette station. Under the leafy chestnuts of Jardin du Ranelagh the drizzle became rain, heavy drops rattling the leaves above me, penetrating my thin jacket and shirt as I ran the last block to the museum entrance.

When I located the little Corot painting, two young women were standing directly in front of it, engaged in conversation and evidently not in any hurry to move on. Despite the wet shoes pinching my feet and a trickle of rainwater sliding down the back of my neck, I was conscious of the beauty of one of the women. When she turned to her friend, I glimpsed large grey eyes and a sprinkle of freckles across the bridge of her nose. Her wheat-coloured hair was pulled back from her oval face into a ponytail. She looked very French—the expressive pouts of her mouth, the way her hands moved in the air as she talked.

At last they became aware of my presence, and moved off. At the doorway the woman with the ponytail looked back at me, with a frank, assessing interest and a hint of flirtation in her eyes. A mischievous smile flitted across her lips.

I had looked at the painting for a long time, lost in that particular mood that Corot's pictures always evoked, as if I had found a long-lost place. But you could not live inside a painting, no matter how much more preferable than real life it seemed. And art was not life. I'd learned that much in Paris.

I went down to the cafeteria and sat near the window, waiting for the rain to stop, already feeling a nostalgia for Paris, as if it were in the past already.

When I had finished my coffee and was about to leave, I noticed at a table nearby the woman who had been in the Corot room. She was sitting with her chin on her hand, gazing out through the rain-streaked window to the soft blur of the street outside. I reached into my pocket for my sketchbook and pencil and began to draw rapidly. The profile and the ponytail were easy, but I struggled to get the mouth right, that expressive pout of the lips.

The next time I glanced up, she had turned in her seat and was looking directly at me. Our eyes met briefly before I looked down, embarrassed to be caught staring. Abruptly, she rose and walked straight over to my table. I quickly covered the sketch with my hand.

"Since you have been sketching me for the last twenty minutes," she said, "I think it is only fair that I at least get to see the drawing."

Caught unawares, I could do nothing but remove my hand from the page. She leaned over and studied the drawing, her ponytail brushing across my cheek.

"Not bad," she said, tracing a fingernail over the drawing. "But you flatter me. It's a little idealized. You idealize women, perhaps?" She said it as a challenge, with an amused smile.

I found myself tongue-tied and could only shrug. She closed the sketchbook and slid it back across the table and turned as if to leave. Somehow I managed to gather my wits about me and I asked her to sit down. She did.

Her name was Claudine Jourdan. I ended up not leaving Paris. I married her instead.

Now, remembering that day also brought back a reminder of everything that I had lost. The hollowness was still inside my heart. I turned away, leaving the dog and the sea and the moon to themselves.

LeBec was unchanged since my visit the other day, a couple of boats in the tiny harbour, a handful of cottages in a row opposite, the same heaps of netting and lobster pots on the quay, but instead of being deserted this time, there were two men in denim overalls bent over an engine on blocks, a little cloud of smoke drifting above their heads from the cigarettes both of them had clamped in the corners of their mouths.

They looked up at my approach and I waved as I walked down the quay.

"Bonjour, I'm looking for the cottage called La Minerve."

"You must be the painter," the older one said—they appeared to be brothers.

"Yes. Leo Millar." I extended a hand to each and they introduced themselves as Benjamin and Simon Grente.

"Père Caron told us you'd be coming. The cottage is the last one along the lane." Simon pointed out the direction.

I'd been told that all the cottages were named after Corsair ships, and I passed La Belle Poule, La Lutine, La Junon, La Jolie Brise, before reaching La Minerve, each one with its name painted on a tile embedded in the stone next to the front doors. The big key Père Caron had given me slipped neatly into the lock. The door opened into a spacious square room. By the light from the doorway I located the windows and unlatched the wooden shutters, flooding the room with sunlight.

I had expected to find something rather ramshackle, but the room was clean and tidy. A much-scrubbed wooden table with four chairs stood in the centre, an armoire in the corner, a chest of drawers beneath the window and a long wooden bench with lumpy cushions in front of a large fireplace. A sink and simple stove were situated against the far wall.

A narrow staircase led up to a bedroom: bare wooden floors, another armoire and a big wooden bed with a nightstand. I opened the windows and shutters, which gave a view onto the sea. Leaving the windows open, for the room was a little musty and would benefit from an airing, I went back downstairs and opened a second door, which led to a long walled garden. I guessed that the small stone hut at the far end was the privy. There were pink and red roses climbing one of the walls and a row of espaliered apple trees, much neglected, against the other.

A big leafy fig tree dominated the end of the garden and for a moment the sight of it made me sad. It was a vivid reminder of rue du Figuier. After Claudine and I got married we moved to an apartment on the top floor of a building between the Seine and rue de Rivoli. An old fig tree stood in the courtyard below our windows, a remnant of the orchard that had grown there when the Marais was just a village. I decided to take the presence of this tree at La Minerve as a good omen, confirming my decision to move into the cottage.

Back in the main room I stood for a moment, savouring the atmosphere. The cottage felt sturdy, safe, welcoming. A refuge.

"Will it do?" Simon was at the door. "Père Caron says you will be using it as your painting studio."

"It's perfect," I answered.

"It's been empty for a couple of years. My wife gives it a cleaning in the spring. Dust and cobwebs and such."

"She did a very good job. I can probably move in tomorrow."

"There are dishes in the cupboards and my wife can let you have some bedding. You'll need a gas cylinder for the stove. You get your water from the well. It's clean, I checked. No electricity out here so we rely on oil lamps and candles." He walked over to the fireplace and crouched down, twisting his head to peer up the chimney. "The crows like to nest up there sometimes but it looks like they didn't bother this year. I'll arrange for a load of firewood. The mists can be cold if the wind comes up, even in summer."

"Thank you."

"If you like, I can have my boat at the harbour on the other side tomorrow afternoon and bring you over with your stuff. There is a tractor at Le Port, but it is much faster by boat."

"That would be great. I appreciate the offer. I'll pay you for your time, of course, and for the wood."

"Not to worry. It will be good to have someone living here again. Too many have left the village and gone over to the mainland to work. Maybe you will have time to make a little painting for us one day. My Maria would like that."

"It's a deal." I shook Simon's hand before he left, pleased at the welcome I'd received.

I turned and surveyed the room again. For most of my life home had been the dormitory at the Guild—my bed, the cupboard where I hung my clothes, the little bedside locker for my few belongings. After the Guild, I'd had a scholarship to art school and I'd lived in a rooming house on Haro Street in Vancouver, then I'd moved into a studio in one of the old buildings on Powell Street in Japantown. There'd been a string of studios over the years, in Vancouver, then New York and then in Paris. Rooms for work, for painting in, with a bed in a corner behind a curtain, second- or third-hand furniture, a hotplate for cooking, usually a bathroom down the hall. I hadn't minded. I was a painter and that was how artists lived. Until I met Claudine.

In the beginning, after we were married and started living on rue du Figuier, it had taken me quite some time to settle in, to be comfortable in any of the rooms except the studio. I'd never had a dining room, or sitting room, much less a proper bedroom. We owned the apartment, bought with an inheritance from Claudine's father, but it still took a couple of years for me to get rid of the feeling of impermanence. I think it was only after Piero was born that I allowed myself to believe that I had a home and a family, that finally I was at home.

And then how quickly it had all changed.

On an impulse, I reached into my jacket pocket for the bleached oyster shells I'd collected on the beach, and arranged them in the sunlight on the windowsill.

CHAPTER 11

RATHER THAN GO BACK TO THE HÔTEL DES ÎLES THE same way I had come, along the route des Matelots, I decided to follow the shoreline towards the headland marked on my map as Le Colombier—the dovecote—where I had seen the house called La Maison du Paradis.

The tide had risen higher while I was seeing to my new cottage and the waves now came right up to the dunes. The white dog was nowhere in sight, and the moon was high in the sky, looking much smaller and less impressive.

The track meandered left, away from the dunes and across a heath, where a flock of crows rose into the sky protesting my presence, black flutterings on blue. Just visible through a dense grove of pines on the far side of the heath was a rooftop, and I made my way in that direction. It was immediately quieter in the trees, away from the breeze and the sound of the waves. Underfoot lay a carpet of dried pine needles. The house I had glimpsed was no longer visible and there was no path here, but I guessed I was heading in the right direction.

I hadn't walked very far when I heard a peculiar sound, a quick squawk, like the choked-off call of a gull. I assumed it was some kind of bird. The sound came again, like a voice, but not a voice, and not a bird either. I stopped. The breeze sighed in the pines softly. Then the sounds came rapidly, from some sort of musical instrument, a clarinet maybe.

Yet these jumbled sounds could hardly be called music. Only once had I heard music remotely similar to this cacophony, and that was on Tenth Street in New York, at a party in a loft belonging to some musicians. They had played what they called "free jazz." Try as I might to be hip, I had heard only a noisy confusion of sounds. It was like looking at the abstract expressionism everybody was painting—I saw no meaning, just a tangle of colours and shapes. Since then, I'd been a few times with Claudine to musical recitals at churches in Paris— Mozart, Vivaldi, that kind of thing—but my tastes ran more to the Mississippi blues of Lightnin' Hopkins and Fred McDowell that I'd first heard in a coffeehouse in Vancouver.

I moved forward, almost tiptoeing, my steps cushioned by the pine needles. But when I stepped on a dried branch the crack of the snapping wood was as loud as a gunshot. The sounds stopped immediately. I remained motionless, holding my breath, peering into the shadows. All was silence.

The afternoon heat rose in waves from the ground at my feet, the resinous smell of the pines thick. I waited. Then the strange otherworldly sounds filled the grove again. Half a dozen goats came into view, foraging among the rocks or stretching their necks to nibble the leaves at the tips of branches. Just past them, a figure was perched on the rocks, holding a clarinet. The boy! He was barefoot and shirtless, wearing only a pair of tattered shorts. The afternoon light fell upon his dark curls and his bare browned shoulders and touched the clarinet so that it shone like gold.

He played on, unaware of my presence. It was a crude and strange music, but music nevertheless. He seemed to be learning as he played, inventing and repeating sequences, finding tones, mostly off-key, but hitting the right notes frequently. Then, for some reason, the goats all raised their heads at the same time and stared across the clearing. The boy stopped playing. He looked directly at me, calmly, confidently, but his expression was inscrutable. Then, with two quick leaps he sprang from the rocks to the floor of the clearing, still watching me.

"Wait," I called.

I went forward a few paces, raising my hand, reaching out. The boy moved farther away.

"Wait, please." I reached into my pocket and my fingers closed around Piero's silver whistle. I raised it to my mouth. I blew softly, pursing my lips, so that the ball inside the chamber barely revolved, and the sound that came was not the shrill metallic signal that Piero liked, but something like the cooing of a dove.

The boy looked at me with curiosity, his eyes moving from my face to the gleaming silver whistle. He took a couple of tentative steps towards me, and his features become more clearly visible. I stared into his face. He resembled Piero, the thick unruly hair, his manner of moving, something about the alert way he held his head. But the eyes that looked back at me were not those of my son.

Holding the whistle on the flat of my palm I extended my hand to the boy. "Here. Take it. Try it. You can have it."

Flecks of grass and pine needles were caught in his dark curls. On his neck there was a welt of lighter skin, a scar, encircling his throat like a necklace. Slowly he came closer and his hand stretched up, tentatively, hovering, reaching for the gleaming silver whistle on my palm.

"Take it," I whispered. His forefinger touched the metal surface.

As his hand opened to grasp the whistle, I reached out and clasped my fingers around his wrist. Without warning he bent his head and sank his teeth into my hand. A sharp nip, as quick as a fox. With a cry, I released him, and he sprang away, bounding towards the trees. The goats scattered and dashed after him.

For a long while I stood there, alone in the silence, in the emptiness, rubbing my fingertips back and forth along the skin of my wrist. Then I bent down and retrieved the whistle from the pine needles where it had fallen.

CHAPTER 12

I HAD NOTHING, I REALIZED, AS I STOOD OUTSIDE A
cluster of buildings near the harbour. On the nearest building, stone walls and slate roof like all the others on the island,
a sign with a painting of a loaf of bread hung over the door.
Below it was written ALIMENTATION GÉNÉRALE. This
was the local *épicerie*, to which I had been directed by Simon
Grente, who was down at the quay on his boat, the *Stella Tilda*,
ready to transport me back to LeBec. In my hand I had a list of
everything I would need to provision the cottage.

I opened the door and entered, to be greeted by a man
wearing a baker's jacket of rough cotton and trousers dusted
with flour.

"*Bonjour.* Monsieur Millar?"

"Yes. Hello." I assumed that everyone on the island must
know who I was by now.

The man smoothed his neat beard with one hand, streaking it with flour. "My name is Martin Levérrier," he said in a
friendly voice, glancing at the paper in my hand. "We sell a

bit of everything here, whatever you need." Gesturing at his floured jacket, he added, "And of course, as you see, fresh bread, croissants and *gâteaux.*"

The crowded interior of the shop was part hardware store, part grocery store and part everything else. On one wall fishing equipment of various purposes hung from floor to ceiling; there were oilcloth raincoats and rubber boots, shovels and pickaxes, newspapers and wine, oil lamps and canned tomatoes.

"I have to check the breads," Martin said. "Let me know when you are ready." He disappeared into the back.

I started to collect my provisions, piling them on the counter: Coffee, a chunk of Comté cheese, rice, sugar and salt, cooking oil, canned sardines, garlic. From a basket near the door I selected potatoes, carrots with the soil still clinging to them, thick leeks and some small yellow apples. The wine and spirits section was well stocked, and I was in the act of reaching for a bottle of cognac when I let my hand fall. Did I need it? Since arriving on the island I had not felt the same need to find oblivion every night. The last item I selected was a woven basket with sturdy handles.

Martin returned with a half dozen loaves in his arms just as I was pensively walking around the store, trying to think if there was anything I had forgotten. I reached for some cans of evaporated milk.

"You won't really need that. Ester Chauvin supplies us from her farm, just chickens and a few cows, but she provides many of the islanders with eggs and milk and butter. Her duck is very good." He went into the back and came back with a glass bottle of milk. "Stop off at her place anytime. It's called Manoir de Soulles; you can see it from the route des Matelots."

From the basket of fresh bread on the counter, I chose a thick crusty loaf while Martin began to total up my purchases on a scrap of paper. Looking up, pencil poised, he said, "Cooking gas?"

"I forgot that. And matches."

As I was paying him I said, "I passed a house earlier, on the other side, a pretty little place called La Maison du Paradis."

"Ah yes, that belongs to Madame DuPlessis."

"I think I might have met her the other day. Black hair, a few years older than me?"

"Non, Madame DuPlessis has not been here for some time. She is an older lady who lives in Paris."

"But the cottage is inhabited? I thought I saw someone there."

"Yes, another lady is staying there. A musician."

That explained the clarinet. "I saw her son too, a boy of about ten?"

He shook his head as he handed me my change. "Non, that lady is alone. She doesn't have any children with her."

Outside, Simon Grente was waiting with a handcart, smoking a cigarette. I loaded my bulging basket onto the cart and Martin lifted up the cylinder of gas.

"Bonne chance," he said and shook my hand. "Remember, the bread is fresh every morning."

THAT EVENING, I COOKED A MEAL of boiled potatoes, fried onions and grilled mackerel that came courtesy of Simon. It wasn't exactly gourmet fare, but at least I was actually making a meal for myself again. For so long I'd eaten in cafés or made do with sandwiches or just spooned something out of a can.

I washed the dishes in water drawn from the well and left them to dry on the counter before going back outside to the garden. The fading sun had covered the east wall in a slanting light that bathed the walls in an orange glow. I sat down on the stone bench near the fig tree, turned my face to the sun and slipped my shoes off, settling my toes into the grass, feeling the warmth of the earth on my soles.

I thought over the encounter with the boy yesterday. I hoped that I hadn't frightened him away completely. What was his relation to the woman? Was it her clarinet that he was playing? I supposed he could be her pupil. No doubt I could have asked Simon or Martin Levérrier if they knew anything about him. But I wanted it to be a sort of secret. I had a sense we would meet again.

All around me was the golden sunset light. The walls of the garden were like an embrace, arms reaching out from the sturdy presence of the house to hold and guard me. I felt alone, but not lonely.

As I sat there, a tiny rust-brown bird landed on the wall a few feet away. It cocked an eye in my direction, then puffed itself up and turned towards the sun. To my delight, it launched into song, its tail wagging up and down as a rapid stream of notes trilled forth from the little body: *chit chit chit cher, chit, chit, chit cher.*

The white breast glowed orange in the falling light, so that the little bird seemed lit up from within. It seemed to sing for no reason other than that it was there, in the warm light, alive. The innocent music of its song took me out of myself, so that I forgot my sadness and felt a brief and unexpected moment of joy. Happiness still existed in the world. It had just lost a place in my heart. In a few minutes the sun dipped below the edge of the wall and suddenly the garden was cast into evening shadow. The glow and the colour faded from the roses. The sparrow ruffled its wings, lifted off and flew away, as if following the sun.

I went back into the house. It felt chilly and dark, so I lit the kindling in the fireplace, then added wood as the flames grew. I perched on the edge of the couch in front of the fireplace with my hands stretched towards the warmth. The shutters were still open and the light framed in the windows was now a deep velvety blue. All was silent, except for the crackle of the fire. Every now and then a gust of sea wind blew over the house and the shutters creaked softly.

Here I am, I thought, an artist with his own little seaside cottage on a picturesque island. This is everything a landscape painter could want. But would I ever paint again? That long-ago day in Vancouver when Brother Adams had taken me to see the Corot had been a moment of revelation, and I had been a disciple ever since. Art had been not only a home and a refuge, but a path that I had always believed I could follow.

I looked over at the two oyster shells on the windowsill. Earlier, they had seemed icons of promise, glowing with light. But now, in the shadows, their brightness was gone and they were just dead objects, and suddenly the notion that beauty meant something seemed a foolish illusion. The old despair came over me again. My selfish absorption in my painting, my attempts to re-create beauty, had led to the death of my wife and child.

A couple of weeks before I'd quit Paris, Serge Bruneau, my friend and dealer, had convinced me to come to lunch with him.

He always had some new discovery, some little out-of-the-way bistro that he wanted to share. The place was south of Place de la République, just near Cirque d'hiver. I don't remember what we ate. I drank quite a few martinis. Serge had sold one of my paintings, a view of the ruined Roman bridge at Pont de la Roque, for quite a lot of money, and the buyer wanted more in the same vein. I told Serge that I hadn't painted since Cyprus and I was not going to take it up again.

He protested that I surely couldn't be serious. No matter how much I'd suffered. It would come back to me.

I said to him, "You know, for me, painting has always been a kind of spiritual activity, and now I've lost my faith. Or seen it for the illusion it always was. In the end a picture is simply a picture, pleasing to the eye. Or not, as the case may be. The rest is just bullshit."

"But my dear Leo," Serge replied, trying for a jovial tone, "of course people like you and I make a religion out of art. What else is there?"

"Only darkness. I can't see the point of art any more."

"I will not agree with you," Serge said emphatically. "I've based my whole career as an art dealer on the belief, the faith you talk about, that art gives something to the world."

"Really?" I said angrily. "Did the Nazis who swarmed through the Louvre gawking at the paintings during the war change their ways? Those bastards who killed my wife and son, did Art matter to them? Art is a sideshow, an entertainment. Nothing more."

"This is your grief talking," Serge said. "You are someone who has been blessed with a special gift. Your paintings give a great deal to people—pleasure, poetry, beauty. Even faith in life. You express what is in all of us, who cannot express it. Are you willing to discard that gift?"

I was faithless now, like a believer who sees that his God was only a shape on a wall, his own shadow cast by a fading light.

I'd always thought of Serge as a sensualist and I told him so. "You enjoy life easily," I said. "All this—the food, the wine, this place, the paintings you surround yourself with. I envy you."

"You think I'm nothing but a hedonist?"

"The appreciation of beauty comes naturally to you. I've always had to struggle to find it."

"And you have found it, Leo. People like me are the ones who struggle to know beauty. We rely on you, the artists, to show it to us."

But now it was I who needed someone to show me the way.

An owl hooted in the gathering darkness. I was very far away from everything, but I was used to being alone. Even as a kid, lying at night in a dormitory full of other boys, I had known that I was alone. Sometimes one of the smaller boys would whimper in the darkness, or sob quietly, crying for something lost. But I never cried, and I wanted to tell that boy that it wouldn't do any good. I never cried. Not even when I wanted to. Not even now.

Remembering those nights at the Guild made me think of Brother Adams. I suppose he was the closest person to a father that I had ever had.

When I left Vancouver, heading to New York to try my hand at being an artist there, I'd gone to say goodbye to Brother Adams and he had given me a little going-away present, a book. It was obviously old. The title was embossed in faded gold letters on the worn leather cover. *The Ideal View.* The pages were yellowed and the illustrations were in black and white, pictures of landscape paintings. By then I knew some of the names: Corot of course, Poussin, Claude Lorain, John Constable, Cézanne and Pissarro. Facing each picture was a line or two of text. I read the words opposite a painting by Corot. "The most perfect landscape painter the world ever saw. All is lovely, all amiable, all is amenity and repose; the calm sunshine of the heart."

"Now that is something to make a picture of, eh?" Brother Adams had said. "'The calm sunshine of the heart.'"

Would he have been disappointed with the way I'd turned out? Of course I'd suffered, maybe more than most people, and he would have understood. But now I had given up art and everything he'd hoped I would become. Would he have understood that?

My thoughts turned to the chapel, to the painting there, and to Père Caron. Something about him reminded me of Brother Adams. He had that same masculine warmth and steadiness that I had longed for so much when I was a boy.

Was I going to disappoint him too?

CHAPTER 13

THE NEXT MORNING, THE FIRST IN MY NEW HOME, when I pulled back the shutters the sea was ragged and choppy with whitecaps, but the rain that had blown across the island all night had stopped. In the little harbour the few boats were swaying back and forth against their moorings, the cleats and buckles on the masts clanking and clattering in the wind.

With Piero's paintbox under my arm, I took the inland path to the chapel, the route des Matelots, which was sheltered from the wind. But where it branched from the chemin des Sirènes I veered off to the right, because it would lead me past La Maison du Paradis. As I was crossing the open heathland, where all the rabbits had wisely decided to stay underground, a strange unfamiliar sound came to my ears, not some primitive music this time but a sort of snarling barking noise from behind the dunes. Remembering that white dog I'd seen in the area a few days ago, I scrambled up the dunes. The wind whipped sand into my face and gusted around my head.

I heard the barking again and just below and to my left I saw a melee of flying sand and twisting bodies. There were three dogs fighting.

Then I saw that it wasn't three dogs but two. The white Labrador I'd seen the other day, and a dark squat mastiff with a thick neck and wide shoulders. The third shape was a child. The boy! They were attacking him. No, he seemed to be trying to separate them. The mastiff appeared to be the aggressor and to have the upper hand, its jaws clamped behind the Labrador's neck. The boy was pulling at the white dog's collar.

I charged into the brawl and aimed a hard kick at the mastiff's flank. The dog released its hold and tumbled sideways and then was up immediately, circling me. A low rumbling snarl came from deep within its chest, audible over the gusts of wind. I was frightened but I stood my ground, putting myself between the dog and the boy. The mastiff leapt at me, going for my throat. I threw up a blocking forearm and with my other hand punched the animal's head as hard as I could. Teeth ripped at my sleeve as the mastiff's mouth fastened on my arm and I punched it hard again between the eyes. It fell and rolled on its back. I kicked at its hindquarters. Regaining its feet, the dog snapped its teeth at my leg, missed, then loped off with its tail between its legs, turning to cast a final glare at me before disappearing over the dunes.

When I looked around, the boy and the other dog were nowhere in sight. There was only the wind whipping across the waves and the sand grains gusting up against my legs. I heard a shout above the moaning of the wind. Just on the crest of the dunes where the dog had slunk away, a figure appeared—the woman from the chapel.

She came skidding down the dune, waving her arms. "What happened?"

"Was that your dog?" I shouted. "It could have killed that boy!"

She slid to an abrupt stop, holding her hair away from her face as the wind flattened her black curls across her cheeks. "What boy? I heard barking and shouts, some kind of awful commotion."

"You should keep that animal leashed! It's a damned menace."

"What are you talking about? I don't have a dog."

"What?" My anger was in full flow, I was hardly listening to her.

"I don't own a dog. It wasn't mine."

"It's not your dog?"

"Of course it wasn't, I just told you."

"Did you see which way the boy went?

"I didn't see anyone."

I bent down with my hands resting on my knees, taking deep breaths. The inside of my mouth tasted metallic.

"Are you all right?" she said.

I shook my head, unable to speak, the anger draining out of me. I sat down on the sand.

"What's happened?" she asked again, her voice softening.

"Two dogs were fighting. The boy was trying to separate them. I managed to get myself between them and one turned on me. A vicious thing." I looked up and down the beach. "You didn't see a boy?"

"No, I just heard those awful sounds." She knelt on the sand next to me. "Your sleeve is torn. If you've been bitten you should have your arm seen to. You can get tetanus from a dog bite."

I looked dazedly at the rip on my denim shirt, then pushed the sleeve up to expose my forearm. The skin was broken, showing a few drops of blood.

"It's nothing."

"My cottage is just on the other side of the dunes. I have a first aid kit there. You'd better come up."

"I'm fine," I said. But I felt very tired. I just wanted to lie down and close my eyes.

"Come on." She held out her hand, as if to a child. "It's not far."

We went over the dunes, bending against the stiff wind and walked up a rocky path. I had not seen the cottage from this angle before, although I'd passed the front side often enough. Like my own cottage, there was a walled garden, where hollyhocks on either side of a blue wooden door were swaying back and forth in the gusts. She led me through the garden into a large room.

Along the wall was a tall Normandy armoire, its shelves displaying a collection of patterned plates. The other walls were covered with photographs and paintings. On the opposite side of the room an old couch was arranged in front of a fireplace where a couple of logs glowed.

"Sit down," she said.

I sank onto the couch, overcome with fatigue, as if I had just run a great distance. From one of the drawers next to the sink she brought out a metal first aid box with a red cross on the lid. "Roll up your sleeve and let's have a look."

There were a couple of small beads of blood along the gash on my forearm. I flexed my hand. "It doesn't look too bad," I told her.

"We should put some disinfectant on it anyway."

It occurred to me that this was the second time she'd seen me injured. What must she think? "I'm not always like this," I said. "In a mess of some kind."

She gave me the smallest of smiles.

Holding my arm by the wrist she wiped the abrasion, then tipped a little alcohol onto the cloth from a small brown bottle and dabbed it on my forearm. I remembered being in a similar sort of occasion, with Père Caron that first day after my climb up the cliff. The same day I had first seen her too. I remembered the bruise on her cheek, which had faded now to a very faint discolouration.

"You are shivering," she said.

When I held my hand out above the surface of the table, palm down, it was trembling. I clenched my fist. "That whole thing with the dog and the boy really shook me up."

She crossed to the counter under the window where a couple of wine bottles stood and poured some out into a glass. "Drink this," she said, bringing the glass over.

I swallowed, washing away the lingering metallic taste in my mouth.

"Who is this boy?" she asked.

"I thought you might know."

"Me?" She gave me a surprised look. "You keep mentioning him. Is he the same one you were searching for that day on the cliff?"

"He reminds me of . . . someone." I ran my hand across the paintbox, which I had placed on the couch next to me. My fingers traced the letters etched into the lid. "This was his. Piero."

"Where is he?"

"I had a wife and a son. Claudine and Piero."

She stared at me. "Where are they now?"

"They're gone."

"Have they left you?" It was almost a whisper.

I put my hands over my face and shook my head.

Touching me lightly on the shoulder, she said, "What has happened? Tell me."

"They are dead."

"Oh, I'm so sorry."

I looked away, at the photographs on the walls. Strangers.

"What happened?" she said.

As I sat there on her couch, shivering, stretching my hands out to the fire, feeling that I would never be warm again, I found myself telling her about what had happened to Claudine and Piero.

When I finished, we were silent for a few moments. "In the end, it was my fault," I said finally.

"You are not to blame," she said. "It was an accident."

"No. If I hadn't persisted in going up to the church, if I hadn't been so selfish, none of it would have happened. All I could think about was the painting I wanted to make."

"None of us can foresee the future."

"I put them in danger, and they suffered for it."

"And now, this other boy, who is he? I don't know the islanders much. I've only been here a short time myself."

"Just a local lad, I suppose. He resembles Piero a bit. That's all. I've been making too much of it."

She frowned at me, as if aware that there was more to it than that. "That day I found you lying on the ground at the cliff edge, what happened? You were in pretty rough shape."

I looked away and reached for my wineglass, draining what was left. "I came here, to this island, because there was nowhere else to go. And I went to the cliff because I had literally reached the end. At the last moment I heard something behind me and I saw the boy in the mist."

"And . . . ?"

"I thought—I thought it was Piero. And then I fell. I landed on a ledge and eventually managed to climb up. That was when you found me."

She blew air out between her pursed lips and shook her head.

"He saved me in a way," I said. "The boy. And I thought it was Piero, that he'd come to stop me, to call me back."

She nodded. "Suffering can make us imagine things, it can make us behave in ways we cannot understand." She sounded like she knew more than I'd told her.

"I know he is not Piero. And I know I haven't imagined him. He is as real as you and me. I've seen him, I've touched him. Just the other day, in fact, practically right outside your door."

"Here? What do you mean?

"The whole thing was quite strange." I told her about hearing the odd musical sounds in the woods. "It was the boy, standing there with his goats like some mythological faun, making this strange music on a clarinet."

"Ah, that explains it," she said.

"What?"

She strode over to an instrument case sitting on the counter, snapped the catches open and brought out a clarinet. "Like this one?"

"It looks exactly the same."

"The other day I came home and found my clarinet lying on the kitchen counter. I never leave it lying about when I'm not playing. This instrument is very precious to me, it has a special history, and I always put it back in its case. I couldn't understand how it came to be on the counter. I'm never absent-minded about it. And you say he was actually playing it?"

"Well, yes and no." I tried to explain what I'd heard.

"How odd. Did you try and talk to him, to find out who he is?"

"I think I went about it in completely the wrong way and frightened him off." I told her about trying to grab and hold onto the boy.

"It's likely he is afraid of you. He must have been terrified when he saw you fall. Too scared to even go for help. And he probably feels some responsibility for what happened on the cliff, even though he's only a child. But I don't understand why a boy that age is not in school. Why is he tending goats and running around shirtless? What about his parents?"

"I don't know," I said.

"Have you tried to find out?"

"Not directly. I wanted to talk to him first. It would seem a bit odd for a stranger to be asking questions about some local boy, don't you think?"

She frowned slightly. "What do you really want from this boy, Leo?"

I wasn't sure myself, but I said, "Do you have children?"

She shook her head.

"Then you can't really understand," I told her.

"I know about loss."

My eyes went again to that faint vestige of the bruise on her cheek. I sank back wearily on the couch. "You're right, of course. But you have to understand that I can't just let it end. I have to know who he is. He is a kind of phantom right now. Maybe just knowing that he is an ordinary boy like any other will help me."

She walked over to the table and picked up a pack of cigarettes. I watched her as she crossed the room. She was wearing a thick oatmeal-coloured sweater and a black skirt that came down to her calves, and a pair of old-fashioned lace-up boots. Her thick hair was disorderly from the wind and she raked it back on each side of her head with her fingers as she sat down. She lit the cigarette with a battered old brass Zippo that gave off a strong smell of lighter fluid, and I picked up the cigarette package.

"Lucky Strike. I used to smoke Luckies for a while when I lived in New York."

"Are you American?"

I shook my head. "Canadian."

She said, "I started smoking these at the end of the war when the American soldiers handed them out."

"Were you here in the war?"

"Paris. Other places." She looked away, gesturing at the cigarettes. "Have one."

"I never took to it," I said. "But I like the smell." I set the package on the cushion between us.

"I really think you should put a bandage on that scrape," she said.

I didn't object when she rummaged in the first aid tin and brought out a roll of adhesive bandage. She tossed her cigarette into the fireplace, then cut off a strip of bandage and removed the backing before pressing it over my wrist. Her face was close to mine as she bent over my arm and I was conscious of the warmth and scent of her body. A hint of lily of the valley perfume. I studied her profile, the smooth tanned skin of her cheek, the sweep of her thick eyelashes, the full mouth as she bit lightly on her lower lip with concentration.

I looked at her hands. They were long-fingered, strong-looking. She wasn't wearing a wedding ring, but there was a band of much lighter skin on the third finger of her left hand and the kind of indentation that the long wearing of a ring leaves. On the underside of her left wrist were two pale lines on the skin, running parallel to the veins. I glanced at her other hand. The same thing there. Cuts, from long ago. I wondered about that. And the bruise. I'd been so consumed with my own story that I hadn't given much thought to who she was and why she was here. There was something out of the ordinary about the situation.

She looked up, meeting my scrutiny. I saw the sudden widening of her pupils as her eyes seemed to become darker and more intense in her face. That moment when we had looked at each other in the chapel came back to me—the almost physical sensation I had felt.

"I don't even know your name," I said.

"It's Lorca," she answered in a thick voice.

"You're not French?"

"I am. Lorca Daubigny. I was named for the Spanish poet."

"I'm Leo Millar."

"I know. You said so that day on the cliff." She let my wrist drop, still looking at me. Then she gave a little shake of her head and got to her feet. She stood leaning on the mantelpiece, busying herself lighting another cigarette.

"And when you find this boy," she said, "and realize that

he is, as you put it, a local lad with a life of his own, what then? What will you do?"

"I don't know." I hadn't thought beyond just wanting to verify who he was. I changed the subject. "Have you seen the old painting in the chapel?"

"No. I've only been to the chapel once. The day I saw you there."

Our eyes met again. Did I imagine that little flare of connection?

"The painting is supposedly by Davide Asmodeus. Do you know his work?"

"Didn't he do that one in the Louvre? It hangs near Géricault's *Raft of the Medusa*?"

"Yes. But this one is in a terrible condition. Père Caron, the priest, has asked me if I could try and clean it."

"You are an artist?" She inclined her head at Piero's paintbox.

"Yes. But not a restorer. Anyway, you should come and look at the painting. That is, if you are interested in Asmodeus."

"Maybe." There was something guarded and pensive in her expression now. Her voice had become impersonal.

"It's called 'Love and the Pilgrim,'" I said.

She raised her eyebrows and gave me that steady, assessing look. I suddenly felt uncomfortable, embarrassed at talking about my life with someone who was, after all, a stranger. And was I completely misinterpreting those glances between us? Was I being foolish, even a little desperate, while she was merely being polite? The logs in the fireplace were throwing off an intense heat, the room seemed smoky, and the taste of the wine was sour on my tongue.

"I should be going." I buttoned my sleeve, stood and picked up the paintbox. "Thank you for your help. And for listening."

She saw me to the door. "Take care of your arm. If I see the boy I'll let you know," she said.

"Thanks. I'm going to be at the chapel most days."

At the end of the path, where it curved into the trees, I glanced back. She was standing in her doorway, staring after me, but I was too far away to read her expression.

CHAPTER 14

"HIS NAME IS TOBIAS."

"Who? You mean him?" I pointed with my brush at the painting.

Père Caron and I were standing in front of "Love and the Pilgrim" examining the newly cleaned section. I had concentrated my efforts so far on the two faces and the two hands reaching for each other.

He shook his head. "The name of the boy is Tobias. The one you have been searching for."

"You know who he is?"

"I have known him all his life. Tobias is an island boy, who has lived here since he was born."

Tobias. It was an unusual name. I only knew it from that exquisite little painting by Elsheimer, *Tobias and the Angel*. I didn't know the subject, just that it was from the Bible. Something about an angel restoring someone's sight.

Père Caron's expression became stern. "He is not your son. Not reincarnated or related or anything else."

I wondered how he knew so much about my quest to find the boy. "How did you know?"

"The woman who is living in the cottage, La Maison du Paradis, came to see me the other day. Lorca Daubigny. She told me your story." His voice softened. "I know of your loss."

I put down the brush I was holding. "You've been discussing me?" I wasn't sure I liked that.

"Leo, I had a feeling that first day about why you were on the cliff. I didn't know anything about you, but now it makes sense. You must not blame yourself for what happened. God forgives us. I'm sure your wife and son would too. They would have wanted you to go on with your life." He smiled kindly. "Perhaps God will show you the way."

Not God, I thought. The only God I had ever known was the crucified figure that hung behind the altar in the chapel at the Guild. The Brothers had taught us the prayers and the hymns and told us the stories of signs and wonders. Sunday after Sunday I had stared up at the face, wanting that dead man to come alive, to prove his power. But he had been powerless, to help himself or to help me. I don't remember exactly when I had stopped praying. Perhaps when I realized that prayers in the chapel did as much good as the tears that the other boys shed in the dormitory at night.

Maybe the priest found solace in his own prayers, but the only hope I held was for moments of mercy. Never absolution.

"Would you like to meet him?"

"The boy?"

"Yes. Tobias. I think you should meet him. You obviously want to."

I hesitated. I had been obsessed with finding him, but now, did I really want to see what lay behind the mists? Did I want mundane reality to replace the illusion I had created?

As if divining my thoughts, Père Caron said, "Best to clear up any misconceptions, *n'est-ce pas?*"

"Of course. Yes, I would like to meet him. "

"I could have told you earlier, I suppose, but I sensed something unresolved in your questions. Your confusion caused me some concern."

"He reminded me so much of my own son. But you needn't worry, I'm not under any sort of delusion."

"In that case, we can go now."

"Now?"

"Unless you prefer to carry on working. We can make it another time."

"No, no. Now is fine. Just let me tidy up."

While I wiped my brushes clean and capped the jars of turpentine and vinegar, Père Caron waited at the door, rolling himself a cigarette. He was wearing his habitual suit of dark blue linen and the ubiquitous beret. Glancing over at his stocky form, I thought that in any another situation he would be taken for a workman. In fact, there was little to distinguish him from the fishermen of the island. A man of the earth, I thought with a measure of envy, a man of the people. And he has his God to comfort him. He belongs. He has a place.

We headed inland, following a path that was marked LES HAUTS-VENTS, which I translated as the "windy heights." There was no wind though, sheltered as we were by the thick pines. I had brought a jacket, but I carried it slung over my shoulder in the warmth. Today I was wearing a white shirt, much wrinkled after being washed in a bucket of well water then hung to dry in the garden of La Minerve.

As the path ascended through the trees, I could hear a faint chugging sound, like one of the outboard motors the fishermen attached to their dories, but it was growing louder by the minute. At the same time I was aware of a strong smoky apple scent in the air. In a minute the path led us to a clearing, where the origin of the sound became evident in the shape of a strange and noisy apparatus that looked like a combination of antique tractor and ancient steam engine. There were pulleys, pipes, tubes and chimneys, two boiler-like tanks, all of it emitting puffs of steam and smoke, the whole machine rumbling and vibrating and appearing to be on the verge of either exploding or collapsing into a heap of sooty metal. At the far end of the apparatus, a tube of copper pipe dripped clear liquid into a cask.

The priest paused and put his hand on my arm. "Tobias is not like other children. If you want to meet him, let him come to you. He is shy of strangers, although not unfriendly. But one thing, Leo, be careful with him. He is happy in his own way. Respect that."

While I was pondering this rather cryptic advice, Père Caron led the way into the clearing. "*Bonjour!*" he called out.

I noticed a stone hut, something like a grain shed or cow byre. I had expected the boy, but a bent-over figure emerged from the doorway. *Leprechaun* was the first description that came to my mind. The man was small, hunched with age, his pants held up with wide suspenders, a floppy beret sitting on top of his white frizz of hair. A pair of sparkling blue eyes looked up at me from a much-wrinkled face.

"May I introduce Étienne Leroux," the priest said.

"*Ça va?*" the man greeted me as I shook his rough callused hand.

"*Ça va bien,*" I answered. It goes well. "And with you?"

"*Pas mal, pas mal.*" Not bad.

"Étienne is distilling Calvados," Père Caron explained, nodding at the machine.

"*Goutez!*" the old man said. Taste it. He handed me a metal cup that was attached to the rumbling contraption with a section of thin chain.

I held the cup under the trickle dripping from the copper tube until there was enough for a mouthful. It was warm and powerfully aromatic. "Phew!" I waved a hand in front of my lips as the fiery liquor surged down my throat. "That must be hundred proof." I blinked rapidly and exhaled again.

The old man rocked back on his heels, chuckling. "*Très fort!*" Very strong. He held up a clenched fist and tapped his chest.

"Étienne supplies the island. The apples mostly come from Ester Chauvin's farm. She has the best varieties of fruit. But we use a few from my own orchard. All this is completely illegal of course. But are we supposed to order from the mainland, from strangers, liquor made from apples we have never tasted?" He shook his head emphatically. "*Non.*"

I wasn't sure what any of this had to do with the boy, Tobias, but decided to be patient.

Étienne was explaining the workings of the still.

"Of course, you have to begin with the best cider and make sure that it ferments properly. The apples are the key. A mixture of sweet, tart and bitter. I use a minimum of five varieties, Bisquet, Marin Onfroy, Binet Rouge, Clos Renaux, Doux Eveque. I won't tell you the recipe, because that is my secret."

"Don't worry, my lips are sealed."

I took another careful sip from the tin cup.

"It has to be aged in oak casks," the old man explained. "Two years at least. But the longer the better."

"Which I can attest to," Père Caron said. "I have a bottle of fourteen-year-old Calva at home. For special occasions." He smacked his lips. "Pure nectar."

"If you are here in the autumn you can come and pick the apples and see how we make cider, in the old ways," Étienne said to me.

"Étienne is Tobias's grandfather," Père Caron said.

"I see. I was wondering why you'd brought me up here. Not that this isn't very interesting. But the boy, isn't he here?"

"*Le petit?*" Père Caron said to the old man. "*Il est où?*" Where is he?

Putting two fingers to his mouth, Étienne emitted a loud whistle. In a minute or so a large ram ambled into the clearing. I recognized it, remembering well my previous encounter with the animal. Just behind it the rest of the goats were visible, but no boy. Étienne held his hands up, palm out, suggesting that he had done what he could and had no idea of his grandson's whereabouts.

On a sudden impulse, I reached into my pocket and brought out Piero's silver whistle. I blew three blasts, modulating the tone to give the impression of three syllables. *To-bi-as.*

This had little effect other than to draw startled looks from Étienne and Père Caron and make the goats scatter. I shrugged and dropped the whistle into my shirt pocket. As I turned back to the two men I heard a soft breathy whistling sound, mimicking the syllables I had just blown. The boy was standing on the edge of the clearing, holding to his lips what looked like a simple reed flute. He blew again, a sound more like the wind than music.

He lowered his flute and smiled at me. I reached quickly into my pocket and brought out the silver whistle again. "I wanted you to have this."

The boy stopped smiling and studied me with a serious look, older than his years. Last time we met, I had tried the same tactic and no doubt scared him badly. I wanted him to forgive me for that.

"It's for you." I held out my offering.

He came forward deliberately and simply lifted the whistle from my hand. I stared at his face, those familiar features. But the eyes that glanced up quickly to mine were those of a stranger. I noticed again that thin necklace of scar tissue around his throat. He tapped my palm once with his forefinger, stepped back towards the trees and, just before he disappeared from sight, smiled again.

SOMEWHERE IN ONE OF THE DRAWERS in the apartment on rue du Figuier there was a photograph taken in Luxembourg Gardens.

There had been snow that morning in Paris, just a dusting like icing sugar on the statues in the Jardin. Piero was in a stroller, only his luminous eyes and the tip of his nose showing beneath the scarf that was bundled around him. At the little kiosk near the entrance, Claudine bought cups of *chocolat chaud* and let Piero taste the thick residue from the bottom of her cup, dipping her finger into the sweet chocolate and placing it in his mouth. When I lifted him out of the stroller and kissed him, his breath was sweet, and when I kissed Claudine she tasted of chocolate too.

I was so in love with her. Every night I wanted to feel her close and warm against me as we fell asleep, and I wanted her face to be the first thing I saw in the morning, like sunlight. When I looked at her across the room, or now in the park, it was with awe, and a kind of reverence at the fact that our beautiful son had come forth from her body. With the birth of Piero I felt for the first time that I belonged to something. My wife and son brought an unexpected grace to my life, like a blessing bestowed on me.

I preferred their company to that of anybody else, or anything else. Even art, I thought. All the treasures of all the museums in Paris were puny compared to the wonders of my wife and son. My own attempts at creation paled next to the radiance of the child. I didn't even draw him in the beginning, I could only stare with wonder.

In the photograph, I am holding Piero up so that he can touch the statue of the little Pan at the east end of the gardens. Piero is smiling and his smile is just like that on the face of that timeless boy of bronze. Art historians call it the "archaic smile," after a style of ancient sculpture. I had first encountered that smile years ago when I moved to New York and discovered the Cloisters, a place constructed to resemble the gardens and buildings of a medieval monastery. I often used to sketch there, and one day I had come upon a small stone head of a smiling boy, his expression both innocent and wise. The eternal smile.

I had seen that smile in the arcades of the Cloisters, on the faces of Etruscan figures in the Louvre, on a statue in Jardin du Luxembourg and on the face of my own son. It is a smile of those who are blessed by the gods, a smile that takes joy as the natural order of things.

And now here it was again, on the face of a living boy beckoning from the woods.

"Tobias!" I called as he slipped away. "My name is Leo."

In reply, two silvery notes from the whistle.

Père Caron said, "That is the only way he will ever be able to answer you."

"What do you mean? Why?"

"He cannot speak. He is mute."

"Mute!"

I realized now that Tobias had not uttered a single word on any of the occasions I had encountered him. During the terrible incident with the dog there had been snarling and barking and my own shouts, but the boy had said nothing. And when he was playing the clarinet in the forest, there were musical sounds but never a voice, never a word. Not even when I grabbed his wrist. Now I understood that strange otherworldliness about the boy. He was surrounded by a profound silence.

"Has he always been like that?" I asked Étienne. "Was he born that way?"

"No, not always. Not in the beginning." Étienne turned to the priest. "You must explain to our friend, Père. It is your story as much as anyone's."

"*Pauvre petit*," Caron said, shaking his head. Poor child.

Étienne brought out an earthenware jug with a cork stopper and three small clay cups. Père Caron sat down on a rough wooden bench beside the hut and waited for the liquor to be poured. He drank, and then reached for his tobacco. He took his time to roll the cigarette and light it with a wooden match.

"About seven years ago, I was over in LeBec one afternoon. I forget why. An errand. I was passing near the harbour when I heard shouting, an argument between a couple who lived in one of the cottages. Stéphanie and Paul Leroux, Tobias's parents."

"Paul was my son," Étienne explained.

"I knew them very well of course, this couple," the priest continued. "They were hard-working when sober, but they both liked to drink. I couldn't hear what they were arguing about as I approached. A stiff wind was blowing across the quay, the sea was quite rough, even within the protected harbour. Paul was standing in his dory, the boat was rocking up and down, his head coming level with the pier on each surge of the waves, then dropping out of sight. Stéphanie was on the quay, shouting down at him. I think they were both drunk. Paul certainly was. As I reached them, I understood the cause of the argument. It was Tobias. He was sitting in the stern, clutching the tiller. He couldn't have been more than three years old at the time. Stéphanie was shouting at Paul that it was too rough to have the boy in the boat. Paul was shouting back that it was never too soon for the son of a fisherman to learn the ways of the sea. I tried to intercede. It wasn't the first time that I'd attempted to settle a quarrel between those two.

"As soon as Paul saw me he pushed off from the pier. Almost immediately, Stéphanie leapt from the quay and landed in the boat. The two of them struggled like maniacs. A wave surged up and the boat tipped on its side. All three of them tumbled into the water."

He cleared his throat and sipped from his cup. "I didn't know what to do. I cannot swim, you see. Isn't that ironic? A man living on an island, surrounded on all sides by water, and he cannot swim. I still can't." He paused and studied the cigarette between his fingers, watching the smoke rise upwards in a thin transparent curl.

"When the boat righted itself, the boy was dangling over the side, caught in a coil of rope. Paul and Stéphanie hadn't come up again. In the meantime the boat was drifting towards the harbour mouth and the child was hanging with his feet in the water and his body trapped in the tangle of rope. I ran to the end of the quay shouting for help. Thank God somebody heard me. A woman name Maria Lundin, who lived in the nearest cottage. She dived in and managed to get to the boat and bring Tobias to safety. I suppose if that rope hadn't been twisted around the boy's neck he would have drowned."

"That explains the scar tissue on his throat," I said.

He nodded. "There were welts around his neck, like red rope, for weeks. They healed eventually. He didn't speak during that time, but we thought it was because of the accident. But when days later he still wouldn't speak, Étienne and I eventually took him over to the mainland. The doctor who examined him said the vocal cords were badly torn. Irreparably so, it turned out."

Étienne Leroux shook his head. "A sad business. My son and his wife were never found."

Père Caron stood up and tilted his head back to look at the sky. His eyes were moist. "There you have it, one of life's tragedies." He dropped the remains of the cigarette at his feet and carefully ground it out with the heel of his boot.

"Poor kid," I said. "I would never have let anything like that happen." I heard my own words, the outrage in them, and I fell silent. Was I any better than Paul and Stéphanie in the end? When I looked over at the priest, I saw the suffering, and the guilt, in his face.

"It was a severe punishment upon them," he continued. "But at least they would never know that their carelessness had deprived their child of his voice for the rest of his life. And that is God's will, I suppose. Which is sometimes hard to comprehend, much less accept." He kicked at the ground with the tip of his boot. "I don't know what Tobias remembers of that day, or of his parents. Maybe nothing. The mind has the ability to erase pain, or at least bury it deep inside. But he has not spoken a word since that day."

"Nothing?"

"Nothing. Believe me, I would know. And I have tried."

"We took him in, of course," Étienne Leroux said, "my wife Thérèse and I. But she passed on herself some years ago. I try to care for him as best as I can, but he goes his own way and I don't have the heart to prevent him. He has a room in my cottage, I feed him, but he roams where he will. The whole island is his house."

Père Caron said, "All of us, everybody on the island, contributes to his care in one way or the other."

"And his schooling?"

"He prefers the company of the goats to other children," Étienne said.

"I tried to place him on the mainland with a family," Père Caron explained, "so that he could go to school there. But he was isolated, mocked by the other children. He ran away and hid aboard a boat coming back here. More than once. Eventually I undertook to educate him myself. As best I could. We have both learned a rudimentary sign language, but he can read and write as well as any other boy his age. Other than that, nature is his teacher."

"But what do the authorities say?"

"It is better not to involve them, don't you think?" He put his hands in his pockets and tilted his head at me. "We don't want him put in an institution or some 'special school' far away. This island is the only home he has ever known."

I did not have to think very hard to imagine what the boy's life was like, the isolation, the loneliness, the confusion. I knew what it was to be an orphan.

Père Caron said, "Tobias has his ways. Someone not familiar with him would naturally be confused by his behaviour. Sometimes I myself am confused by him. But he is a very intelligent boy. Nothing is wrong with him, except for the fact that he doesn't speak."

On the way back down the hill we walked in silence. Eventually, I said, "Thank you for letting me meet Tobias." I was grateful for the kindness of the priest. I understood now how much he cared for the boy.

When we parted and I continued on to the chapel, I was wondering if there was a way to help Tobias. It was all very well to run around like Pan with his goats, but later, when he grew up? What then? But what could I do? What right had I to interfere?

I wished I had Claudine to talk to. She'd always known the right thing to do. And that thought brought back all my old feelings of despair.

CHAPTER 15

THAT AFTERNOON I CROSSED THE CHANNEL between the main island and the chapel, and walked across the dry kelp-littered sand in my bare feet, carrying my shoes in my hand. The tide had been out since the morning, although it would turn soon and come flooding back. Reaching the chapel, I went immediately to the painting. My eyes took in the details again, the two people moving across the landscape, the woman with the lyre, stretching a hand back to the man who came behind. And beyond them, the humble little building, the chapel of Notre-Dame de la Victoire.

In the last few days I had done a substantial amount of cleaning on the surface, especially on the two figures, which were now illuminated against the surrounding shadows like actors spotlit on a stage. What drama were they enacting? In the gap between the two outstretched hands was all the abyss of loss. Would it ever be bridged? Would they ever reach each other? Where did that path lead? What awaited in the building on the hill? Standing closer, I searched the darkness that still shrouded the rest of the landscape. Was there another shape hidden in the obscurity? For a moment I looked for the outline of a boy, watching from the trees.

"Who are they?" a voice said from the shadows.

I spun around with surprise. A figure rose from a pew in the first row near the altar.

"Sorry, I didn't mean to startle you," Lorca Daubigny said.

"I didn't see you there. I thought I was alone."

"I was going to announce myself when you came in, but you seemed so engrossed in the painting that I didn't want to disturb you."

She stepped towards me, and I was better able to see her in the light from the doorway. Her hair was pushed back from her face, a little unruly, and she carried a straw hat in one hand. She was wearing a white linen shirt with the sleeves rolled up and a dark skirt that came down to her knees. Her sandals were white leather with very thin straps. I noticed that her toenails were painted crimson.

"I came to tell you that I talked to Père Caron," she said.

"He told me you'd been to see him the other day."

"You don't mind? You did ask me to try to find out about the boy."

"Yes, I did. And thank you."

"So you know who he is, at last."

"Tobias. Tobias Leroux. I've met him now."

"The priest was worried about you."

"Did he explain what happened to Tobias? That he is mute?"

She nodded. "It's awful. The poor child. What will become of him in the long run?"

"You know, that day when I heard him trying to play your clarinet, I really had the impression that he had some innate musical talent."

"Oh?"

"Perhaps the fact that he doesn't speak has made his hearing develop more acutely."

"It's possible."

"I don't know much about music, but what I heard touched me." A sudden idea occurred to me. "Maybe you could listen to him? You could even give him a few lessons."

"I don't know about that," she said slowly.

"You're planning to stay on La Mouche for a while, aren't you?" I realized that I wanted her to remain on the island. "It would be a challenge for you, if nothing else."

"Are you repainting this picture?" she asked, obviously wanting to change the subject.

"No, just giving it a cleaning. Or trying to."

I had earlier lifted the painting down from its place above the door and positioned it against the wall near the entrance where the light was better. She stood next to me, leaning forward a bit to look at the picture, a faint scent of her soap reaching my nostrils, sweet against the oil paint smell that had become a permanent part of the chapel's atmosphere since I'd started work in here.

"I said I would do it as a favour for Père Caron. He hopes I can restore it, but the painting is in terrible condition really. Years of exposure to the sea air have degraded the pigments so that I've no idea what the original colours were."

She squatted in front of it, peering at the area I had cleaned. "And the subject, is it a variation on Orpheus and Eurydice?"

"Why do you say that?"

"Well, two figures moving out of what looks like a cave, which could be the underworld, one of them carrying a lyre. Do you know the story?"

I nodded. "I suppose it is a story that most musicians would be familiar with."

"Naturally. It flatters us, that music can bring back someone from Hades. But in the original myth Orpheus carries the lyre when he comes to rescue Eurydice. Here, the roles are reversed—the woman looks like she is leading the man out of the underworld."

"Apparently an expert from Paris came before the war and said it should be called 'Love and the Pilgrim.'"

"I like that title better." She put her finger over the space between the outstretched hands of the two figures.

"Bold Lover, never, never canst thou kiss,
Though winning near the goal—yet, do not grieve;
She cannot fade, though thou has not thy bliss,
For ever wilt thou love, and she be fair!"

She had spoken the lines in English, and I said, "Keats."

"We studied the poem in school. I had to memorize the whole thing and it stuck in my mind forever."

I responded with the last couplet of the poem. "Beauty is truth, truth beauty—that is all / Ye know on earth, and all ye need to know."

"Do you think that is true?" she said.

"I used to. Once."

"I understand," she replied softly.

She reached into her pocket for her Lucky Strikes and lit one, crossing her arms casually as she contemplated the painting. "'Love and the Pilgrim.' Who is which, do you think?"

"I assumed he was the Pilgrim, reaching towards Love," I said.

"Not necessarily. Love is always personified as a woman in art, as if only men can have an object of longing and desire. Perhaps she is the pilgrim here, and she is reaching out for love."

"That would make it a very different picture."

"It would." She took a drag of her cigarette and exhaled. The smile she gave me through the smoke was enigmatic.

I ran a finger across the canvas and examined the tip.

"Having to clean all of this seems like an immense job," Lorca said.

"It is. And I'm not sure it's possible. Too bad, though. Père Caron is so enthusiastic about it."

"If you think restoring this painting is impossible, why don't you make a new one?"

"A new painting?" I raised my eyebrows "For this chapel?" The idea had never occurred to me. I shook my head. "No, I'm finished with all that. I have no inspiration any more."

"Because of what happened?"

"Art doesn't change anything." I remembered saying something similar to Serge Bruneau once.

"It could brighten this chapel," she said. "Think of it as something for others, seen only by those who come here seeking peace or consolation. A little bit of beauty is not such a bad thing."

"Is that how you approach your music, as the creation of beauty?"

"In a way," she said. "I just want to make one small true thing in this world. Like that Grecian urn in Keats's poem. It's a worthy aspiration for an artist."

I looked down at the dark painting. "I wouldn't know what to paint. Besides, it would take months."

"Do you have somewhere else to be? Paris? Canada? Maybe you need to be here."

Père Caron had asked me the same thing. Had they been discussing me? Or was it just obvious that I needed something or someplace to belong to?

"And what would my subject be?"

"Paint this place."

"What, the chapel?"

"The island." Almost to herself she said, "There is a strange beauty here. So quiet, somber in a way. Yet always with the sensation that something is about to happen. Something strange and beautiful."

"I could paint you," I said.

"Me! I didn't mean that."

"I'm serious." I didn't know why I'd made the suggestion. As a way to keep her here? "If I painted the island landscape I'd have to put some people in it. Just like this artist, Asmodeus, has done."

"And how would you like me to pose?" she said. "Not as a fleeing Eurydice, I hope."

"Just the way you are now," I said. "But more in the light. Without light there is nothing."

"You mean like this?" With a smile she assumed a pin-up posture, hands on her cocked hips, a coy smile, making a game of it. "Venus on the half-shell?"

"Then you'd have to be nude."

"Ah, but that would be a different painting entirely."

An image came to my mind, unbidden, of her standing naked. I'd painted many nudes in art school, and Claudine at one time also posed for me, but the image I saw now had nothing to do with art. She smiled again, but her eyes had an expression I couldn't decipher.

"That would be altogether different," she repeated, as if aware of my thoughts.

Embarrassed, as if I had been caught peering through a window, I looked away. "I haven't painted in a long time. It's as if I have forgotten how."

"Why don't you try?"

"What good would that do? Being an artist belongs to another life."

"It might take you away from yourself." There was something caring in her face when I looked at her again, not the bantering attitude of a few minutes ago. She said, "Why don't you attempt a quick little sketch? I don't mind posing for a few minutes."

Her seriousness prompted me to consider the proposal. Stepping to one side, I studied her, and as she turned to face me the light was behind her, streaming, just as it had that very first time on the cliff when I'd come back to consciousness and seen her as an apparition. That is what I should attempt to paint. But I felt incapable of using paint and brushes for my own purposes, as if I had no right to be a painter any longer. I reached for a pencil.

"All right, why not?" I said. "Turn a little more to the side. To your left. Just relax in a normal position." Approaching, I gently touched her chin, adjusting the tilt of her head a degree. My fingers lingered, then I stepped back.

The sunlight from the open doorway fell on one side of her face, contrasting the flesh tones with the darkness of her hair, an inky black with highlights that seemed blue. She was beautiful, but in an unusual way. Her features were angular, chiselled almost, but also a little worn, as if she had lived intensely. Claudine had been pretty and very feminine. This was a face that was beautiful in a much different way.

I directed my attention to the page. A few lines appeared as my pencil moved, roughing in the general shape of her head. A little mark for the eye line, a dot where the tip of the nose sat, another line for the lips. With the side of the pencil I blocked in patches of light and shade, drawing her hair. Then I set to work on the features. It was like being in the portrait class in art school again: visually measuring the proportions, judging one form against another, paying particular attention to the shape of the upper eyes and the corners of the mouth. For some reason, if you got those right you were well on your way to getting a reasonable likeness. I had always been good at faces, ever since those long-ago days at the Guild, and I'd retained that facility despite the fact that I chose to paint landscapes and not people.

Taking my time, I constructed her features, erasing, adding, subtracting, noting the strong angle of her chin, the very slight curve of her nose, the elongated teardrop shape of the nostril, her straight eyebrows and her dark eyes. I worked on the mouth, the little upward curve hinting at a smile, the full sensual lower lip. I stopped drawing and stared at her, my pencil hovering over the paper. My eyes went to her hands, the pale scars on her wrists. What had happened there?

She turned her head and met my gaze. Unblinking. Intense. Her forefinger toyed with the strap of her watch, an unconscious gesture betraying an inner tension.

I made a few more quick adjustments, a little shadow beneath the chin, and sat back. Lorca relaxed and sat down next to me, her shoulder touching mine as she studied the drawing.

"How very strange," she said.

"You don't like it?"

"I don't mean that. It's a very good likeness. I just mean how strange to see myself so unexpectedly, through someone else's eyes. I've never had my portrait done before."

I leaned forward and with the tip of my eraser made a tiny highlight on the black iris of an eye. The expression came alive. Just that one small touch made all the difference.

"And is that who I am?"

"Maybe," I replied. "Although with a portrait it's always more the artist's interpretation than a real likeness. We can never really understand how we look to others."

"Have you flattered me? I see something tender in the eyes. But the mouth is seductive."

An image flashed through my mind—a different occasion, a different woman asking to see my drawing, a different portrait. I had not thought of Claudine as much lately. Sometimes I forgot her. Piero was still alive in my mind, because of Tobias, but Claudine seemed to be receding further into the past.

For long seconds Lorca contemplated the drawing in silence. I was aware of her scent—tobacco and soap, Lucky Strikes and lily of the valley. I could also detect the flintiness of the stone walls and traces of furniture polish from the pews, a familiar smell from long, long ago.

"Maybe it's how you want me to be," she said at last, turning to me, her voice a little hoarse, smoky. Our faces were only inches apart.

I put a finger on her cheekbone, where the faintest hint of colour, barely perceptible, as if a smudge from my own brush, showed the remnant of her bruise. "I know nothing about you," I said.

She gave a slight shake of her head, forestalling questions.

I ran my finger across her lips, felt the softness of her skin, the warmth of her breath on the back of my hand, heard the sound of her breathing. She tilted her head up so that her lips brushed across my fingers and nuzzled into my palm. Then she lifted her face and kissed me.

The touch of her mouth on mine came as a shock, as if I had been dreaming and this was suddenly real. It lasted a minute, and then she broke away, placing her hands on my chest, palms flat, pushing, separating from me. She stood up and moved to the window, remaining there with her back to the room.

"The tide is coming in," her voice said. Beyond the walls of the church the ocean sighed, the sandpipers called on the beach. When she turned again, she studied me with a serious expression, as if regarding a stranger.

"What is it?" I said.

"I wonder if I should have done that."

"Are you regretting it?"

"No. No. But still."

I said to her, "Would you pose for me again?"

She walked over to the door and opened it wider. Light entered, the smell of the ocean, the sound of the incoming tide.

When she spoke, her voice was flat. "Don't have any illusions about who I am, Leo. Or what I can be." She stepped out through the doorway. Holding her sandals she quickly crossed the sand, skipping past the puddles, lifting her skirt high on her thighs when her feet splashed the water up around her legs. On the other side she bent to slip her sandals on before turning to look back—like the woman in "Love and the Pilgrim." But she did not stretch out her hand, and she was quickly gone.

I turned back to the painting. And there, as my eyes adjusted to the darker interior, the scent of Lucky Strike cigarettes hanging in the air touched some chord in me and I was plunged into another world.

THE PINK AND ROUNDED CURVE of the woman's breast was a few inches from my face. I was naked, so was she. We had not exchanged a word in the last hour. I hadn't even seen much of her face, just her pink nipple and the curve of her breast rising and falling very slightly with her breathing. The overhead lights were bright, without shadows, and beneath her skin I could see the line of two bluish veins.

When I glanced down and to the left I noticed a slight sheen of perspiration in the space between her breasts, and below, her navel and the gentle swell of her belly. A fold of white sheet was draped over one of her thighs, and the contrast of pink skin and white cloth and her dark pubic hair drew my attention. I knew I shouldn't look. All I could think about was that I must not get an erection because fifteen other people were staring at us intently.

The woman and I were arranged on a platform in a complicated pose based on the figures in Rubens's painting *The Union of Earth and Water*. The people peering at us so attentively were students in Don Jarvis's life drawing class in the art school on Hamilton Street in Vancouver. Usually I would have been among them. But to earn a bit of extra income, I sometimes sat as a model in the portrait drawing sessions. Always clothed, though, and never practically entwined with a naked woman.

By avoiding all eye contact with the other students in the room, and by keeping my eyes on the far wall, and by not looking at the woman's body, I managed to get through the next hour.

After the session was over, and we were dressed, she surprised me by asking if I wanted to go for a beer at the Alcazar, the pub two blocks away that was favoured by art students. Her name was Hollis and she was a painter. She had a thin nose and a wide expressive mouth framed by short untidy hair, and she was quite a few years older than me, at least in her mid-twenties. Her eyes were outlined with heavy mascara. She smoked Lucky Strike cigarettes and wore a leather jacket, like Marlon Brando's in *The Wild One*, with metal studs and zippered pockets and a buckled waist.

I told her I painted landscapes. She gave me a look, half disbelieving, down her nose, raising her eyebrows. Her scrutiny made me uncomfortable. Her gestures were animated, quick, her bony fingers fluttering in the air, the numerous rings on her fingers sparkling, both wrists jangling with bracelets. She wore red lipstick, and she looked gypsy-like in the hazy light of the bar. When she asked whose work I liked and I mentioned Edward Hopper and Andrew Wyeth and Corot, she laughed and asked me what century I thought I was living in. I hadn't heard of any of the artists she talked about—de Kooning, Kline, Joan Mitchell. I was eighteen years old, living on my own for the first time, and I wanted to be an artist. She made me feel ignorant, inexperienced, out of my depth. And completely fascinated.

In those days, if people asked me about myself, my past, I usually made up a story about my parents dying in an automobile accident and being brought up by an aunt. But this time, when Holly asked, I told her the truth, that I had grown up in the Guild Home for Boys, up on 44th Avenue in Kerrisdale. Her manner changed then. She leaned across the table and touched my cheek and told me I had sad-poet eyes. Later in life, when I was a little older, I understood that change, and how my story would affect women, and sometimes I took advantage of it.

Holly and I talked a long time in the bar. She switched from beer to bourbon. And then she took me to her loft above a Japanese grocery store on Powell Street. When she opened the door and flipped the light switch the whole room lit up and the colour hit me like a physical blow. An enormous abstract painting leaned against the opposite wall. Thick yellows bright as exotic flowers, brilliant jungle greens, slashes of reds and pinks like the feathers of tropical parrots. I was stunned.

There were other paintings in the room, all of them big and bold. Slabs of midnight blue over smears of charcoal black, jagged orange gestures breaking through fields of deep purples. They were shocking, violent, almost alive. I'd never seen anything like them before. Everything on the canvases seemed a chaos, a random clamour of savage colour and primitive shapes. But with a meaning to it, a hidden meaning that seemed just beyond my ability to understand. I was lost, overwhelmed. But I was also impressed.

When I asked her what they were about, she answered that they weren't pictures of something, like the landscapes I painted, and they weren't for decoration either. They were facts, she told me. Not a copy of reality, but reality itself.

"I don't paint nature," she said. "I am nature. Think about that one when you're doing one of your landscapes." Then she had turned off the lights, plunging the paintings into darkness, leaving a burning afterimage like fireworks on my retina.

She took me to her bed, in that room with its sweet scent of oil paint and tangy turpentine, and kissed me with a mouth that tasted of bourbon and tobacco. My real education had begun there, in art as well as in love.

CHAPTER 16

To work, I told myself, as I headed to the chapel, hurrying across the damp sand and straight up to "Love and the Pilgrim." I focused on the technical problems presented by the darkened varnish and the fragile pigments. But I had held the brush and cloths for only a few minutes before I set them down, unable to lose myself today in the painting's shadows. I could not stop thinking of Lorca.

I reached for my sketchbook and opened it to the portrait I'd made of her yesterday. With my penknife I cut the page from the sketchbook. Finding a couple of thumbtacks in my paintbox I pinned the drawing to the wall. I remembered each stroke of the pencil, each little smudge and erasure, and what had taken place between us here in the chapel. I ran my fingers over the paper, remembering her eyes and her voice and her mouth. Then I turned away from the drawing and left.

My restlessness took me up the ridge and over to Ester Chauvin's farm, Manoir de Soulles, where I sometimes stopped for milk and cheese and on occasion took away a cooked dish of lamb stew or roast chicken. I passed the big stone barn with its smells of hay and manure just as Ester appeared from a side door, two buckets of feed in her hands, chickens clucking towards her skirts, a smile of greeting on her face as she caught sight of me.

"*Bonjour*, Monsieur Millar." She set the buckets down and we shook hands. "Something for you today? Milk, eggs?"

"No, thank you. I was just passing."

"I have a *canard* cooking in the kitchen if you need something for dinner tonight."

"Thank you, madame, but I already have sardines from Simon Grente."

"Ah. Well, next time. I will give them to Madame Daubigny."

"Madame Daubigny?"

"Yes, she was here the other day when I was butchering a duck. I told her I would be making confit today and she ordered one. It was a large duck. The two of you could have had dinner together. Both of you eating alone like that in your separate cottages is a shame."

An image flashed across my mind, of the two of us sitting down to a dinner outside in my garden, candles and moonlight. I would like nothing better, I felt like telling Ester.

After drinking a cup of coffee and a small glass of pommeau with Ester, I took my leave, resisting the urge to wander past La Maison du Paradis. Instead, I decided to head up to the Hôtel des Îles.

Coming up the path I heard voices behind the garden hedge, one in particular that I recognized, and I opened the gate hopefully. Four people were sitting in the sunshine at one of the tables, a bottle of cider between them, the dark green glass beaded with moisture. They turned at the sound of the gate. Two couples, strangers, tourists probably. I looked around. She was not here. I heard the similarity in one of the women's voices, the slight huskiness and the Parisian accent. Sticking my head into the kitchen I said hello to Victor and Linda.

"Leo. *Bonjour*," Linda said. "*Ça va?* How are you?" She gave me a quick embrace and a peck on each cheek. Victor set down the knife on the cutting board where he was chopping parsley and shook my hand.

"You have some visitors, I see."

"*Oui*, off the yacht in the harbour. Did you notice it?"

"No, I haven't been down that way."

"They came up from Brest last night. I'm just making lunch for them. You'll stay? I'm making a cheese and walnut salad."

"Thanks, but no. I had a big breakfast this morning. I need to walk it off before I think of food again. But I will have a glass of cider."

"Go and sit in the garden," Linda told me. "I'll bring you some."

I took a seat at a table on the opposite side of the garden, sitting at an angle to the visitors. Linda brought me a tall glass of amber cider and a saucer of roasted almonds.

While I sipped the cider, I listened to the visitors' conversation. But it was the one woman's voice I listened to, not the words but the timbre. She was in her fifties, petite, hair cut short into bangs that framed her face. Not at all like Lorca. But if I looked away, I could imagine it was she, and I could almost see her.

From the Hôtel des Îles I took the path that led to Les Hauts-Vents and the clearing where I'd been the other day with Père Caron. The mechanical contraption for distilling apple brandy was in place outside the little stone hut, but today it was silent, just a faint smoky apple aroma lingering in the air. Étienne was nowhere in sight. I sat down on the rough-hewn log bench. I wished Tobias would appear. If it was just the two of us here, in the daylight, not in mysterious fogs or shaded woods, we could get to know each other.

When I thought of his injury, his burden, I asked myself again if there wasn't something I could do to help him. But what? Money? I certainly had more than I needed now. For some reason, when I stopped painting, my prices went up. Serge had probably engineered it in some way, I supposed, but in any case my bank balance was healthy. But what could money do for Tobias? Did he need better care? A private tutor perhaps, or trips to the mainland, Paris even? Would that be wise? What about music lessons? Hadn't he shown some kind of talent when I heard him that day in the forest?

And then my thoughts returned to Lorca. Always back to her. I didn't know what I felt, really. Was it just loneliness? Was it sexual desire?

I opened my sketchbook and reached into my pocket for a pencil. I felt rusty, the way I imagined a musician must feel coming back to an instrument after a long absence, the fingering of chords no longer automatic.

Lorca's suggestion that I make a new painting for the chapel was still in the back of my mind, growing like a seed but not yet showing any buds. There ought to be figures in the painting, I thought, like in "Love and the Pilgrim." But what figures, and in what relation to each other? There would need to be a story, but I had no ideas. Placing the sketchbook in my pocket I headed back to the chapel.

My footsteps from earlier in the day were still visible in the sand, like those of a solitary Crusoe. The two blue herons that liked to feed along the ponds left by the tide took flight as I walked across. They made a big loop round the side of the chapel and swept down again behind me.

She was there. But not as I wanted her. She was there only as an image, the portrait drawing, still pinned to the wall. The likeness was very good, I realized. So good that I found it a bit unnerving, sitting alone with this face in front of me, her and not her at the same time. The drawing was also powerful, I saw. Precisely because it showed my desire. Had she seen that? Was that the illusion she had referred to?

I turned away, hiding her face from my gaze, and went back outside, round to the back side of the chapel. The tide had started its gradual and inexorable approach. Soon my footsteps would be erased. I took off my shirt and pants and walked naked down the sloping shelf of rock and into the warm sea, wading out to knee height, and then I dove in, feeling the clean clear water wash over me. I turned over onto my back and floated. The outline of the chapel was like a ship in the water, an ark. I thought of the blank white wall above the doorway. In my mind's eye I imagined a scene there. A landscape, vague and unformed, like a place hidden in mist, a memory or a hope.

CHAPTER 17

THE NEXT MORNING, THE TIDE MADE ACCESS TO the chapel impossible. My wandering took me in the direction of the presbytery. Perhaps Père Caron would be home. We could have a coffee together.

Coming up to his house on the west side I took a shortcut by climbing over the low stone fence and cutting through the apple orchard, past the tall mauve hollyhocks on the south wall, and was just crossing the lawn when a strange figure appeared from the side of the house, dressed in a canvas smock and wide straw hat with a veil hanging down from the brim. Two hands covered in a pair of long canvas gloves were extended as it advanced towards me.

"Are you looking for me?" a voice said.

"Père Caron?"

"Yes, somewhere underneath all of this."

The veil was lifted to reveal the priest's face. "I was just about to visit my bees. Which is why I'm wearing all this. Would you like to come and help me with the gathering of the honey?"

"I don't know anything about bees." I indicated my bare arms. "I'm not exactly dressed for it, either."

"No matter. Come with me back to the house. I've got some extra gear."

Five minutes later I emerged wearing a long raincoat, a veiled straw hat like the priest's and a pair of gardening gloves on my hands.

"They don't usually sting," he explained as we walked down towards a cleared area near the trees where a number of rectangular wooden hives were arranged in a semicircle. "At least not me, after all this time. But they might be disturbed by the presence of a stranger, so keep your movements slow."

As we drew closer to the hives I could see the bees, little black dots in the air, hovering around the structures or moving back and forth to the trees in a steady stream.

"I sometimes use a smoker to pacify them," Caron said, "but it leaves them confused and agitated. Don't worry, you're well protected. Bees are actually quite docile. The stories of people being attacked by swarms are mostly myth. They're not going to mind sharing a bit of their honey with us."

I could now distinguish the black dots as individual bees. A steady hum buzzed from the interior of the structures, like the sound made by plucking rapidly on a stretched rubber band.

"They have their own music," Père Caron said. "Each individual bee is insignificant on its own, but together, all those wings moving in unison create a voice. The voice of the hive." He puts a hand on my arm. "Stand here and listen a moment."

There were fluctuations in the sound, slight variations in volume, a little more intense on one side, a momentary pocket of silence on the other.

"Like an orchestra," I said.

"Directed by the same conductor that guides our own actions."

"Whom you call God?"

"Something more than chance, perhaps?" he answered. "The buzzing sounds monotonous to most people, but I can hear the differences in the voices. Mostly they are content, happy to have sunshine and flowers. When a storm is approaching you will hear a tone of anxiety. If a wasp or a mouse gets into the hive the buzzing becomes angry."

"And today?"

"The sounds of harmony. All is right in their world. You see that they are flying back and forth towards those trees?" He pointed a gloved hand. "Just on the other side is a meadow of lavender. A lot of nectar is being brought back. The voice of the hive today is one of industriousness too."

Some of the bees had discovered my presence and were buzzing around my veil, a couple of them settling on the cloth and crawling about just inches from my nose. I raised a hand to brush them away.

Père Caron touched my arm. "Keep your movements calm and slow. These are the guards of the hive. They are curious about you, nothing more." He lifted the lid from a hive, set it on the ground and then slid out one of the flats on which the bees had constructed a comb. Gently, he shook the bees loose. "Ah, nice and full of honey."

While I watched, he removed his glove and used his fingers to break off a small piece of comb. "Taste this. Just chew it lightly and spit out the wax when the honey is gone."

I lifted my veil, slipped the piece of comb into my mouth and chewed. "I can taste the lavender."

"I would like to have an orange blossom honey, like the one I tasted in Provence once, but orange trees will not take to our climate. Twice I've imported seedlings from the mainland, only to have them wither at the first touch of the east winds."

Taking up a pail and a wooden spatula, he began to ease the honey gently from the flat, the golden syrup pouring out in a thick slow stream. "Is that not a miracle?"

"If you believe that miracles are possible," I said.

The priest gave me an inquiring look. "I often think that the bees can teach us something."

"Harmony, order, co-operation?"

"Yes, of course the hive is a model of a good society. But I was thinking that when you take an interest in something other than yourself, even something as apparently insignificant as a hive of bees, the world becomes a much more remarkable place. There is a chain of events from the pollen in the flower to that honey on your tongue which goes far far beyond this little meadow. And you are a link in the chain. You have a part to play as well."

"And what would that be?"

He smiled. "Have you settled down in the cottage?"

"I don't really think I can restore the damage to the painting in the chapel, Père. It needs the hand of a professional. I'm not even sure I'm going about the cleaning process in the correct way."

"I see." He busied himself with the honey flat, but I'd heard the disappointment in his voice.

"I had a visit from Madame Daubigny," I said.

"Ah."

"She made an interesting suggestion. That I should make a brand-new painting for the chapel."

"To replace our 'Love and the Pilgrim'?" He took up the pail of honey and moved in the direction of the house. I followed, removing my hat and gloves, which were becoming uncomfortably hot. "And this new painting, can you accomplish such a thing?"

"I can try. With your permission."

"By all means, my boy. Of course."

"I can't replace the Asmodeus. And I'm certainly not as talented as he was."

"One never knows what a painting can accomplish. And what will be the subject?"

"I don't know."

"Maybe it will be an island landscape, with figures. Like the original. Pilgrims and lovers?"

"Maybe."

We walked for a few moments in silence, and then I said, "I wanted to talk to you about Tobias. Do you think he would take to some music lessons?" I told him about hearing Tobias trying to play the clarinet.

"Have you put the idea to Madame Daubigny?"

"Sort of. She didn't discount it entirely."

"I know you want to help him in some way, Leo, but I honestly don't think Tobias has much talent in that direction. I have tried to get him interested in the piano more than once." He shook his head. "But I have a better idea. Why don't you be the one to give Tobias lessons? In drawing."

"Really? Do you think he would be interested?"

"He likes to draw. He is a bit of a wild boy, but when he is drawing he becomes very serene. The activity seems to give him pleasure. His whole face changes."

"Of course I'd be more than happy to help him." I was thinking of how important drawing had been for me when I was Tobias's age, how it had allowed me to forget my loneliness.

Père Caron said, "I'll put it to him so that he understands. The answer will be his alone, though. Now, I must give you a jar of honey to take home." He took me through to a pantry where two of the shelves contained rows of neatly arranged jars.

"My treasure trove. Each of these is from my bees—collected, strained and bottled by my own hand. As a painter, you will appreciate the varieties of colour." There were transparent golds, silky ambers, dark malty-looking syrups. He ran his fingers over the jars, "Now, let's see. Ah, here. I think you will like this one." He unscrewed the cap, lifted out a seal of white wax and reached for a teaspoon in the drawer. Dipping it into the honey he offered the spoon to me. "Taste it."

The flavour was immediate and powerful. I ran the honey back and forth over my tongue and swallowed. "Something grassy, summery?"

"Wild thyme. Last summer. It was growing everywhere." He handed me the jar. "And you must take one for Madame Daubigny as well. This one." He reached for a second jar. "It's not a grand cru, but not ordinary either. Perfectly suitable for a gift."

He could just as easily have given it to her himself, I thought. Was he trying to steer us together? I shot a sharp look him, and received a curious smile in return. I felt myself colour slightly.

As I left, the two jars of honey in my pocket, the priest called, "And, Leo, let the boy come to you, if he wants to. Who knows, perhaps miracles are possible, even if they are only small ones."

CHAPTER 18

I WANTED TO SEE LORCA AGAIN BUT I DID NOT GO TO
her. In fact, I avoided that side of the island completely, only
travelling between my cottage in LeBec and the chapel, and
sticking to the route des Matelots, or walking along the eastern
shore if the tides made it possible.

Of course, it would have been easy enough to just stroll over
to La Maison du Paradis and knock on the door. There was that
jar of honey from Père Caron, which I'd promised him I'd give to
her. A suitable excuse. Not that any excuse or reason was necessary. We were practically neighbours, after all, and what could
be more natural than a neighbourly hello on the way to the shop.

But then I would think again of the almost cold way she
had spoken when she left the chapel. I remembered also that
black eye on the day I first saw her, and the band of lighter skin
on her finger where a ring had recently been removed, and her
seeming reluctance to say anything about herself.

There were other reasons why I did not go to her. For so
long I had lived with a heart of ice and now I feared a thaw. I

had another motivation for staying close to the chapel, one that had nothing to do with Lorca, or even my work there. I was waiting for Tobias. It was clear to me now that until I met him normally, in a way that would let me see him as an ordinary boy, my lingering illusions, or confusions, between him and Piero, would continue. I wanted to know him for himself.

The restoration of the painting progressed slowly and methodically. For hours I lost myself in the careful removal of grime and yellowed varnish from the surface of the canvas. The two figures were now fully visible and I was working my way outwards, as if the light emanated from them, pushing the shadows back.

When my hands or my eyes became tired I would sit back on one of the pews and look up to the blank wall where the painting had hung. In my mind I painted scenes there, but only in my mind, for still I had no ideas or inspiration.

Lorca had said something when she was encouraging me to paint a scene of the island, that the landscape had the hush before a storm, that it gave her a sense of something about to happen, something strange and beautiful. So I waited. Not for a storm but for the beauty.

In the meantime I drew. Once, my sketchbooks had always been in use, had always been in my pocket when I left the apartment, a pencil in my hand. The book and the pencil had been instruments of joy. And then the covers had shut, and remained shut, until the other day when I drew Lorca's portrait.

I sat now with the book on my lap, doodling, drawing faces, some invented, some familiar, like Linda and Victor at the hotel, or Simon, testing my visual memory. Flipping over to a fresh page I started to draw Père Caron with his bushy moustache and the ever-present floppy beret. It was a face that could have lent itself to caricature, but I resisted, because it was a kind face that I did not want to insult.

A memory came to me, of the time at the Guild when I'd made that drawing of Brother Adams and instead of punishing me he'd given me a book on how to draw. Thinking of Brother Adams always evoked a complex mixture of emotions: loss, guilt, gratitude never expressed. It was through his generosity and faith in me that I had been able to leave Vancouver and continue my studies in New York, and it was through his grace that I had gone to Paris.

The last time I saw him was after I had left the Guild, although I was still living in Vancouver, in the studio that had been passed on to me by Hollis when she left for San Francisco. Adams had told me that he'd put my name in for a scholarship and I'd been awarded a grant to further my studies at the Art Students League of New York. I was immensely grateful to him, but after moving I didn't stay in touch as much as I should have, only sending the occasional postcard. Grateful as I was to Adams, the Guild was a place I wanted to forget. Being an outcast and an outsider, the shame of it, was no longer a part of my picture of myself. I never mentioned the Guild to new acquaintances; instead I used a story about being raised by grandparents after my parents were killed in a car crash. In New York no one really cared about your past, anyway.

When news came of Brother Adams's death, I had changed studios a number of times and the announcement took three weeks to be forwarded to me. There was also a letter from the headmaster of the Guild explaining that Brother Adams had remembered me in his will. The amount was quite a bit. He'd requested that I use the money to go to Paris—he'd been there once himself as a young man, and he always said it was the only place in the world for a painter to be. Of course, I was told, I also had the right to do whatever I wanted with the money.

That evening, as I sat at the window of my studio on Coenties Slip, down at the tip of Manhattan, watching the daylight fade and the lights of the cars moving along the Brooklyn Bridge, my heart broke and I wept. I'd never lost anyone before. Even when Hollis announced that she was leaving I'd gotten over it soon enough. Not having known my parents, I'd always felt that I had nobody to lose. Now I knew that was not true. There had been times over the years when Brother Adams had been kind to me and I'd fantasized that he was my father, concocting stories in my mind about secrets and hidden identities. I had known him all my life. I wept now because I had never felt more of an orphan.

Adams used to have a little painting of mine, one I'd given to him during my first year of art school. A little landscape done in Stanley Park. It was always in the same place on the wall of his office when I visited. He'd said to me once about the painting, "Who needs a view when you can see a world as beautiful as this?" Maybe that was one of the reasons why I'd become a landscape painter. For the joy it gave.

That night I'd had a dream.

I found myself standing alone on a desolate and wild shore. I'd been shipwrecked. In the far distance I glimpsed the faint shape of an island. I knew that I had to find a way to get to that island. The only things I had with me were my paintings. It occurred to me that I might be able to use the wooden stretcher bars and frames to construct some kind of raft. I could then use the actual painted canvas to rig up a sail. Somehow I managed to do this. As I built my craft, the sea became rough and a thick mist began to envelop everything. I was afraid to venture out, that my raft would fall apart, that I would lose my paintings, and even my life. But then I heard what sounded like Brother Adams's voice in the mist, repeating his favourite bit of advice. *Faith and hope, my boy. Faith and hope.*

I managed to get the raft through the surf and then I twisted the sail into the wind and in a few moments I had surged out beyond the breakers. Soon the wind fell, and there was nothing around me, no shore in sight, not a breeze or a current, and I kept thinking I should have stayed on the land because at least there had been water and fruit and a chance at rescue.

Gradually sunlight began to show through the mist, and I could feel a slight breeze picking up. My raft began to move again. And then I saw other rafts. They were strange-looking things, of odd shapes and unusual colours. One of them swept by me, all deep earth tones and soft golds like an aged oriental carpet. A man who looked like Rembrandt sat at the tiller. Another raft skimmed by, black and white and all jagged shapes and angles. A stocky bald man in a striped T-shirt waved. Picasso. Other boats joined the fleet. There was van Gogh in a raft with sails of bright corn yellow and intense blue. Matisse steered past in a blaze of red. I looked up at my own sails as they filled with wind and they were glowing, all silvery light and soft dove greys and milky whites, as beautiful as anything I'd ever seen.

THE NEXT MORNING I HAD BOOKED MY PASSAGE on a real ship, the SS *Volendam*, bound for Le Havre, with a connecting train to Paris.

CHAPTER 19

I ENTERED THE CHAPEL CRADLING AN OVERFLOW-
ing bouquet of wildflowers in my arms and let them slide
onto the table, where they spilled out in a spray of yellow and
orange. In the little vestry where Père Caron kept the objects
necessary for Mass, and where I stored my painting equipment during services, I found a wide-mouthed pewter vase on
a shelf. I filled it halfway from one of the water bottles I kept
behind the door.

With my pocketknife I snipped the ends of the stalks from
the flowers before arranging the bouquet. I placed the vase in
the sunlight flooding in through the window. The bright yellow of the petals, glowing so intensely in the floating array
of flowers, made me feel almost dizzy, intoxicated, as if the
colour were some honeyed wine that I had been drinking. The
flowers were *marguerites jaunes.* Brown-eyed Susans. Claudine
had taught me the name during our first summer in Montmartin when I used to bring her bouquets of wildflowers after my
painting excursions.

In most ways, she had been a practical and down-to-earth person, but she also had a romantic side to her. Once, I had been sitting in the garden of her mother's house, sketching a blue flower that grew near the wall. "Aquilegia vulgaris," Claudine had said, coming up behind me. "Commonly known as the columbine. From the Latin for 'dove.' See here, this little spur at the top is a bit like a dove's neck." She touched the blossom delicately with the tip of her pink fingernail. "And the petals fold out like wings. When Mary, mother of Jesus, was pregnant, she went to visit her cousin Elizabeth, who somehow knew that the child was going to be the promised Messiah. Elizabeth is the one who says, 'Blessed art thou among women, and blessed is the fruit of thy womb.' I love the sound of that phrase. So beautiful. When these parts here, the spurs or dove's neck, wilt and fall to the ground, they resemble shoes. So in medieval times the story grew that wherever Mary's foot touched the ground during that visit, columbines sprang up."

Then Claudine reached forward and plucked the flower from its stem, and with the side of her thumbnail sliced the blossom open. "Pistil, stigma, stamen, style, ovary," she said, reciting the names of the parts. "It's kind of a secret, isn't it, these hidden chambers inside a flower? When I see the harmony and the logic inside a flower I think of our own hearts and maybe that the reason they beat is not just an accident of nature."

I remembered touching her upper lip, where a little dusting of yellow pollen had somehow lodged. "Powdered sunlight," she said as I rubbed it between my fingertips.

Would I ever paint a bouquet with the same sense of joy that I once had? I turned away now from the flowers to the big piece of canvas that was tacked up on the east wall. I had obtained it through Simon Grente, who'd fetched it from a sail-maker on the mainland. The canvas was of a rougher quality than I would usually select, but it would do for the new painting I intended to make. When I had a subject.

A couple of small boards, painted white, sat on the table. I had asked Simon Grente for any scraps that might be lying around, and he had cut them to size. They were for Tobias— when he came, if he came.

As if in answer to my hopes, three notes from a whistle sounded in the quiet of the morning. Looking out, I saw Père Caron and Tobias making their way across the causeway. The priest waved. Tobias blew the whistle again.

Père Caron entered first, taking off his floppy beret and shaking my hand. "*Bonjour.* Tobias has come to see how one goes about making a painting."

The boy hovered behind the priest, giving me a shy look. He leaned forward to sniff the flowers, then studied the paint-box with its gleaming brass fittings. He was wearing a short-sleeved shirt with a check pattern of green and white and a pair of khaki pants, both of which looked freshly laundered. In fact, he was altogether cleaner than I had seen him before. When he stepped past me, his curls gave off a scent of shampoo.

He ran his fingers across the paintbox, tracing the letters engraved there, a smile on his face, that familiar enigmatic smile.

"That box used to belong to another little boy," I said. "His name was Piero." A sudden impulse came over me, to give the box to Tobias. But I couldn't, I couldn't part with it; it was all I had left of my son.

"I have something for you," I said, opening the paintbox and bringing out a small cardboard carton. Inside were four tubes of paint. On each one was the name of the manufacturer, Liquitex. They were labelled with the names of the pigments: *titanium white, cadmium yellow, alizarin crimson, ultramarine blue.*

They were something new called "acrylic," a paint that could be mixed with water instead of linseed oil and turpentine. They had come from André Jocelyn, the store where I had bought my materials for years. Piero often came with me and they made much of him there, calling him *le petit maître*, always taking his questions seriously and treating him with professional dignity.

The last time I'd been to the shop was in the months after Claudine and Piero died, when I'd taken to roaming the streets of Paris, obsessively revisiting the places where we used to go. I'd been standing outside the store window, remembering happier times, when André came out to greet me. He asked after the boy and I lied, saying he was fine and I'd bring him for a visit soon. The box of paints had been a gift for *le petit*. Never used.

"The paints are for you," I said now to Tobias.

He reached for them, hesitated with a glance at Père Caron, who nodded, then gathered them up.

"They're very easy to use—all you have to do is mix them with water. I'll show you."

I poured some water into a jam jar before uncapping the tubes and squeezing a bit of each colour onto the palette. I handed him a brush and pointed to one of the whitewashed panels.

"What shall we paint?"

Tobias pointed at the bouquet.

"The flowers? Good idea." I dipped a brush into the yellow paint and made an outline of the petals. Adding a little red and a touch of black to make a dark brown, I dabbed it in the centre of the flower. "You give it a try."

Tobias drew a flower shape, quite accurately I noticed, then filled in the petals with yellow as I had done. He rinsed the brush and squeezed the excess water from the bristles with thumb and forefinger, mimicking me, and then mixed the brown for the dark centres of the flowers.

"Very good. And if you want to lighten the colours, just mix in a little white."

The tip of his tongue showed between his lips as he concentrated. I smiled. Piero had done exactly the same thing when he bent over his drawing.

Watching the sure way Tobias applied himself, I said to Père Caron, "It's not the first time he's painted?"

"No. As I mentioned, he loves to draw, and sometimes he uses some tubes of gouache I have at home."

We stood silently for a time, watching Tobias work. My eyes moved up from the boy's painting to the pale scar that encircled his neck. He was still too young to know fully the extent of his tragedy. Yet he seemed content, and today his expression even showed a hint of pleasure. Children are like that, I thought, they can forget. But the suffering will come later.

"He has some talent, *n'est-ce pas?*" the priest commented. "An artist in the making."

"*Le petit maître,*" I murmured. The little master.

Piero had shown early promise. He might even have gone on to develop into an artist. He was often in a corner of the studio when I worked, silently painting his own little pictures, sometimes humming tunelessly. His presence had been comforting to me, a sign that all was right with the world.

Once, when Piero was at school, I had looked through his sketchbook and amongst the drawings of dinosaurs and rocket ships I was surprised to come upon a rendering of my own face. It had some basic errors in proportion, but the likeness was uncanny; the angle of my nose, the particular shape of my upper lip, the intensity of my gaze.

I'd felt a surge of pride when I realized that Piero had drawn me from memory, for I certainly had never posed for him. I'd had no particular desire for my son to follow in my footsteps, the life of an artist was uncertain at best, but nevertheless, his skill and interest had pleased me.

And what of this boy, I wondered. Did he have a talent? And did it matter? Although if I could teach him something, a means of expression, it might help him later. Maybe I could help him find a voice. If words would always fail him, perhaps pictures would not.

Père Caron had discovered the portrait sketch of Lorca, which I'd pinned up again. "This is very good," he said.

"Thank you. She was here the other day and I did that. I'm sorry but I haven't had a chance to take that jar of honey over to her yet."

He was stroking his chin in a thoughtful manner while he studied the picture. "You are friends with her, *non?*"

I didn't answer and moved over to where Tobias was painting. The boy looked up at me expectantly.

"Not bad," I told him. "Your picture looks just like the flowers." In truth, the boy had made an admirable little painting that not only resembled the bouquet of *marguerites*, but also had a quality that was more than just childish enthusiasm. Of course he knows nature, I told myself. These flowers are an everyday part of his world.

"You like these paints, don't you? I can show you how to paint all sorts of things. You could even help me with the painting I'm going to do for the chapel." I pointed to the canvas tacked to the wall. "We'll work on it together."

He nodded vigorously, as if the matter was settled, and went back to his painting.

"Any more ideas on what the new picture will be?" the priest asked.

I ran my hand across the unpainted cotton and shook my head. "I'll have to give it some more thought."

He said, "I don't know what your true feelings are for Madame Daubigny." He paused and it took a moment for me to realize his meaning. "But with Tobias it is different because he is my responsibility."

I looked over at Tobias. "I want to help him."

"Leo, you might think I am meddling, but you ought to be clear in your mind what your relationship is to these two individuals. I don't mean this"—he tapped the drawing of Lorca—"but to the real people. Let me meddle a little further and say accept her, and the boy, for who they are. Do not let yourself substitute them for what you have lost."

I knew what he was telling me. *Don't hurt them. You are not the only one who can be disappointed.*

I folded my arms and nodded. When I turned round to look at Tobias he was no longer there. "He's gone," I said, not bothering to hide my disappointment.

"But look, he took the paints with him. That's a good

sign." Pushing back the sleeve of his jacket, Père Caron tapped his watch. "And I must go too. Time and tide wait for no man."

"Will he come back?" I asked, more to myself than to the priest.

At that very moment the chapel door opened and Tobias reappeared. He walked straight over to me and held up his painting. On the bottom edge, in lettering very similar to that on Piero's paintbox, was the name TOBIAS. He placed the painting in my hand and stepped back with a solemn little nod, and then he left the chapel again.

"There is your answer," Père Caron said.

Chapter 20

I WAS STARING INTO AN EYE; DARK, LIQUID, LONG-lashed and shining.

I crouched forward, closer, seeing a patch of light blue reflected on the surface of the eye, and in the blue a fleck of corn yellow. As I moved back, the reflection changed and I realized that the blue was the sky and the yellow was the mirrored image of the yellow kerchief I wore round my neck.

I stretched out my hand and the donkey, who seemed to be just as curious about me, tossed its head, blinking those wonderful large brown feminine eyes. The thought occurred to me that I had been seeing what the donkey itself saw—me. If I painted that reflection I would be making not only a picture of the donkey and its eye, I would in essence also be making a self-portrait. The notion struck me as a revelation about the whole enterprise of painting. A truth about the nature of seeing.

But how to paint such a truth?

I remembered the donkey painted by Caravaggio, in that wonderful unfinished *Adoration of the Shepherds*, where it is not the infant Christ, but the mild and kind and long-suffering face of the donkey in the background that carries the true meaning of the picture.

Yesterday, after Tobias and Père Caron had left the chapel, I'd set to work immediately on the big sheet of canvas tacked to the wall, wanting to capture a moment of inspiration I'd experienced as Tobias paused in the doorway, suspended between light and shadow. Using just a stick of charcoal, and not worrying too much about accuracy, I'd roughed in a sketch of a boy, his body turned away in the act of leaving, but his face still looking at me. The details of the face would come later—the smile—that would be easy enough, but sometimes a movement is so particular, conveying some essential quality, but also so fleeting, that it can be lost if not recorded right then.

This morning I'd come back. The image still pleased me, but it wasn't enough. I had no idea what else to include. Taking up the stick of charcoal, I roughed in the outlines of a building—the chapel—spending a half-hour getting the proportions right, adjusting a line, correcting an angle, erasing with a rag and starting over. Then, without even being conscious of what I was doing, I sketched in the shape of a woman. In the end I had two figures and a building, but only emptiness around them. It would have been easy enough to fill the canvas with all sorts of things—I could make up landscapes and buildings and people on the spot—but I realized that I wanted this picture to be special. I needed it to be the truest thing I'd ever done.

The unpainted expanse of canvas was like a white mist, hiding a tableau, or had the events not taken place yet? Once again

Lorca's words came back to me, of the sensation on the island that something was about to happen. An air of suspension.

I dropped the cloth and charcoal on the table, grabbed my paintbox and went out.

By now I was familiar with most of the routes criss-crossing the island, some more than others, and I headed northwest along a lesser known path, Circuit du Phare, in the direction of the lighthouse, Phare du Monde. Maybe a fresh landscape would inspire me. I was determined to make a painting. Not a portrait, or a still life of flowers, but a land-scape, like I used to do.

The fields were mostly uncultivated, although some of them were fenced or boxed in with that particular dense hedge-row, bocage, that I knew from the area around Montmartin. In one of the fields I passed a herd of white cows, perhaps belong-ing to Ester Chauvin. They were like sculptures, as if made of clay, the warm light falling on their flanks in the same way that it fell on the bleached oyster shells that sat on my windowsill in La Minerve. They all stopped their grazing and raised their heads to observe me, turning in unison as I passed, as if a man in a field were a strange sight indeed.

Before doing that portrait of Lorca I would have said I was incapable of summoning the resources to undertake a task like making a new painting for the chapel, but now, for the first time since that day in Cyprus, I felt that I was seeing the land-scape as an artist, with the eyes of the painter I had once been.

I wanted to know the island. To be an artist is to know as well as to look, to know the names of the birds, the trees, the phases of the moon, the shells on the beach, even the clouds and why the sky is blue in the morning and red at dusk, so that one can paint with faith and hope and worship. I wanted that worship again.

And then I had come upon the little grey donkey standing alone in a pasture surrounded by a low stone wall. He seemed so alone and forlorn that I stopped. I clicked my tongue and said hello and the donkey's beautiful long ears swivelled towards me and he immediately ambled over, pushing his head over the wall to snuffle at my sleeve. When I stroked my palm down the long nose I was surprised at the coarseness of the animal's fur, having expected it to be soft, like a child's toy.

The grass in the pasture had been cropped low to the ground, but on the other side of the wall it was long and green and thick, out of the donkey's reach, so I crouched down and pulled a handful free, then extended it towards the questing muzzle. The black lips were soft on my palm as the animal took the grass from me. I reached over and stroked the hide again, the rough hide, listening to the satisfying crunch of the animal's teeth on the fresh grass, aware of its warmth under my palm, the beat of its life.

A wave of affection came over me for this mild and gentle creature. I was struck by the fact that it existed at all, and that out of all the moments in time, I and it should be here together. I'd often felt the same way when I looked at Piero. That from nothing could come such a miracle was astounding. How beautiful the world could be, how strange and wonderful.

What was the name of the man in A Midsummer Night's Dream, the one whose head is transformed into that of a donkey? Bottom. That was it. Poor fellow, wandering lost and bewildered in the woods, but a princess had loved him. And then there was Puck. The magical sprite. I remembered him flying over the stage. It had been one of those few times when some of us Guild boys were taken on an excursion into the city. I must have been about nine years old. The play was at the Orpheum Theatre on Granville Street. The afternoon had been rainy, dark, with the pink and green neon signs and car headlights making it all seem magical. And even though the wires suspending Puck as he flew back and forth were clearly visible, it was still thrilling—a boy who could fly and make magic.

Why had I never taken Piero to see that play? It must have been on countless times in Paris.

The donkey wandered off a few metres, nibbling at the grass, and I perched on the wall, opening my paintbox and setting my sketchbook in the lid. Using a palette knife I mixed yellow ochre with touches of iron oxide black and crimson until I had a suitable mid-grey. Additions of white in varying degrees gave me a range of cool and warm tones that were similar to the various aspects of light and shade that made up the colour of the donkey, a grey violet like the hue of wet beach sand, almost monochrome but full of subtleties.

I moistened a flat-bristle brush in turpentine and touched it to a mound of colour. My hand, holding the loaded brush, hovered with anticipation, but also anxiety, almost with dread. Then I applied the brush to the paper, rapidly smudging greys to define the shapes. No detail, no indication of what the shapes were or would be as I pushed the brush, dragged it, twisted the bristles hard against the paper, creating a language of marks to describe what I saw, what I felt.

Once the schematic block-in was done I laid in some washes, thin umber to define the earth, a hint of blue for the sky, then I switched to a smaller softer sable brush for the details, the patches of white on the ears, the dark almost brown stripe down the back. For the grass in the foreground I used pale yellow, which became a muted green with touches of black.

I worked in a kind of trance, quickly, without conscious thought, to forestall doubt, to let my emotions make the picture, putting into it all my fear and longing and uncertainty. When the shapes became a form, and when the forms became an object, and when the object suggested life, the donkey itself, I sat back. But one more thing. Switching to my smallest sable, its tip not much thicker than one of the donkey's eyelashes, I touched a tiny dab of pure cadmium yellow on the eye. Too small to mean anything to a viewer, but I would know what it was. A kind of self-portrait in a fleck of colour.

There it was. Just a little painting of a donkey, nothing really, but the sight of it almost broke my heart. And at the same time I felt such joy.

I wanted to share this feeling; I wanted to show the picture to one person in particular.

CHAPTER 21

THE ROUTE TO THE HEADLAND KNOWN AS LE COLOMbier was familiar to me by now and I was soon walking along the chemin des Sirènes in a green silence broken only by the softest rustling of the drizzle in the leaves overhead. As I caught sight of the cottage roof I remembered her parting words. Not a warning exactly but definitely a caution. My steps faltered. A sense of foolishness came over me and I felt just like a schoolboy bringing his handiwork home to be praised. I wished I'd brought the jar of honey from Père Caron instead. At least that would be a legitimate reason for appearing at her door.

When the cottage came into view, a slow curl of white smoke hanging above the chimney, I veered off to the left instead of going to the front door, following a little sandy track that I remembered from a previous walk. Here, a patch of wild barley grew and I unfolded my pocketknife, then kneeled to cut a bundle of stalks until I had enough for a loose bouquet, the feathery ears thick with plump seeds. Low to the ground in the barley were small poppies, crimson and black. I knew that they were prone to wilt within the day when picked, but nevertheless I gathered a handful to insert among the stalks of barley.

The bouquet was cool and moist in my hand. At the cottage gate, with its sign LA MAISON DU PARADIS, just as I lifted the latch, a burst of music poured out from one of the open windows—a cascade of notes ascending and descending in a torrent of sound, whirling, frenzied, passionate, wild.

And just as suddenly as it had burst forth, the music stopped. Silence. The soft patter of raindrops. My own breathing. I willed the music to come again, wanting that rapid cluster of notes to fill the air. I knew this was not Tobias, but Lorca. This was real music.

The clarinet started up again in a different cadence, embellished with quick lilting flourishes. Now there was something hauntingly familiar in what I heard, harking back over the years, and I recognized that fast dissonance, the high trills held longer than breath seemed possible. Hollis. In her studio that first time, when she'd put on some strange music and awakened a fire in me. "Do you dig Stravinsky?" she had asked. I remembered the painting on the sleeve of the LP. A phoenix rising from the ashes—the Firebird. She'd played it often, and I'd listened with her, reading the words on the back of the record sleeve, so often that they had fixed themselves in my memory like a poem learned by heart.

> In that land where a princess sits under lock and key,
> Pining behind massive walls.
> There gardens surround a palace all of glass;
> There Firebirds sing by night. . . .

For some reason, a mental slip of the tongue, I had mis-read the first word of the second line as *Painting*. Perhaps that was why I still remembered the little poem.

Even as these memories were running through my head, the music changed. Slow now, pulsing, permeated with melancholy. I heard it and understood it—that striving for completeness, for union, for wholeness. It was music made not for the listener but for the creator, articulating something deep inside the soul.

When the music ended, it did so not with a conclusion but a trickling away, a weariness, almost defeat. As if there were nothing more to say.

Gradually I became aware of other sounds that had been there all the time but seemed to have paused for the music. The soft hiss of the waves on the beach below the cottage, the faint bleating of sheep, the caw of a crow. A gutter was trickling somewhere beside the house, and the smoky scent of burning logs hung in the air.

I felt as if I'd been under a spell. There was only the memory of the music. Ephemeral. Not like a painting or a book, objects that could be touched, but like water, slipping out of your grasp as you tried to hold it. I walked softly up the path, stopping just short of the door when I glimpsed Lorca through the window. She was sitting on the couch in front of the fireplace, hunched forward, the clarinet across her knees glowing in the light of the flickering flames. The fingers of her right hand were rub-bing back and forth across her lips. The mournful desolation of the music was still on her face.

I knocked. Her expression was troubled when she opened the door, but it changed into something hopeful when she rec-ognized me, and then noticed the bouquet in my hands.

"Leo." She took the flowers and as I leaned forward to kiss her she turned her head so that the kiss landed on her cheek. "Is it raining?" she said. "You look chilled. Come and sit by the fire." Taking my hand she drew me into the warmth of the house. She was wearing a black blouse with pearl buttons and a dark suede skirt. Her feet were bare.

I placed my paintbox and sketchbook on the couch as I sat down and extended my hands towards the warming flames. On the side table stood a carafe, her Lucky Strikes and a glass with an inch of red wine in the bottom. When she had arranged the bouquet in a vase and set it on the windowsill, she brought a fresh glass, filled it for me, topped up her own and sat down at the other end of the couch.

"Have you been out painting?"

"One small thing."

"Can I see?"

I handed her the sketchbook. A gust of damp air from the open window swept across the room, blowing her hair across her face and fluttering the pages of the sketchbook. She flattened her hand over the painting.

"What a noble little creature," she said. "Pure of heart." She smiled sadly. "It's very good."

"Other than that portrait sketch of you, this is the first time I have really painted since, since Cyprus." I found that I could say the word without the usual upsurge of pain in my heart. "You inspired it."

"Really? Am I to be your muse, then?"

"I've been avoiding you," I said. "Or trying to."

She took her Lucky Strikes and went to the open window, shaking a cigarette loose from the pack and lighting it. I wandered over to the middle of the room by the big oak table. Some books lay scattered next to sheets of music manuscript paper. I don't read music, but at the top of the sheet were the handwritten words *Contra Mortem et Tempus.* I spoke them aloud.

"A quote from a painter, actually," she said. "Ernst Joseph-son. In reference to his painting *Näcken*, of a boy sitting in a waterfall playing a violin. I saw it in Stockholm once."

"Like Tobias, in the forest with your clarinet. What do the words mean?"

"'Against Death and Time.' Isn't that the point of art?"

The manuscript had a number of crossings-out and corrections. In her own hand, I assumed. "Are you composing something?"

She nodded. "Trying to."

"I was outside earlier, I heard you playing. The second part sounded very tragic. Was it this music?"

"Yes, it was."

"Why was it so sad?"

"It's an old piece that was never finished. From the war years."

I had guessed that there was a ten-year gap in our ages. When the war ended twenty years ago she would have been about twenty. "Was it hard for you, that time?"

She drew on her cigarette and turned to blow smoke out the window. "Life is hard, Leo. You know that, better than most people."

"Tell me something about yourself," I said. "Why . . . why did you have a black eye when I met you?"

"Oh, Leo," she answered softly, but said nothing more.

I looked down at the books on the table: *Les larmes viendront plus tard*, with a cover picturing an African landscape, George Sand's *Un hiver à Majorque* with Delacroix's portrait of Chopin on the cover. Lying open and face down was *Pensées Morales* of Marcus Aurelius. I picked this one up and turned it over. A passage had been marked in red ink. I read the underlined words out loud: "'The sexual embrace can only be compared with music and with prayer.'" I put the book down. "Do you believe that is true?"

"Don't you?"

She stubbed out her cigarette in a scallop shell and closed the window. Leaning back against the sill she looked at me. That same considered look from the first day in the chapel, part curiosity, part defiance, part something else entirely. A log shifted in the fireplace with a flurry of red sparks. The rain rattled against the window. Her eyes were deep and impenetrable. Minutes seemed to pass.

Then she crossed the floor and took me by the hand. Her eyes were shining. "Come," she said, leading me to the stairway.

Her bedroom was shadowy in the muted light from outside. A white chest of drawers with a mirror, the glass draped with a curtain of lace. The bed was large, covered by a white quilt. Kindling and newspaper had been laid in the small fireplace. Lorca took a box of matches and lit the fire, then one of the candles in the black wrought-iron chandelier on the mantel.

"Come," she said again, taking my hand, pulling me to the bed.

The rain rattled against the window. Outside the circle of light and warmth from the fireplace, the darkening room seemed to enclose us, folding us into its glow. When I kissed her it was like sinking into black water. I held my breath. And then I exhaled, drowning.

AFTERWARDS, WE LAY APART, our faces close, gazing at each other without speaking. There were fine smile lines on the skin at the outer corners of her eyes. I was aware of the difference in our ages again. And in our lives.

"What?" she said after a while, responding to the intensity of my stare.

"I want to know you."

"Isn't this enough?"

"Not only like this. More."

"You mustn't love me, Leo." Her expression changed, she got up and went into the bathroom. A tap ran, the toilet flushed.

She came out wearing a red and white kimono and sat down on the corner of the bed with her back to me, the kimono sliding down her shoulders. Like an odalisque, I thought, looking at her long back, like Ingres's *La Grande Baigneuse* in the Louvre.

As she stretched for her cigarettes on the bedside table I immediately noticed the ring on her left hand. A simple unadorned gold band. It had not been there when she went into the bathroom.

"You found your ring."

"I never lost it."

"I noticed you weren't wearing one before."

"I decided not to wear it. For a while."

She lit the cigarette, her back still to me, head turned away, the smoke making a lingering spiral towards the ceiling. I heard the pattering of the rain, the crackle of the flames, the thudding of my heart.

She turned to look at me. "I am married. My husband is Armand Daubigny. He's the conductor of the Orchestre de Paris. In which I play. He is twenty years older than me. I was his pupil. We've been married for fifteen years. Satisfied?"

I was disappointed, but not really surprised. A woman of her age and beauty would not be single. "And the black eye?"

She looked away. The rain was a continuous tapping at the window accompanied by a gurgling from the gutter outside. She sighed. "He hit me when he found out I was having an affair. With another musician. Not from the orchestra. A jazz musician. He despises jazz." The casual way she said this, as if it were hardly of consequence, surprised me. She raised a hand to her cheek.

"It's gone. It's over."

"The affair? Your marriage?"

"The bruise."

I looked at the scars on her wrists. "Is that something you do often? Have affairs?"

A shrug.

"Is that what I am? An affair? Or not even that?"

She leaned forward and flicked cigarette ash towards the fireplace.

"Do you love your husband?" I said.

"It's complicated."

Neither of us spoke for a time.

Then I asked, "Why *did* you make love to me?"

"Because it was pure. Without questions or answers."

"Was this a revenge on your husband?" I knew I sounded bitter.

"Don't be cheap, Leo. It doesn't suit you."

"We just made love. Is that cheap?"

"Do you think you can fall in love so easily? With a stranger. You want to know about me? Well, where should I start? The day I was born? Or is it my husband who interests you?"

"Sorry." I stroked the warm skin of her back, already desiring her again. "Perhaps you were just being kind to a lonely man. Is my desperation that obvious?" When she didn't answer, I said, "Or did you just need a little recreation to relieve the tedium of a rainy afternoon." I said it to provoke her, to get a reaction.

She spun round and glared at me. "What do you want from me, Leo? Someone to replace your dead wife?" She jerked away, pulling the kimono over her shoulders.

For a second I was speechless. Then I was getting up, pulling my pants on, grabbing my shoes and shirt, already going down the stairs, face hot with anger, shame, humiliation.

I heard her calling, "Leo! I didn't mean that."

Too late.

As I passed the table and grabbed my sketchbook, I noticed that the poppies in the bouquet were already wilted.

CHAPTER 22

I walked back along the chemin des Sirènes feeling used. And foolish for letting myself be used. For feeling anything. Was it all a game to her? A little fling that she'd instantly regretted?

The leaves around me were dripping but the rain had stopped, although the sky was dark with sullen clouds. At the junction with the route des Matelots I paused. I wanted a drink. I wanted several. But I didn't want to talk to anyone, or see anyone, which meant the hotel was out. There was an almost full bottle of Étienne's Calvados in my cottage. That would do. Then I remembered the bottle of wine I had taken to the chapel after Lorca's last visit. She'd wanted a drink and I hadn't had anything to offer her, so I'd stowed away a Beaujolais with my painting gear. I headed for the chapel; it was closer than my cottage.

A thin sheen of water covered the sand of the causeway. The tide was coming in. The sandpipers were gone. I took off my shoes and socks and rolled up the bottoms of my trousers, my feet throwing up splashes as I crossed.

Inside, I tossed my sketchbook and paintbox onto the table and lit the oil lamp. It hissed into life. I sat down on one of the pews to dry my feet before crossing over to the canvas tacked on the east wall. I stood for a moment looking at it, then with the damp cloth I'd used to dry my feet, scrubbed out most of the charcoal drawing of the woman. In the bright light of the lamp my shadow fluttered across the walls. Who was I kidding, thinking I could make a painting for this place?

I turned and looked at the little portrait of Lorca, which I'd left on the table propped against a jar. What I saw made me gasp. There was a slash of red paint right across the face and a coarse grimace had been drawn over the mouth.

I stared, dumbfounded. The smear was like a gash, a bleeding wound. For a second I had the absurd idea that Lorca herself had done this. But it was as if my own anger had manifested itself in this crude disfigurement. As if one of my long-ago caricatures had come back to haunt me.

A round object whipped past my head and rebounded off the wall with a thud. I jerked around. A second apple came flying across the room, narrowly missing my head.

A figure was framed in the window—a figure with a scowling face.

"Tobias!" I shouted.

The face dropped out of sight as I rushed to the window. I ran back to the door and flung it open. But in the gloom I saw nothing against the dark shape of the island.

"Tobias!"

Then I heard a strange guttural cry and the sound of splashing, like an animal galloping across the causeway. The boy was briefly silhouetted on the ridge as he vanished into the dusk. I didn't call out again.

I looked at the two apples lying on the floor, the portrait with its lurid streak of red paint, and the whole thing in the harsh light from the lamp was like the scene of a crime. I couldn't bring myself to even try to remove the paint. Why bother now?

I noticed too that the painting of the flowers was gone, the one Tobias had signed and given to me. Had he seen me carrying flowers to Lorca's door? Had he seen more? The shutters had been open. Is that why he had slashed paint across her portrait? To hurt her? Or me? I had not given him a thought all day. I'd wanted to paint, and I'd wanted Lorca. My promises to teach the boy had been forgotten.

Lorca had said I shouldn't have any illusions about her. But this whole place was an illusion, and I was the self-deluded fool in the middle of it. What did I think I could accomplish here? This wasn't a real studio. Lorca and Tobias and Père Caron were strangers to me, and I was using them as actors in some misguided personal drama.

I picked up my paintbrushes and hurled them across the room.

AT A CERTAIN DISTANCE from the shore there is a place of emptiness, where neither the island nor the distant mainland is visible. One either goes forward, or turns back. I looked back from the deck of the *Stella Tilda* to where La Mouche had sunk over the horizon. The boat's engine rumbled and vibrated beneath my feet and the sharp breeze blew a waft of diesel smoke across the deck.

Simon Grente, steering from the wheelhouse, raised his eyebrows in an unspoken question, indicating that it was still possible to turn around. I shook my head and faced in the other direction. I did not look back again, not even when the mainland appeared, nor when I disembarked in Saint-Alban, nor after I had pressed a handful of franc notes on the protesting Simon and walked up the slope to the town with my bag in my hand.

CHAPTER 23

I STOOD IN THE HALLWAY OF THE APARTMENT ON rue du Figuier with the keys bunched in my hand. I inhaled, and all the familiar smells overcame me, a thousand memories flooding my senses so that I seemed to inhabit not only this particular point in time but all the moments that had ever taken place in these rooms.

But was there anything left of that old life? I flicked on the light switch and shut the door. Nothing had changed here, except for the film of dust that had appeared on surfaces. Where did dust come from, I wondered, and how did it penetrate rooms when the doors and windows were shut? A pile of mail had accumulated on the floor and I pushed it aside with my foot, not bothering to even glance at the envelopes.

This was the only real home I had known in Paris, or anywhere else, for that matter. This *quartier*, this street, these rooms, had been my life—the birthdays, the Christmases, the dinners, the happy times.

As I wandered from room to room again, the strangeness of the apartment struck me. Everything appeared unfamiliar, unrecognized, like the belongings of people I had never met. I could not even bring myself to sit down in one of the armchairs.

I wanted a drink.

The kitchen sink was full of empty wine bottles. In the cupboards there was nothing. I'd long ago finished off the Calvados and the brandy, and even a bottle of gin, which I hated. Just behind the sauces I spied the label of a pommeau bottle. Uncorking it and lifting the neck to my mouth, I swallowed. Oh that familiar taste! In a moment I was standing in the garden of the house on rue Pierre des Touches in Montmartin, listing to the cooing of the turtledoves in the pine trees, in my hand a small fine crystal glass containing my first taste of that sweet sherry-like drink made from cider and apple brandy. It was my first visit there. We had known each other less than two months.

Was that the day we'd cycled down to the dunes? Yes, it must have been. We had wheeled the bikes up the gravel driveway to the street. Within two minutes we were at the edges of the small village, past the houses of grey stone and slate roofs, on a flat stretch of road. Claudine rose on her seat and pedalled hard, shooting ahead. I raced to catch her. She was wearing a yellow summer dress cinched at the waist with a white belt, and a pair of espadrilles on her feet. Her dress billowed around the tops of her thighs as I caught up to her, whistling in appreciation. She laughed and made no effort to cover her legs.

As we rounded a curve, the sea appeared, spread below like a carpet of blue light fringed by white sand, immense and wide to the distant horizon. The road twisted and curved down through the fields, crossed a narrow river and ended at the dunes. The tide was high. Not a soul was in sight on the long beach. To the right, at the mouth of the estuary, stood a green lighthouse on a point of land.

Oystercatchers with long red beaks scurried along the shoreline, heads bobbing up and down as they dug at the wet beach. Claudine dropped her bike on the sand and ran down to the water, her hair streaming behind her like a horse's mane. The birds took to the air in a wave of flashing black and white. She bent down and picked up something and when I approached she held her hand out to me, fingers closed over her palm.

"For you," she said.

But first, I said I had something serious to tell her, and I confessed that the story about my parents dying in a car crash was a lie. I told her the truth about my upbringing.

"Why did you lie to me, Leo?" she responded. "You say you love me. I tell you everything that is in my heart. Everything. I don't hold anything back."

"It's a lie I've always told. A kid once told me my mother was a prostitute. It hurt me. Maybe it was true. I'm ashamed that I had no parents. I didn't want anybody to think that my parents gave me up, that they didn't want me. For whatever reason."

"I don't care about your parents, Leo. But if you could tell me this lie, what others? How can I believe anything now?"

I took her hand, the one she had held out, and she opened her fingers. In the centre of her palm lay a small pink shell, worn smooth by time and the ocean into a perfect heart shape. Then she pulled her hand away and was running up into the long grasses on the dunes.

When I crested the slope she was nowhere in sight. It took me five long minutes of searching and calling to find her. She was reclining on her back in a little hollow nestled and sheltered between two higher dunes, one arm flung back above her head, a clasped hand resting lightly across her breasts. Her eyes were shut. Her dress was bunched above her knees, showing her long thighs. I could smell the warmth of the earth.

I lay down next to her and she opened her eyes. When I saw her expression I thought I had lost her. But then she whispered, "I forgive you," and she pressed the small heart-shaped shell into my hand. "You can have my heart now," she said.

A half-hour later, under that clear blue sky, with the sun warm on our naked bodies, I asked her to marry me.

Replacing the cork in the bottle of pommeau I set it back on the cupboard shelf. I no longer had the desire or need to obliterate my memories with alcohol. I still had that little shell, treasured in a small velvet-lined box among Claudine's jewellery. We can never forget, I thought, but perhaps we can learn not to regret.

From the kitchen I walked down the long hallway to my studio at the back of the apartment. I opened the door but did not enter. Bare walls, a blank canvas on the easel, two drawings lying on the worktable. Two faces. A boy and a woman. I closed the door.

In the living room I opened the windows onto the street. Startled by the sudden noise of the neighbourhood intruding in this place of memory, I quickly slammed the window shut.

The coffee table in front of the couch was littered with magazines and books that I had not looked at in over a year. Sitting on top of Zola's *L'oeuvre* was my paperback copy of Balzac's short story *The Unknown Masterpiece*, the one illustrated with etchings by Picasso. I'd bought it my first year here because it was the story of a painter and took place in Paris. Some of it was set on rue des Grands-Augustins, in a building that Picasso had eventually rented and where he had painted *Guernica*. I hadn't known then that the book was about a painter who works on the same picture for years, unable to finish it, never showing it to anybody, and after his death his friends find a canvas covered in incomprehensible scribbles. For an artist, the story was a chilling one.

I set the book on the shelf and as I did so a sheet of folded paper slipped out from between the pages. It was an article that had been torn from a magazine, and though I knew what it said, I read the words again.

In Leo Millar's paintings now showing at Galerie Serge Bruneau, we have the sensation that time has ceased, or is suspended. Pastoral is the word that comes to mind. These are landscapes of eternity. We feel these are places we might know, and if not, we want to know them, we want to be there and experience that comforting light, that timeless serenity, that beauty.

There are no figures in Millar's landscapes, but rather than making them seem uninhabited, this absence avoids all storytelling. His mysterious terrains are "ideal landscapes."

But there is a disquiet here too, a certain anguish and longing. For all their calm and tranquility, Millar's pictures evoke melancholy as well. His ideal pastorals of order and harmony are also precarious, and because they exist only in art, we feel their absence in our own world as tragic.

Most noticeable in the exhibition is The Church at Pont de la Roque. Here, the view of an ancient ruined bridge and a church silhouetted

*on a hill in the morning light is elegiac, but it is also an image of hope, and,
one might add, of a profoundly expressed love for the beauty of the world.*

I smiled bitterly rereading these words. A review of my first
exhibition at Serge's gallery. Written by someone named Dan-
iel du Courjan in *ArtVue* magazine, which coincidentally was
where Claudine worked as an assistant editor. Perhaps that
should have made me suspicious, but I was too pleased to give
it a second thought when Claudine presented me with a copy.
I am good at anagrams and crossword puzzles, so maybe that
was why the name suddenly clicked in my mind some hours
later, and out of the blue the letters rearranged themselves in
my mind as an anagram of *Claudine Jourdan*. I confronted her
and she confessed that the article was her work.

I was extremely angry. I didn't need my wife puffing up my
work under a false name, and if the word got out I would be
the laughingstock of my contemporaries. I was humiliated. We
argued. Claudine pleaded that she'd meant well, but I wouldn't
even speak to her. I tore the article out of the magazine and
locked myself in the studio.

Later, only after reading the review over and over again, did
I see that this was a wonderful description of my paintings. I
couldn't have articulated it so well myself no matter how much
I had tried. I realized that Claudine understood me, deeply,
which meant that she loved me, deeply. My anger evaporated
instantly. I apologized, we forgave each other, and I took her
that night to Bofinger for oysters and champagne. Was that the
night we conceived Piero?

Folding the paper up again I slipped it back between the
pages of the Balzac and placed it on the bookshelf. Perhaps one

day I would read the story once more, and find the article again.

Across the hall I could see Piero's bedroom, and the colourful wooden mobile hanging from the ceiling. I'd made it of balsa wood in the studio, painting the shapes in bright primary colours, then putting it up on the morning the three of us came home from the hospital a few days after Piero's birth. The first time we were together here as a family. I remember him lying on his back, looking up at the mobile, his chubby little legs making pedalling motions in the air.

For the first days Piero mostly slept. When he opened his eyes they were a luminous dark blue, and their extraordinary beauty, their absolute purity, had made me weep. Life had been serene here, mother and child like gifts to me from heaven. Days and nights of contentment. Was there any better definition of happiness?

Those first months Claudine had been resplendent with an inner light, her skin glowing, a beatific smile on her lips as she sat with Piero at her breast. I'd never painted them like that, mother and child, because by then I was doing landscapes exclusively.

Before Piero, in the months after our marriage, I had done some nude studies of Claudine, but one day while I was drawing her, she had said to me, "Leo, I don't want to pose any more."

"Why not?" I asked, disappointed.

"It's too unnerving," she said. "The way you stare at me, almost taking me apart piece by piece and reassembling a version of me on your canvas. You look at me as if I am nothing more than a tree or a table. I don't recognize you when you stare like that. You become someone else."

"It's just concentration," I explained. "I have to look very carefully."

"You want to capture me. Isn't that what artists say, that they want to capture a likeness, capture a moment?"

"Well, yes, in a way." What I wanted was to hold back time, to make permanent what was as transient as the light passing through the air. I wanted to keep us like this, together and happy, forever.

She explained. "When I am naked in front of you I want it to be a special experience between us, one that we share. I don't want to become a picture. It is the living woman you get, Leo, not a representation. Maybe it is just vanity, but I want to age with the face I have. I want to look at your work, now and in the future, with joy, not with regret. Stick with your landscapes."

A few months later I was working at my easel when the door of the studio opened. Claudine stepped into the room wearing a white lace robe. She stopped a few feet away and let the robe slip from her shoulders and fall into a soft heap at her feet, revealing her naked body.

"Look at me," she said.

The early light falling through the windows had a warm rosy tint, touching her breasts, the curve of her stomach and her bare feet with a dusting of gold. The robe at her feet was a creamy foaming wave. A faint blush like the bloom on a peach spread across her cheeks as I stared at her. I was astounded by her beauty. It was as if I were seeing her for the first time. A radiance emanated from her. I felt humbled, in the presence of a beauty no art could match. I was also confused. Had she changed her mind and was she going to pose for me? Or did she want me to make love to her?

She smiled—the first time I'd seen that odd inscrutable smile, filled with a secret inward knowledge that I could not apprehend. Then she said. "I'm pregnant, Leo."

My eyes blurred now at the memory, the knowledge that her radiance was lost and gone forever. I crossed into our bedroom and flung myself down on the bed, burying my face in the pillows, inhaling deeply, trying to find again some lost essence. But only a slight musty odour came to my nostrils. Would I ever be able to sleep in this bed again? How many times had I made love with Claudine in this room? I pressed myself down on the bed, willing her memory back, wanting her.

But it was Lorca I saw, her long limbs and white skin in the rainy light of her room in La Maison du Paradis, her dark eyes fixed on mine, clouding as she cried out and the rain beat at the window.

I leapt off the bed and grabbed at the cover and sheets, stripping them from the mattress and bundling them up into a ball, which I threw into the corner. Collecting my keys from the kitchen counter I hurried from the apartment and strode down to the little Monoprix supermarket on rue Saint-Antoine. I asked one of the clerks for any empty cardboard cartons and he gave me a stack, which I carried back up rue Charlemagne to the apartment.

I started my packing in the bedroom, with Claudine's clothes, not bothering to fold, to examine, to check the pockets, or even to allow myself the recollection of her in some dress or coat. Everything went rapidly into the boxes. Only once did I falter, when I came upon a wine-coloured paisley blouse by Mary Quant that I'd bought for Claudine, along with a set of red lucite earrings, at Bazaar on King's Road when we had visited London to see the big Pop Art exhibition. Our only holiday abroad other than the last journey to Cyprus. With the cloth pressed to my face, I inhaled deeply, smelling her body, the memory of it. And then I thrust it away.

The entire contents of the closet went into the cardboard boxes—coats, dresses, blouses, underwear, shoes, shirts, pants, hats, gloves, scarves. What I could not throw away— the photograph albums, Claudine's jewellery, some special mementos and souvenirs—I placed into two boxes that I shoved to the back of the bedroom closet. I taped the boxes shut and stacked them in the corridor outside the front door.

Next, I went to Piero's room and began the same process; clothes, books and toys. One or two items had special memories and these I set aside—his favourite book called Boo, about the boy who was afraid of the dark; the small cast-iron model of a Citroën *deux chevaux* that Piero had won in a raffle; the sketchbooks; and the dusty wooden mobile of animal shapes painted in primary colours. When Piero's room was cleared, I added those boxes to the stack in the hallway. At the end of my packing, all that remained was a lingering scent on my hands from handling Claudine's clothing, faint traces of her. Only that, and the memories.

I telephoned the charity run by the nuns at the nearby church of Saint-Gervais and arranged for the boxes to be collected by them.

What would I do now? What would Claudine want me to do? I imagined her voice telling me to act, not to just turn my back and walk away. My departure from La Mouche had been sudden and without goodbyes. In a way, I'd fled from the island, just as I'd fled there in the first place. Would I be fleeing for the rest of my life? Perhaps it had been cowardly to leave like that, without even a word to Père Caron. I wished I had never agreed to restore the painting in the chapel, or offered to make a new one. He would be very disappointed. Yet, as I thought of the island it was with longing. For the first time in ages, I'd felt alive there. The restoration of "Love and the Pilgrim" had given me pleasure and a purpose.

And Tobias, his presence, just knowing he was there somewhere on the island, had stilled a yearning that I'd thought of as permanent. But I'd failed him. Especially now. And when I thought of Lorca, and my ambition to paint something new for the chapel, I felt that I'd failed there too. They were the living, not the dead, and was there anything more than my own grief and my own needs that I could offer either of them? Perhaps.

I needed advice. The only person I could call was Serge Bruneau. I dialled his number on the phone. We spoke for a few minutes and then I asked him if he knew of a doctor in Paris who could answer some questions I had.

When I'd hung up I walked through the apartment. The place resembled that of a bachelor—a man who lived alone and always had done so. In the bathroom I washed my hands, soaping off the dust and traces of the past. For a long while I examined my reflection in the mirror, my fingers twisting the wedding band on my finger.

Who is that man? I asked myself. Who did he used to be?

I turned on the taps again and reached for the soap, lathering it up around my ring finger until I could work the wedding ring off. I dried the ring on a towel and carried it in my palm to the bedroom where I retrieved Claudine's jewellery case from the back of the closet. From my pocket I took the gold ring I'd placed on Claudine's finger on the day we were married. I set it on the bed of velvet and placed my own matching ring next to it. Then I closed the box gently, put it back on the shelf and left the apartment, locking the door with a final twist of the key.

I looked at the scrap of paper on which I'd written the address Serge had given me. I had one more stop to make.

CHAPTER 24

"Can you smell that?"

I lifted my chin and inhaled. "Flowers?"

Simon Grente nodded and smiled.

I inhaled again, trying to separate the scent from the diesel oil and fishy odour of the boat. "Honeysuckle?" I said.

"Right you are." Taking one hand from the wheel, he pointed to a blur of green on the horizon ahead. "You can always smell the island before you see it. Sometimes from kilometres away."

The smells became more intense as we drew closer, thick as perfume: the fresh loamy scent of earth, something floral, an elusive tang of wood smoke, even a hint of cow manure. And all the while the blue-green shape ahead grew, becoming land. La Mouche. Now the top of the lighthouse was visible, and the white walls of the Hôtel des Îles above the harbour.

Simon steered us towards Le Port, the harbour below the hotel, and the stone quay, where a long wooden motor launch was moored. I wondered if there were guests at the hotel.

Earlier, after I'd arrived in Saint-Alban on the mainland, I had gone down to the harbour, hoping to hire someone to ferry me over to La Mouche. As luck would have it I found Simon drinking a coffee in the little café next to the harbourmaster's office. He was in town to collect the weekly mail. I didn't volunteer any information about where I'd been and Simon asked no questions.

"Do you want to stop here," he asked now, nodding towards Le Port, "or go on to LeBec?"

"Take me home, please." Realizing what I'd just said, I smiled to myself.

He manoeuvred the boat past the opening to the harbour. Looking up at the hotel where the tricolour fluttered on its pole above the blue shutters of the upper floor, I picked out the room that had been mine. A few minutes later when the boat swung wide to the east, bringing the chapel of Notre-Dame de la Victoire into view like a white schooner anchored against the coast, I felt a warm sense of recognition, of welcome.

The boat glided into the shade of the steep rocky shore that was dotted with low shrubs of gorse, flowers of yellow and purple, dark pines. We rounded a bend in the shoreline and there was the simple stone quay, a few boats tied up at buoys, the scattering of cottages. LeBec. A gull sitting on a lobster pot took to the air squawking indignantly as the boat bumped against the quay. I walked up to La Minerve with my bag and parcels. Nothing had changed in the days I had been away. I made myself a cup of black coffee and sweetened it with two cubes of sugar, then carried it out to the little garden at the back.

On the journey down from Paris I had questioned myself many times about my reasons for coming back. And when La

Mouche appeared on the horizon, I'd re-examined my motives again. I had tried to be clear-headed in my thoughts, and even if my feelings were complex, I hoped I was being honest with myself. But even so, I still had doubts.

One thing I did know was that this was my life in the present tense, this island and the people on it. I did not want a parallel life, I wanted the here and now.

I had come back for Tobias. I had come back for Lorca. I had come back for Père Caron. At the very least, I owed them all an apology. But I had also come back for the painting in the chapel. Not "Love and the Pilgrim" but the new one I was now determined to make. I swallowed the rest of my coffee down and carried the cup to the sink. I wanted to go to the chapel immediately. The barrenness of the room on rue du Figuier had made me realize how much I now thought of the chapel as my studio. I wanted to see my sketches, I wanted to touch my brushes and smell the oil and turpentine. I wanted to see that big expanse of canvas with the outlines of a boy, a woman and a building. I ought to see the priest first, though, and explain my sudden departure, for I'd left everything in the chapel as is, without a word of farewell, and Père Caron must be wondering what had happened. I might very well find that all my equipment had been removed.

Although it was almost evening, I set out along the route des Matelots. But as the chapel came into view I saw the band of blue water surrounding it and realized I had forgotten the tide, which was now full, cutting off the chapel. Frustrated, I stood looking across the sheet of water. I even considered swimming across. It wasn't deep and the evening was warm. If only I had a boat. Come to think of it, why hadn't I arranged for one a long time ago? I had been at the whim of the tides often enough. Just a little skiff and a pair of oars would do. Tomorrow, first thing, I would ask around.

Rather than return to the cottage, I struck off along the route de la Croix towards the priest's house, where I hoped to find Père Caron. If he wasn't home, then there was always the Hôtel des Îles, where I might as well have a drink and dinner, since the pantry at home was quite bare.

To the west, above the treetops, the sky was turning cerulean blue and rose. The day's warmth lingered, rising from the ground. Crickets thrummed in the tall barley. Where the path neared the junction with La Garenne, I caught the scent of wood smoke again, but this time carrying with it the aroma of grilling meat. Realizing how hungry I was, I turned my footsteps towards Manoir de Soulles. I hadn't eaten anything for hours other than a stale sandwich in Saint-Alban. Ester Chauvin often cooked something for the bachelors on the island and I hoped there might be a couple of lamb chops available for me to take home. I grew hungrier by the minute as the aroma of grilled lamb grew stronger.

Just as the farm's chimneys came into view a shift in the evening breeze brought the strains of music to my ears. Not just one instrument but what sounded like a number of musicians playing a lively jig. La Mouche was generally a silent place, with only the sounds of birds and livestock and the occasional boat disturbing the peace, so the music was something unusual.

Hearing a clarinet among the fiddles made me think of Lorca, and then something occurred to me. What if she had left the island too? All the optimism I'd felt on returning evaporated. A cloud of smoke and noise and aromas enveloped me the moment I rounded the corner of the big stone barn and entered the courtyard behind the farmhouse. Figures moved in the haze while others sat at the tables and at the far end under coloured lanterns a group of musicians were adding to the festive atmosphere. It all looked like one of those celebrations painted by Bruegel.

A number of tables had been set out on the cobblestones and off to the left a long iron grill laden with cuts of lamb was the source of the grilled meat aroma. A figure waved and called my name. I made out Père Caron at a nearby table on which tall green cider bottles stood. An elegant white-haired woman was seated next to him.

"Leo! Come and join us."

I walked over and shook hands with him. He was wearing his usual dark blue linen jacket, but tonight he also had on a tie. His moustache had been trimmed, I noticed. The woman, who wore cluster pearl earrings and a Spanish shawl draped over her shoulders, was introduced as Jeanette DuPlessis. I remembered that the owner of La Maison du Paradis was a Madame DuPlessis. I wondered if that was her motor launch in the harbour. Judging by her elegant clothes it could very well be.

I recognized a number of other villagers at the nearby tables, including Linda and Victor from the hotel, but there was no sign of Lorca.

"So you are back," Père Caron said.

"I'm sorry I didn't let you know I was leaving. It was a sudden impulse. And then there was no time to wait for the tide."

"Yes, Simon told me. I assumed something important called you away. But I knew you would be back since your work in the chapel isn't finished."

Turning to the woman, whom I judged to be in her late sixties, the priest said, "Leo is the painter who is making a new picture for Notre-Dame de la Victoire."

"What a good idea," she said. "The chapel could certainly use something other than that dark old picture that hangs over the door."

"And Leo is the man to do it," the priest said. "He is going to surprise us with something magnificent."

"What's the occasion tonight?" I asked. "Someone's birthday?"

"It's a celebration for the arrival of the *moules de bouchot*. We have it every year at this time, on the full moon." Père Caron pointed, indicating a brick outdoor stove on which two enormous copper pots rested over the flames. The woman tending the stove used her apron to remove a lid and reached through the steam with a long wooden spoon to give the contents a stir. Then two men lifted the pot and carried it to a table, where Ester Chauvin began to spoon heaps of steaming mussels into bowls.

Jeanette DuPlessis, who had been regarding the festivities with a look of fondness, now spoke up. "Ah, here are our musicians. Just in time for dinner."

A dignified man with wavy white hair, dressed in a beige linen suit and holding a violin, appeared at the table.

"Bravo, Armand," Madame DuPlessis said, clapping.

"The praise should go to my talented accompanist." The man stepped aside and made a mock bow towards the woman behind him. Lorca.

I couldn't help giving a start—of surprise and pleasure. Our eyes met, and I tried, unsuccessfully, to read her expression. She wore a low-cut dress with a single black pearl on a silver chain around her neck. Her lipstick was red and so were the thin leather straps of her sandals. She had fastened one side of her hair up with a tortoiseshell comb and over her shoulder she'd draped a black crocheted shawl. She was holding her clarinet.

Madame DuPlessis said to me, "I believe you've met Lorca already, but not her husband, Armand."

The man leaned across the table, stretching out a hand, gold cufflinks showing on his white shirt. I saw the thin gold wedding band on his finger, identical to the one Lorca wore. His name had come as a shock, but I had enough composure to stand and shake Armand Daubigny's hand.

"Leo Millar," I said.

Père Caron said to Daubigny, "Leo is a painter from Paris. He's staying over in LeBec while he works on a new picture for the chapel."

Further conversation was forestalled by the arrival of Ester Chauvin bearing a large tray. The bowls of mussels were passed around the table, a basket of roughly cut baguette chunks was distributed and our glasses were replenished with foaming cider.

"*Bon appétit!*" Ester told us, bustling away.

I used an empty mussel shell as a set of pincers to remove the flesh from a large specimen. The taste was garlic and onion, cream, with something fruity underlying the tang of the sea.

"You haven't had our *moules de bouchot* before, have you, Monsieur Daubigny?" Père Caron asked.

"Never. And they are truly sumptuous."

"See, the flesh is orange." He extracted a plump morsel from its shell. "And they are smaller than the usual mussels. But you will never find any as flavourful. The secret is the cider and Calvados. You splash a bit of both in when you add the mussels to the broth. More cider than Calva, of course."

The dusk had faded to a deep blue darkness and someone brought a big wrought-iron candelabra to the table. Père Caron used his matches to ignite the candles, and a warm yellow light bathed our faces. My eyes kept returning to Lorca. Her black hair was lost in the blackness of the surrounding night, her eyes were pools of shadow, her cheekbones sharply defined. I watched an orange mussel being raised to her lips, her white teeth taking it, the mouth closing, the tip of her tongue licking away the creamy sauce from her upper lip. I looked away.

One of the farmhands trundled a wheelbarrow from table to table, tipping in the empty mussel shells. The bowls and cider bottles were cleared away, to be replaced by *pichets* of red wine. Cuts of grilled lamb were served with small boiled potatoes.

"I enjoyed the music," I said, addressing the space between Lorca and Daubigny. "In fact, it drew me here, from across the fields. I had no idea there was a fête in progress. I've just returned from Paris."

"It was composed by Lorca," Armand Daubigny said.

"It's nothing," she replied. "A variation on *Un premier amour*. Which is not my composition at all."

"I thought there was something familiar to it," I said to her. The song had been a big hit for a while, sung by Isabelle Aubret and played on radios everywhere.

"But you are composing other things, my dear," Jeanette DuPlessis commented, leaning forward into the candlelight. "Important things."

Daubigny smiled at Lorca. "And you have made some progress, haven't you, *chérie?* That's why you came here, not so?"

"Do we have to talk about it now? It's bad luck to talk about something before it's finished."

"As you wish." Daubigny sat back and withdrew a cigarette case from an inside pocket. He offered it around. Lorca and Père Caron each took a cigarette.

I wondered if Madame DuPlessis was referring to that music I'd heard coming from Lorca's cottage.

"It doesn't even have a title yet, anyway," Lorca said.

"What about *Nocturne?*" Jeanette DuPlessis suggested, waving her hand to encompass the night around us.

Lorca was silent. Then she said, "Yes, *Nocturne*. Why not?" Leaning forward into the glow she lit her cigarette from a candle flame. "A *Nocturne for Lovers*." Then she sat back, her face claimed by shadow again.

The way she had said this, almost harshly, left a moment of uncomfortable silence. I remembered the music she'd been playing when I arrived at her cottage, how melancholy and inward it had seemed.

"Well now," Père Caron said. He took the *pichet* and topped up the wineglasses.

Daubigny sipped and then said, "This wine is very suitable. Although, for lamb generally, there is nothing better than a Coteaux du Languedoc. Lamb is essentially a southern meat, so you need the Spanish influence in the wine."

For a moment I was reminded of Serge Bruneau, who also liked to make pronouncements at dinners, but in no other way did this man remind me of my friend.

I studied Lorca and Daubigny. They didn't seem like a married couple at all, yet neither did there seem to be any ill feeling between them. But there was some kind of tension. So why was

Daubigny here? For a reconciliation? Questions and doubts rushed through my mind. I had to talk to her alone.

From the far side of the courtyard, music started up again, accordion and fiddle. Under the red and green lanterns, figures were coming together in a waltz. A grog station had been set up near the grill, where the local men were pouring hot water from a battered old kettle into clay cups of Calvados and topping these with a cube of sugar. Père Caron lit a hand-rolled Caporal and the smell of the black tobacco mingled pleasantly with all the other aromas. The moon drifted into sight behind the farmhouse, full and round and yellow.

"What about it, *chérie*?" Daubigny said to Lorca, nodding towards the musicians. "Shall we join in again?"

"You go ahead. I want to digest my meal."

"I think I will. It's not often I get to make music in such rustic surroundings." He took up his violin from where he'd placed it on a vacant chair and left the company with another little formal bow.

"Armand usually plays at the Salle Pleyel," Jeanette DuPlessis said. "He leads the Orchestre de Paris." Leaning across the table she touched Lorca's hand. "And Lorca is his star soloist."

"Or his second fiddle." There was a note of bitterness in her voice. "But he won't ever play the compositions I write."

"He will, he will. That is why you must finish your new piece."

"My unfinished *Nocturne for Lovers*?" She stood abruptly, steadying herself on the chair back. "I think I will dance now with Mr. Millar instead."

"Of course." I moved around the table and let her take

my arm. "Excuse us, please," I said to Madame DuPlessis and Père Caron.

On the edge of the paving where the lantern light was soft, she placed her hand in mine and let me draw her close around the waist. That hour I'd spent with her in her cottage, in her bed, had become dreamlike in my recollection, as if it were something that I had longed for and imagined, but that had not really taken place.

I'd left angry with her, and I'd left the island disillusioned with myself. But being in Paris had given me some clarity and I felt that I'd come back with a better perspective. I had told myself that I was coming back for Tobias; there was no reason to have expected that Lorca would still be on the island, although I had just assumed it. Now, holding her in my arms again brought back such an intense physical feeling that it was all I could do not to kiss her right there in front of everybody.

I glanced over her shoulder and saw her husband with the musicians, and my desire was replaced with the need for some answers.

"How long has he been here?"

"Since yesterday," she said matter-of-factly.

"Is he staying with you in La Maison du Paradis?"

"I told you I was married, Leo." She was silent a moment, then said, "He's staying at the hotel. They both are, even though the house I'm in belongs to Jeanette."

We passed under the coloured lanterns strung overhead, her face ruddy, then green, then orange, and back into the flickering candlelight on the edge of the dance floor.

"Why is he here?" I asked. "To take you back?"

She laughed. "To make sure I'm not drinking and smoking

too much. To make sure I haven't fallen into the ocean. I'm supposed to be composing."

"Is he staying long?"

"They are leaving tomorrow afternoon."

Père Caron passed us, protesting as Ester Chauvin led him among the dancers. We moved back into the shadows again.

She said, "Why did you smear paint all over my portrait and then just leave without a word? Was I that cruel to you?" I didn't answer and she continued, "I'm sorry for what I said, about your wife."

"Did it mean anything to you? Being with me."

"Of course it did." Then she shook her head. "The whole thing is so complicated, Leo. For you as well as for me."

"Are you going back with him?" I asked.

"I thought you had left for good. I looked for you, in the chapel and at your house. Nobody knew where you were these past few days."

"It wasn't me who disfigured your portrait. I'm pretty sure it was Tobias."

"Tobias? But why would he do that?"

"I don't know. Maybe he saw us together. Maybe he was jealous."

She laughed, but with irony. "All these jealous men!"

"Have you seen Tobias around at all? Has he come back to play your clarinet?"

"Yes, actually. Once. I let him play a bit. He didn't stay long."

"Well, it's obvious then that his anger was directed at me and not you."

We took another turn around the dance floor.

"Where did you go?" she asked. "To Paris?"

"I had to buy paints. And take care of a few other things."

Linda and Victor from the hotel swirled by light-footedly. "*Bonsoir*, Leo! *Bonsoir*, madame." I nodded to them.

I pulled her close again so that the softness of her body was against me. Her mouth brushed my cheek. Across the dance floor, Armand Daubigny was concentrating on the other musicians, seemingly unaware that his wife was dancing with me.

"I want to see you, Lorca. Tomorrow."

"I need to sit down for a minute," she said. "I'm a little dizzy."

"Come to my cottage in LeBec," I said.

She shook her head. "No," she said in a low voice.

"I want you."

She glanced over my shoulder towards the musicians. "Oh, Leo." Her eyes searched my face. "All right. But not in the village. And don't come to my house." She thought a moment. "I'll meet you at the lighthouse. Tomorrow at eleven." Her hand briefly slipped into mine, squeezed, and then she moved around the table and sat down next to Madame DuPlessis.

I didn't remain much longer. The fatigue of the long journey had caught up with me and it was all I could do to suppress my yawns. When I saw Armand Daubigny approaching the table, mopping his brow with a blue handkerchief, I said good night and walked home, hearing the fading rhythms of the fiddle and accordion coming across fields of corn and wheat bright under the moon.

She had said it was complicated, and I realized that I was on the verge of complicating things even further, possibly even bringing pain to all of us. But it didn't matter. I wanted the moon to fade and the sun to rise and bring morning, so that I could go to her again.

CHAPTER 25

IN THE MORNING, THE BEDROOM SHUTTERS WERE rattling from a wind and the room was chilly. Pulling on jeans and a thick wool sweater, I hurried downstairs and got a fire going. From the stone jug on the counter I drank two glasses of water in quick succession, then lit the stove to make coffee.

Once the coffee had bubbled up in the percolator and the room was aromatic with the scent of the strong brew and the pine cones were crackling in the fireplace, I opened the seaward-side windows. Beyond the harbour, where the masts of the fishing boats were jerking from side to side above the quay, the sea was slate grey, rough with broken spume whipping off the waves, and the sky was only marginally lighter than the water, grey on grey.

I looked at my watch. Too early for my rendezvous with Lorca at the lighthouse. Would she even come in this weather?

And what of Tobias? I knew I had disappointed him in some way, but I had no real idea what he expected from me. Neither did I know exactly what Père Caron had communicated to him about painting lessons. His removing his little flower picture and defacing the sketch of Lorca were obvious signs of anger, though. Maybe he was just jealous of me having another attachment. Piero had been like that for a period. Whenever visitors came to the apartment he would glue himself to Claudine, wanting to sit in her lap, or hang onto her hand, demanding attention. But I would make it up to Tobias.

I dressed for the weather in a woollen hat and a fisherman's raincoat that I'd found hanging in the wardrobe. The air was moist as I made my way along the route des Matelots and down the path from the ridge that overlooked the chapel, wet air blowing in from the sea and mixing with the drizzle falling from the grey sky. Towards the horizon a threatening bank of cloud was slowly spreading. I wondered if it would reach La Mouche, and if it would be a passing squall or a full storm.

A light was on in the chapel. I halted at the top of the path, surprised, studying the white glow framed in the windows. Other than during Sunday Mass, the building was mine alone and not even Père Caron disturbed me. My first hope was that Lorca had come to meet me. But that made no sense when we had a rendezvous in an hour on the other side of the island. It was probably the priest, come to attend to some business or other. I hoped it might be him since there was something important I needed to discuss.

With my head bent against the wind, I hurried across the causeway. I opened the door into the light and the familiar smells of stone and oil paint to find Armand Daubigny standing in front of the big canvas. He turned towards me.

"*Bonjour,*" he said. He was wearing tweed trousers and sturdy boots and a thigh-length brown leather coat. A plaid scarf was knotted around his neck and he wore a soft cap on his head. Very much the country gentleman, I thought.

"I hope you don't mind," Daubigny said, waving a hand at the painting. "Père Caron told me about your intention to redecorate the chapel and I was curious."

"I'm hardly proposing to redecorate. Mostly I'm making an attempt to restore that painting."

"Ah yes, the Asmodeus. He mentioned it." He crouched and looked at the area I had cleaned, the woman and the man revealed now, as if illuminated by a beam of light in their landscape of darkness.

"'Love and the Pilgrim,'" I said.

"And which is which?" Daubigny asked, looking up at me, holding my glance a moment. He turned back to the painting. "But then, we are all pilgrims when it comes to love."

He rose to his feet and moved over to the other painting, the big one I was working on, a building and two figures, one of them partly erased. He leaned forward as if trying to discern the identity of the face hidden in the smudges of charcoal. And then he saw the small portrait of Lorca, which still had the smear of red across it.

Standing with his hands behind his back he bent and studied the portrait. "Well. Unusual. And is my wife to be your model?"

When he glanced up at me, I shrugged.

"It's very lifelike," Daubigny said. "But you're not pleased with it?" He pointed at the red streak.

"I didn't do that. A local boy is responsible."

"Ah yes, Lorca mentioned a mute boy. Something of a tragic figure."

I tilted the picture so that it caught the light better. "Of course, I haven't been totally accurate in this rendition of Lorca," I said.

"How so?"

"I didn't paint the black eye she had when I first met her."

He laughed.

"I don't see the joke," I said.

"Did she tell you that I gave her that black eye?"

I glared at him. He held up his hands defensively. "I don't blame you for wanting to beat me up, Monsieur Millar, assuming that you do, but before it comes to that, I should tell you that Lorca got that black eye from walking into a lamp post."

"Isn't that what your type always says? That or a cupboard door. Why should I believe you and not her?"

"She was drunk, Monsieur Millar. It happened outside a restaurant, Bofinger. We had just left dinner."

I shook my head, disbelieving.

"It was witnessed by the manager of the restaurant, and two of the waiters who were seeing us off." My face must have showed my skepticism. "Next time you are in Paris you can go and ask them," Daubigny said. "Bofinger is on rue de la Bastille. I am known there. My wife and I dine there often."

"I know where it is. I live nearby."

"In fact," he said, "why don't you ask Lorca again?"

If what he said was true, why would she invent such a lie?

"I don't know how well you know Lorca, Monsieur Millar—not well I suspect, since she has only been here a short time—but you might have noticed she likes a drink."

I remained silent, noncommittal.

"Alcohol gives her solace. And sometimes she overesti-mates her need for consolation." He stepped past me. "There never was a jazz musician by the way. Or an affair." At the door, he turned and said, "You won't be the first young man to become infatuated with Lorca, Monsieur Millar. She is one of those 'dramatic' women. But I wonder if you will be able to cope with her demons." He buttoned his jacket and made a half bow. "*Au revoir.* Good luck with your picture."

I was left with the sound of the wind and the hissing of the oil lamp. I felt out of my depth, like an actor alone on the stage not knowing what his role is, what his lines are. Was Lorca playing some sort of complicated game with her husband, and I was the unwitting pawn?

Pushing back the sleeve of my raincoat, I looked at my watch. Almost eleven. I hurried from the chapel.

CHAPTER 26

THE LIGHTHOUSE STOOD ON THE NORTHWESTERN tip of La Mouche. I had only been past it once, on my initial exploration of the island. To reach it, I retraced my steps along the route des Matelots in the direction of LeBec, then turned off along the path marked LE CIRCUIT DU PHARE. As the track rose I could see to my left the fields and buildings of Manoir de Soulles. All the cattle were huddled in a corner of one field, sheltering under the spreading boughs of the oaks. The light was fading, although it was only mid-morning, and the landscape was almost monochrome, trees and fields and buildings painted in tones of muted green grey. Green umber, I thought, automatically selecting in my mind the key pigment I would use if I were to paint the scene.

The path veered away to the shore, bringing the ocean into view. Beyond the long empty beach, the water was a dark green, almost black, the sky now a solid wall of cloud. Terns and gulls wheeled above the sand, their cries plaintive.

The lighthouse came into view, its rotating yellow lantern a feeble gleam against the immensity of the black sky. The building was a cylinder of stone blocks with the light contained in a green-painted lantern house at the top. A gallery enclosed by iron railings, painted red, circled the base. I walked right around the tower and tried the door. Locked. Since there was no keeper's cottage, I assumed the light was automated. A glance at my watch showed that it was ten minutes past eleven. Would she come?

I paced back and forth in front of the lighthouse, anger rising when I thought of what Daubigny had told me. I was a fool to let myself be toyed with this way. I imagined myself shouting at her, demanding that she explain herself. I imagined myself slapping her. Then I was ashamed of the notion. Jealousy was making my thoughts bitter.

Finding a spot that was sheltered from the wind, I sat down with my back against the stone of the tower. Gusts of wet air wafted in from the ocean, the dark sea heaved and broke, booming on the shore. I looked at my watch again.

Far along the shore I glimpsed a figure. I got up quickly and hurried down the slippery steps. A sudden, low flash of lightning creased the sky, bleaching everything in a magnesium flair of impossibly white light. Then the sky broke and the deluge came, bending the dune grass and pockmarking the sand. I ran towards her.

I was close enough now to see her face and I felt my heart turn over in my chest. The rain battered down as I reached her, and I grabbed her hand, pulling her towards a derelict boat upended near the dunes. Her black hair framed her face in wet tendrils like seaweed and her sodden dress was plastered against her body. She didn't even have a raincoat, just a light cotton windbreaker against the stinging needles of rain. On hands and knees we scurried under the hull and crawled onto a heap of old fishing nets half buried in the sand.

Lorca leaned against the shell of the boat, pulling her knees up to her chest, breathing hard. Neither of us spoke. Anger had been welling in me since I'd left the chapel and perhaps she saw it in my face. There was a kind of fear in her eyes. Her pupils were round and shining. My heart softened.

"You're soaking wet," I said, slipping out of my raincoat and spreading it flat. "Sit here." Reaching into my pocket I took out a handkerchief and wiped her face. There were goose-bumps along her bare legs.

I pulled off my sweater. "Put this on." My shirt had come loose and she scrambled to me, thrusting her icy hands under the cloth, up around my back. I awkwardly tried to fold the sweater over her.

I held her trembling shoulders, felt her wet hair against my cheek. My hands searched her face and my fingers ran over her features like a blind man exploring. When I found her lips I bent my head and kissed her, tasting there the salt of the ocean. Her hands were under my shirt again, moving across my chest as if seeking out the warm beating life in me. Silent lightning flashed, illuminating the ribs of the boat, throwing shadows onto the bleached wood. Then we heard the thunder, and the rain drummed furiously on the boat's hull, the old wood creaking and rocking in the wind. We were buffeted and thrown, our grasps urgent, her breath loud against my ear, her skin white in the blue flashes of lightning between sand and hull.

The storm broke in us.

I LISTENED to the dripping of water running down the sides of the boat. Lorca was still asleep, curled up in the crook of my arm. The musk of our bodies mingled with the smell of the sea.

"The rain has stopped," I murmured, waking her.

Lorca sat up and reached for her dress, grimaced to find it still damp, and pulled it on. We scrambled out from under the boat. A slash of clear blue sky showed in the purple clouds. The ocean breathed in long gentle swells. On the shoreline a solitary long-legged curlew skittered across the damp sand. Lorca took out her cigarettes and lit one.

I watched her smoke, and when she looked over at me, I said, "I spoke to your husband this morning. In the chapel."

"Ah."

"He saw the portrait I did of you."

"Mmm."

My earlier anger came back in a rush. "He told me that he never did hit you, that you got that black eye from walking into a lamp post. He said you were drunk."

She laughed.

"Is it true?"

"Yes. It was just like something out of a Charlie Chaplin movie."

"Why did you tell me that he beat you? That you were having an affair with a jazz musician?"

Taking her time, she extinguished her cigarette by pushing it into the sand until it was buried. Then a shrug. "Maybe I wanted to scare you off," she said.

"Am I part of a little game the two of you are playing? King versus Queen, Pawn in the middle?"

"No," she said emphatically, twisting round to face me. "It's not like that."

"Was there a jazz musician?"

"No. I made that up." She ran both hands through her hair. "It sounds stupid now."

"He said I wouldn't be the first young man to become infatuated with you."

"I don't have affairs, Leo."

"So what am I?"

"You're something else." A small repentant smile on her face, a look of tenderness.

"Your husband also asked me if I would be able to cope with your demons. What did he mean by that?" I took her hand and touched my fingers across the underside of her wrist, feeling the slight difference in texture where the white scars ran. "This?"

She pulled her hand away, grasped a handful of the fine white sand and, holding it tight in her fist, let the grains trickle out in a thin stream. Opening her hand, she blew the last grains from her palm.

"I was his student. Students fall in love with their teachers. It's a cliché, no? Distinguished and accomplished older man, impressionable young woman. Ambitious too. We hit it off musically. Eventually I was promoted, so to speak, and he gave me a place in the orchestra." She glanced up at me sharply. "I was good enough. Better than that, even. Well, to make the story short, we married and lived happily ever after."

"Except?"

She gave a long sigh and shook her head. "I've always been under his spell in a way. Hard not to be with a man like that—talented, charismatic, cultured, famous in his field. I've become trapped in that orchestra. I've always wanted to compose. I do compose, but what I write is not for the Orchestre de Paris. Armand is of the old school—a musician should become technically perfect and stick to the known repertoire. He's looked at my compositions, even advised me on them, but he's never offered to play a single one. Nobody takes a woman composer seriously. Maybe I'm no good. I have no confidence in that regard."

"Why don't you leave? The orchestra, I mean. Find other musicians to play your work."

"It would be a betrayal. Make no mistake, Leo, I owe Armand a great deal. Not only musically. It was a difficult time in my life when we met. The war, all that . . . He rescued me in a way."

"But that was a long time ago. And you don't have any children together."

She let out a long sigh. "I didn't want children. After the war I couldn't imagine a world with children in it."

"And now?"

"And now I am too old."

"Hardly."

"I'm forty-one, Leo." She shrugged. "*C'est la vie.*"

When she continued speaking she kept her face averted. "I had a crisis a while ago. A sort of breakdown. That drunken evening when I walked into the lamp post was the culmination. Armand challenged me to finally finish the composition I have been working on for many years. He said the orchestra would play it, *if* it was good enough." She looked across at me and sighed again, blowing the air out between pursed lips. "So I came here. To get away. To think. To work. To be alone. I didn't know I would meet you."

Reaching out for my hand she pulled it to her mouth and kissed my palm. "I don't want to fall in love with you," she said. "I can't. It's too complicated. I can't even begin to explain how complicated everything is. And it's not fair to you. But I want you. I want you all the time. Now. Again. I don't understand it." She pushed my hand down between her thighs, to the surprising heat there. "Feel!"

"I love *you*," I said. I took her in my arms again and pulled her down to the sand.

She kept her eyes on me the whole time, and afterwards, her look was anguished. "I can't heal you, Leo. I can't. I'll drown."

I didn't know how to reply. I knew that what she said was true.

"You'll forgive me, won't you?" she asked.

"Yes," I whispered, but in my heart I wanted to win her, to win her for at least a little while longer before losing her.

She ran her hands through her hair, shaking it free of sand, then stood looking out to sea. Her face was soft and melancholy. The sight of her was too beautiful to bear. I bent down to lace up my boots.

"I'll go back alone, Leo. It's better that way."

"Yes," I said.

CHAPTER 27

I HAD ONLY BEEN WALKING FOR ABOUT TEN MIN-
utes, following a meandering track that wound its way up the
rocky shore, and had just reached the main path at the top
when I came upon someone sitting on a wide ledge that gave a
view down across the beach towards the lighthouse. A woman
wearing a green plastic raincoat, with a sturdy walking stick
resting across her knees. Madame Jeanette DuPlessis.

"Ah, Monsieur Millar. *Bonjour.*"

She didn't seem surprised to see me and I realized that I
must have been visible from a long way off. I greeted her, and
lingered a moment, feeling it would be rude to just carry on to
my destination without exchanging a few pleasantries.

"Wasn't that a magnificent storm?" she said. "Luckily I
found refuge in an old cattle byre. But you are quite dry too.
Did you find a place to shelter?"

"Yes. I managed to sit it out under an old wrecked boat."

"Then you must have seen Lorca."

"Uh, no. Is she around?"

"I just talked to her. She came up the same way as you just did. And she also sheltered under a boat."

She was looking at me very directly and I felt my face flushing.

"Both of you seem to have weathered out the storm quite well."

I glanced back, saw the lighthouse, the beach beyond, but the boat was out of sight, although anyone coming round the headland would be easily seen from up here. She knows, I thought. It is probably obvious on my face. As it must have been on Lorca's.

"Sit down a moment, Monsieur Millar. The rock here is quite dry already."

"Please call me Leo, madame."

"And you must call me Jeanette. The way you pronounce 'madame' makes me sound like a concierge."

"I thought I had an impeccable accent," I answered with a smile.

"*Ah non*, you sound like one of those G.I. soldiers we met at the end of the war."

We sat silently for a minute. The passing of the storm had left the sky a rich cerulean blue and the sea was tranquil again. Flocks of black and white gulls were bobbing on the swells offshore.

"It's a view one could paint," she said, indicating the tall lighthouse, the black rocks above the white beach.

"A little too picturesque for me," I replied.

"I went and looked at the portrait you drew of Lorca. Armand told me about it."

I waited to hear what else she might say. I had a feeling she was leading the conversation somewhere.

"It is not a pretty portrait," Jeanette said. "And I don't mean what that boy did to it. Lorca is not a pretty woman."

I looked at her with surprise.

"She is beautiful, though, in a way that few women are beautiful. I suppose it takes an artist to see that. Her face is too real, too much personality for most men. She can be almost sphinx-like sometimes. Impassive. Inaccessible. But she also bares her emotions. Like a wound." She paused. "Lorca and I are old friends, you know. I can read her face."

I toyed with the buttons on my raincoat, feeling out of my depth, not knowing if she was sympathetic or disapproving. She had a transparent rain scarf on her head and she took it off now. Her hair was very fine and white, held in place by two mother-of-pearl barrettes on either side of the central parting. She wore no makeup and her skin seemed very clean and silky to me. She smiled, her eyes kindly. If I'd known one of my grandmothers, I thought, she would be about this age.

"Lorca and I came here often in the years after the war. The house belonged to an aunt of mine, but we named it La Maison du Paradis. After what we had experienced in Rosshalde, this was a real paradise. We came here to recover. To heal."

"Rosshalde?"

Her eyes studied my face. "Of course you were too young then. But not by much. They took children too."

"Who did?"

"Rosshalde was a camp. In Germany. A concentration camp. For women. Lorca and I met there."

"A death camp?" I asked.

"Weren't they all?"

In my experience, the war was not much mentioned by

the French. It was something they would rather put behind them. Even Claudine's mother had spoken of it only in passing, despite the fact that the bridge at Pont de la Roque had been bombed and a Canadian flyer had lost his life in the raid. I sensed that scarcely anyone had been left untouched by the war years. What had it been like for Lorca?

"But weren't you a civilian?" I asked. "And why a camp for women? Or were you in the Resistance?"

A wry smile greeted my question. "Nothing so heroic. We were simply Jews. Lorca, myself. Millions of us."

"Ah." I understood now. "What about her family?"

"*Non.*" Jeanette shook her head. "But we survived. We are here."

I was still wondering why she was telling me this.

"We met in the camp. Lorca was already a talented and aspiring musician, but really nothing more than a girl. We even had a little quintet at Rosshalde, with three other women, Betsie and Michelle and Brigitte. But afterwards, when we came back to Paris, Lorca was no longer able to play music. The years in the camp almost broke her. She had lost faith—in life as well as art. And who could blame her? I managed to coax her into enrolling with Armand Daubigny. He was the one who really brought her back. He showed her the value of music. And its purpose."

I was silent.

"She fell in love with him. Love can take many forms, it's not only the romance of novels and films. We can love out of lust, out of admiration, even envy. We can love out of gratitude. We can love simply because we meet someone who understands us." She paused. "Let me tell you something more about

Lorca. You're an artist, you'll understand what I mean. I have known her a long time now—as a musician, as a woman, as a friend. She is one of those few who can bring beauty into the world. She can make beauty for those who cannot. She has the gift. You know what I mean?"

I nodded.

"Call it what you will—talent or ability or whatever. Not genius. That is given to the very, very few. The Mozarts and the Beethovens. Still, what she has . . . I don't have it. Daubigny doesn't have it. Even though he has reached the pinnacle of his career. Sometimes I wonder if he knows what Lorca has. Nevertheless, she has not realized her talent yet."

"Does she agree with this assessment of her ability?" I asked, thinking of the music I had heard her playing.

"Oh, I think so. Every true artist knows it on some level. Lorca's problems lie elsewhere—lack of confidence, guilt, misplaced loyalty. But she must finish what she has come here to do. She must put her music first. That is why she is here, Monsieur Millar."

I stretched my legs out and sat up straighter, easing a kink in my back. "I think I understand what you are telling me, and I'm sympathetic, of course I am. But isn't it up to Lorca to decide what she wants to do?"

"It is hard for a woman to be an artist, Leo. I don't know if you understand this. I speak from experience. A lot stands in our way—society, men, our own hearts. Sometimes it's very difficult for us to put art first, as male artists have always done. The heart can be an obstacle."

"Do you think it is only women that feel that way?" I thought of Claudine, Piero.

"Perhaps." She shook her head. "Lorca has told me a bit about you. About your loss. Sometimes a woman confuses pity with love."

Now I shook my head. "It's not pity."

"You must not harm her," she said emphatically.

"I would never do anything like that. Of course not."

"I don't mean physically," Jeanette said. "Her entire soul is in that music. If it fails, her soul will break and her demons will consume her."

It was the second time in a few hours that someone had mentioned Lorca's demons.

"I think you understand me, Leo," Madame DuPlessis said, and gave me a penetrating look.

I glanced away, watching gulls drifting above the waves. I thought about the painting in the chapel, the blank canvas waiting there. I remembered the day I had sketched the little donkey, and my resolve to make a painting that would be the truest thing I had ever done. And what if I failed? What demons awaited me?

Jeanette was looking at me, waiting for me to say something. "Yes, I understand," I told her.

She nodded. "Good. We are leaving this afternoon."

"You're taking her away?" I asked, shocked.

"No, Daubigny and I are leaving. Lorca will be on her own here."

"And her husband is fine with this? What does he know?"

"Armand has been many things to Lorca. Mentor, saviour, protector, lover. Husband, of course. But even he understands now she has a destiny that might take her away from him. From all of us."

"Are you suggesting that I should leave too?" I asked her.

"The tide is coming in," she said. She stood up. "I ought to get back to the hotel. Now that the storm is over Armand will be wanting to cast off and catch the current." She offered me her hand. "Au revoir. I don't know if we will see each other again."

"You've given me a lot to think about."

I sensed a hesitation in her, as if she wanted to say more. Then she did. "Lorca is a different person since she came here, Leo. I saw something in her face today that I have never seen before. Under different circumstances . . . well." She shrugged. "You know what the situation is. What will become of it is up to you. And Lorca. But I hope you will think seriously about what I said."

"I will. Bon voyage, madame."

FROM A VANTAGE POINT ABOVE LE BASSIN, standing just out of sight among the pines, I watched the long motor launch ease away from the stone quay, heard the throaty rumble of the engines. I had watched the boarding of Armand Daubigny and Jeanette, seen the farewells to Victor and Linda and Père Caron. I'd watched the brief embrace of husband and wife, the kissing of each cheek, not on the mouth, more like friends than anything else. I'd watched because I had not believed until now, seeing Lorca waving from the quay and the boat raising a small wake as it left the harbour, that she would not leave too.

After a suitable interval, I set off along the route de la Croix. The chapel on its islet was inaccessible, isolated by the tide. It was time I found a boat so that I could ferry myself back and forth. Cutting back inland I headed for LeBec, hoping to find Simon Grente there.

A couple of hours later Simon and I were tying up a little yellow dory on the shore across from the chapel. Simon had towed it there behind the *Stella Tilda*, and he explained that the best time to cross was at full tide. If it was ebbing or flooding the strong current would carry me either up or down the shore, or even out to sea. Simon asked if I wanted to moor at the chapel, but I said no, I had some errands to do first.

Once he had left, I headed along the now-familiar chemin des Sirènes towards La Maison du Paradis. My jacket pocket contained the jar of honey that Père Caron had asked me to give to Lorca. The storm had left the path underfoot thick with fallen acorns and the leaves of the oaks and elms were still dripping onto the ferns despite the sunlight filtering from the clear blue sky overhead. I would tell her I understood now. There need not be any secrets between us. Jeanette said she had seen the transformation in Lorca's face. I knew she loved me. As for Jeanette's cautions, I no longer believed that love and art were incompatible.

I heard the music before I was in sight of the cottage and my steps slowed, then came to a stop. I could imagine her feelings, coming back after being in the company of others and wanting only a return to her music. Many times I'd felt the same emotion, as if the studio were the only place in which I could be myself.

I heard a long sombre note on the clarinet, held for something like ten seconds, before it flowed seamlessly into the next one, and the next, eleven in all, seeming to hang suspended in the air. A sudden shrill burst of sound followed. Violent.

Painful. Then the melody, slow, serious, almost world-weary, disappointed. The tune went on in this way, climbing and falling, anxious, hesitant at times, without resolution.

As had happened the last time I listened to the sounds of the clarinet coming from the cottage, I experienced a feeling of being excluded. This was inward-looking music, private, solitary.

I waited, wanting to hear a change in the mood and spirit, something hopeful. Where was that striving for liberation, for wholeness, I had heard the first time? The music wandered on, repeating, searching, until it returned to that sudden harsh, angry flurry again, as if rejecting its own ennui. The emotion in the music was almost unbearable to listen to. Thinking about what Jeanette DuPlessis had told me, I felt helpless. Did I understand anything about the complexities of Lorca's life with Daubigny, or about what had happened in the camp at Rosshalde? Did I even understand what she was trying to do in her music?

Much as I wanted to see her, to coax her to tell me about the demons she was wrestling with and to rescue her from them, I knew that this was not the moment to intrude. I stepped back and retraced my way along the path between the trees, the sound of the music becoming less and less distinct until it was indistinguishable from the sounds of distant birds.

CHAPTER 28

THE NEXT DAY I WAS IN THE CHAPEL EARLY. BUT I did not paint. At least not a picture. I made a colour wheel, which was something that I had not done since my first painting classes at art school. Three things—more accurately, three people—diverted me from working on either "Love and the Pilgrim" or on my own picture, which had no name yet. *Untitled. Or Unknown.*

Père Caron arrived at the chapel shortly after me. The tide was out and I had not had to use the dory Simon had provided. I made us each a coffee on the little spirit stove. We talked in a general way about the fête, about the visitors, even about Paris. Every now and then I caught him giving me curious, frowning glances. I had the impression that he had come to check up on me. But he didn't ask any direct questions, not about why I had left the island so suddenly, nor about why I had come back. I didn't explain my reasons either, for the present. He was a perceptive man and it was probably clear to him that I'd returned to see Lorca. And Tobias.

While he smoked one of his cigarettes, sipping from the coffee in his other hand, he stood gazing at Lorca's portrait, which I'd pinned up on the wall. I had not attempted to remove the smear of red paint, nor to erase the grimacing caricatured mouth. Père Caron must have seen the picture already while I was away, but he remained silent. Only his frown deepened.

I told him what had happened, that in all likelihood Tobias had done it. "He was probably here waiting for me and got upset when I never showed up."

"Hmm."

I almost said, *I was with Lorca*, but I had a feeling he knew.

"He took away that little flower painting too."

"Ah," Père Caron said, setting his coffee cup down. "I think I need to talk to him. Explain things. I'm going over to see Étienne later. Tobias will probably be there."

"Père, I have something important to discuss with you."

"By all means." He made as if to sit down on a pew.

"It concerns Tobias, and Étienne. I wonder if we could meet for dinner tonight at the Hôtel des Îles? Could you ask Étienne if he will come too?"

He looked mystified but agreed readily. As he left he saw the bottle of his honey sitting with my painting equipment. It was the one intended for Lorca. "Oh, you still have that," he said.

"I'll make sure she gets it today."

He seemed about to say something, but must have decided against it.

The storm of the previous day had left unsettled weather in its wake and the sky was full of broken white clouds scudding northwest. The sunlight had a different quality, white

rather than the usual yellow tint. I had not been fully aware of
it, but there had been a turn in the season. The cusp of summer was past.

APPROACHING LA MAISON DU PARADIS, I was glad not
to hear any music coming through the trees. I don't know if
I could have taken a repetition of yesterday's emotions. The
moment I knocked, I knew she wasn't there, something
about the echoing sound created by my hand on the wood.
After placing the jar of honey on the doorstep, I knocked
again, making sure, and then walked down the path and shut
the iron gate behind me.

From there, I walked round the side of the garden and
down to the top of the dunes behind her house. Just to have
a glance at the ocean, I told myself. Passing seabirds often
paused on this side of the island and I had sometimes glimpsed
small flocks of rare black gulls along these shores. There were
no gulls today, but the beach was full of those razor clam shells
the French call *couteau*. I gathered up a few of the more attrac-
tive ones to add to the growing collection of seashells on my
windowsill in La Minerve. It was almost impossible to resist
picking up shells when I walked along the beaches. I'd never
seen two exactly the same. I thought of them as jewellery, a
kind of sculpture hand-made by the oceans.

When I looked up from my beachcombing, I saw Lorca and
Tobias. They were quite close to me, on a small headland, both
looking away at something inland. The way they stood, in stillness, like two figures in a painting, set off such a familiar echo
that my heart felt as if a hand had just given it a squeeze. They

were like mother and child isolated in an elemental landscape, looking at something only they could perceive, that I would never know. I wasn't disturbed or pained by the memories flashing through my mind. The sight of them together gave me a strange sense of comfort. I watched a moment longer, then, without disturbing them, went back the way I'd come.

WHEN I GOT BACK TO THE CHAPEL after visiting the hotel and alerting Linda and Victor to expect us for dinner, the first thing I saw was Tobias's flower painting propped up on the table. The second was Tobias himself, standing by the far wall, looking like he might flee at any moment. He had on a battered straw hat and a pair of trousers that were rolled up to the knees.

Without saying anything, I took the painting and hung it on a nail in the wall. Then I removed the portrait of Lorca and placed it under my sketchbook. He watched me from beneath his hat with a mixture of shyness and curiosity. Still ignoring him, I took the big wooden palette I'd brought with me from Paris, and began to lay out pigments along the outer edge. I sensed him approaching, his bare feet silent on the stone floor, and then I could feel him standing just behind my left side. Once the paints were set out, I stepped back and turned to him.

"I think we should begin with the colour wheel."

He frowned and made a round shape with his mouth and then formed a circle with his hands.

"Imagine a rainbow—you know what that is, of course you do—imagine a rainbow bent into a wheel shape, so that the colours flow into one another. Here, let me show you."

With a pencil I drew a large circle on one of the flat boards, then reached for a brush and pulled the palette closer. "The rainbow has yellow, then orange next to it, then red to purple to blue to green and back to yellow. What we call the spectrum." I placed cadmium yellow, vermilion and cobalt blue at equidistant points on the circle. "Now we mix the yellow and red to get orange." I showed him. "Next we mix the blue and yellow to make green." This time I handed him the brush. "And finally, making a mixture of cobalt blue with red will give us a purple. And there we have the rainbow arranged into a wheel."

We spent the next few hours refining the wheel, adding white to some mixtures, creating further colours with the secondary hues we had just mixed. Tobias took to it quickly. And when I showed him how colours opposite each other on the wheel could be used to make a whole range of subtle greys, from a faded sunset violet to the green of a tree in the mist, he understood almost intuitively. Of course, he lives very much through his eyes, I told myself. These are the colours with which his world is painted.

When it was time to finish for the day, for the tide would be coming in soon, Tobias took the colour wheel and tapped himself on the chest with eyebrows raised in a question.

"Take it with you," I said. "Do you have your paints?" He nodded and I gave him a few more boards. "You can practise on these."

We walked back across the causeway together just as the first questing rivulets of the sea began to touch the sand between us and the main island. I let my hand rest on his shoulder and he looked up quickly. Oh, how that look touched me. The gratitude in it. And, for the first time since I had set eyes on him, affection too. I squeezed his shoulder and blinked away the sudden tears that stung my eyes.

CANDLES ILLUMINATED THE TABLE in the still air, the sky was starry overhead and the whisper of waves breaking along the shore came up through the darkness. I was sitting in the garden of the Hôtel des Îles. Also at the table were Père Caron and Étienne, along with Linda and Victor. We had just finished eating a sea bass wonderfully cooked in white wine and shallots.

"I've missed your cooking since moving to the other side of the island," I said to Linda.

She put on a face of mock disappointment. "Ah, but I hear you favour Ester's *grillades* now."

"Not the same. There is absolutely no comparison. In fact, I'm thinking of moving back here just for the dinners."

"You flatter me too much," she replied with a pleased smile.

Since the departure of Daubigny and Jeanette, the hotel was without guests, although Victor had mentioned that a party of birdwatchers was expected for the weekend.

Père Caron had been the first to arrive, and as we drank an aperitif together, I told him about my afternoon in the chapel.

He'd nodded and smiled. "Tobias was with Madame Daubigny this morning," he said. "I met them at her house. I think he is becoming quite fond of her. Anyway, I managed to clarify things for him. We are all forgiven." He then told me that Lorca had sent her thanks for the gift. I thought of Lorca, alone in her cottage, and I wished she were here. But when I remembered the music I'd heard, I knew her attention was elsewhere at the moment.

The dishes were cleared away and the cheese platter was placed on the table. I said, "I went to see a doctor while I was in Paris."

The priest raised his eyebrows. "Nothing serious, I hope."

I smiled, shaking my head. "Not for myself, for Tobias. I talked to a throat specialist."

"A throat specialist?" He was frowning now.

"I wanted to know more about his condition. Whether it is actually permanent or not."

"What did you find out?" Étienne asked.

"Well, obviously nothing can be determined unless Tobias is actually examined. But the specialist did say that in some cases where there has been an injury to the vocal cords, it can possibly be reversed. Depending on the extent of the damage, of course."

"You think there is a possibility?" Étienne said.

Père Caron rolled a cigarette pensively. He lit it, cleared his throat and said, "What exactly do you have in mind, Leo?"

"Has Tobias been off the island much?"

"No, not really. As I told you, we tried to send him to school in Saint-Alban but he always found a way back. We went to Rennes once or twice over the years."

"How did he react?"

"We went by train, which he seemed to like."

"He wasn't frightened of the traffic, all the people, the noise?"

Père Caron shook his head. "Honestly, I think he enjoyed himself. Once he understood that I wasn't going to leave him there."

"I think we should take Tobias to Paris," I declared.

"Paris?"

"A friend of mine, Serge Bruneau, my art dealer, made some inquiries for me. There is someone at L'hôpital de la Salpêtrière, a Dr. Felix Dault, who specializes in these sorts of ailments. I went to see him. He said that in some cases where there has been external trauma to the throat—he used the example of someone who tries to hang himself—gruesome, I know—but in a way that's what happened to Tobias, the rope around the neck . . . Anyway, Dr. Dault said that when the vocal cords are torn they form a kind of scar tissue, just the way skin will do after a cut."

"Like the scar around his neck," Caron murmured.

"This scar tissue can grow to the extent where it makes speech impossible, especially in children. But sometimes it can be removed."

Père Caron said softly, "After his accident, we took him to the clinic in Saint-Alban. You remember, Étienne? The doctor said it was useless to hope that the boy would ever speak. All these years I've never thought to question that." He leaned forward, head bowed. "I've grown too lazy here."

Linda interrupted. "You have cared for Tobias as if he were your own son. That is more important than anything else."

The priest, who was frowning deeply, said, "It has been seven years since the accident. How can any damage be repaired now?"

"I don't want to get anyone's hopes up, least of all Tobias's, if we put this to him, but Dr. Dault is willing to examine him and make a diagnosis. And if it's possible, he'll perform the necessary surgery."

"This is a risky idea, Leo. We are talking about a boy who has barely left this island. What do you think, Étienne? You are his legal guardian."

The old man sighed and raised his hands in a helpless gesture. "What of the cost?"

"I'll pay all the costs," I said quickly. "And I have an apartment where we can all stay."

"I don't know about these things. You will have to explain this to the boy, Père."

Turning to Linda and Victor, I said, "You have no immediate stake in the matter, but you also know Tobias. What is your opinion?"

"Unless you try," said Linda, "you will never know."

"How can this be explained to him?" Père Caron asked. "If the doctor can't help him it would be horribly cruel."

"Well, is he better off as he is?" I said. "What kind of life will he have as he grows older? He will face an isolation far greater than he knows now."

The priest sighed. "It's a big responsibility to take on."

"Who will take it on if not us?" I said.

"Of course we must try, whatever the difficulties. It is the right thing to do. It might work. God willing."

"You have to be the one to put forward the suggestion, Père," I said urgently, leaning forward.

"Of course. And I will come to Paris with you."

"Good," I said, nodding, something like hope stirring in me. "I really feel that this is something I can do for him."

"God willing," Père Caron repeated. He crossed himself, the first time I had seen him do this outside of the church. Then he leaned forward and touched my hand.

"I know what this means to you, Leo. But please, do this for the right reasons. Do this for Tobias."

CHAPTER 29

"WELL, YOUR SON IS IN GOOD SHAPE. AREN'T YOU, young man? Except for that little problem in your throat. But we will soon fix that."

I wondered if I should correct the doctor's slip of the tongue. I glanced at Lorca. She gave me a little smile in response. I let the doctor's assumption pass without comment.

We were in an office on the third floor of L'hôpital de la Salpêtrière in Paris, with the throat specialist Dr. Dault. When I first consulted him, I hadn't actually said that Tobias was my son, but neither had I said he wasn't. It didn't matter now, though, since I had a notarized letter from Étienne giving me permission to make any decisions.

"Have a seat on the couch, Tobias," the doctor said, dropping the wooden tongue depressor into a trashcan and lifting Tobias down from the examining table. He took a jar of lollipops from his desk and offered it to the boy, then to Lorca and me. We both declined. He unwrapped one for himself and tucked it in his cheek.

Tobias installed himself on the long leather couch with the copy of *Les Aventures de Tintin: Les Bijoux de la Castafiore* that I had bought for him at the railway station in Saint-Alban. He was wearing a pair of new khaki jeans with zippered pockets and a striped shirt with long sleeves. His hair was newly cut. Looking at him, I reflected that he seemed no different from any of the other boys we'd seen on the streets since we arrived.

When I first proposed bringing Tobias to Paris, I had expected Père Caron would accompany us. The priest had explained everything to the boy, and then I had done my best to lay out an idea of what a visit to the doctor would entail, of the possibility of an operation. I had stopped short of telling Tobias that he might or might not regain his speech. Père Caron remained somewhat doubtful about how much Tobias understood. Knowing that the boy had an affection for Lorca, he had discussed my plan with her. To his surprise, and mine, she had offered to accompany us. He needs a woman with him, she'd said.

Étienne had not come with us. He was too old, he said, and it was too far, and he had too much work to do. I didn't argue. A further surprise came when Père Caron announced that he would travel no farther than Saint-Alban. His presence was superfluous, he said. Tobias was quite comfortable with Lorca and me, and the journey was too tiring for an old man. It was also a needless expense. I was unsure of the priest's motives, whether he was just trying for the easiest way, or whether he was contriving to place the three of us in an intimate situation. But either way I was touched that he, and Étienne too, trusted me with the boy.

Watching Tobias now, as he sat with his legs swinging and his head bent over the Tintin book, the lollipop shifting noisily from one cheek to the other, I felt a pang of sympathy for him. He'd been very brave so far, even though he'd looked unsure when the train pulled out of the Saint-Alban station and the waving Père Caron disappeared from sight. But then he settled himself on the leather seat, looking up at me with eyes that showed the trust and the affection I now valued so much. Soon he was pressed against the window again, watching everything with wide-eyed interest.

Lorca and I hadn't talked much during the journey. For most of the trip she busied herself with her music manuscript, reading it over, sometimes tapping out a rhythm with her pencil or making corrections to a line. I looked at her often, trying not to be too obvious about it, trying to absorb everything I had learned about her in the past week, wondering whether things had changed between us since our encounter during the storm. In all the excitement of preparing for the trip to Paris, she and I had not had an opportunity to talk properly. And now, the time was not right. I turned my attention back to Tobias.

When we arrived at Gare Saint-Lazare, we were too late to stop off at my apartment, so we took a taxi directly to the hospital. Once we'd been let off at the gates, we walked up to the imposing building. Only then did Tobias's footsteps slow and his hand clutch my arm. Noticing, Lorca kneeled down and explained that both she and I would be with him the whole time. After that, he'd seemed more curious than anything else, and the doctor had soon set him at ease.

Now, Dr. Dault placed his lollipop in an ashtray on the desk and glanced over at Tobias before addressing me. "Tobias's condition is what we refer to as 'aphonia.' It literally means 'no voice.' The situation, to put it simply, is that some nodes have formed over Tobias's vocal cords. It's uncommon in children. I usually see it in people who sing for a living. These nodes, which are a kind of growth on the vocal folds, prevent a proper adjustment to the airflow, making normal speech difficult, and sometimes impossible. Obviously, it is as a result of that first trauma to his throat."

"Can you do anything about it?" asked Lorca.

"It's a safe and relatively minor surgery. I've done a number of them." He paused. "Whether your boy will talk afterwards or not is another question. However, I don't see why he should not be able to learn. He is young, his body is still growing and changing, and he is intelligent. I know of a speech therapist in Rennes who can help you with that. However, all I can say with any confidence is that from a physical point of view, after the operation the boy will have the *means* to speak. If he is prevented from doing so by any psychological damage from the accident, then that is out of my sphere."

"Will he have to stay in hospital for long?" Lorca said.

"We can do it late this afternoon. I reserved a surgery room when you telephoned yesterday, Monsieur Millar. He will stay overnight, of course, so that we can keep him under observation. There will be an incision in his throat, which will take a while to heal, and his meals will be liquid in the first few days. As with any medical procedure, some time and patience will be needed during the healing process, but his doctor in Saint-Alban should be able to handle that as well as taking out the stitches."

I glanced across at Tobias, then at Lorca. "Well then, I think we should go ahead."

I had brought the consent forms, signed by Étienne, and

I gave them to the doctor now. He read them through, raised an eyebrow at Lorca and me, then shrugged and signed the forms.

"Tobias hasn't eaten today, has he?" he asked.

"Only water since last night," I replied. "As you instructed."

The doctor consulted his watch. "I will see you later this afternoon, eh, Tobias?" The boy looked up and nodded.

Once all the forms had been filled in and a blood sample taken, we walked through the hospital grounds to the street. I took Tobias's hand. Being on these familiar streets, I couldn't help thinking of Piero. The Jardin des Plantes where we had spent many hours kicking a football around was nearby. Yet the memory didn't bring on the usual pang of regret and loss.

As we passed a news kiosk, I set down the suitcase I'd bought for Tobias. The newspaper headlines on the racks outside the kiosk were all about President de Gaulle's meeting with the Soviet premier, Alexei Kosygin, and his anti-American speech in Cambodia earlier.

"What about going to a movie," I said, pointing at the big poster showing the comedians de Funès and Bouvril dressed up in German army uniforms. "*La Grande Vadrouille*. It looks like fun. What about it, Tobias? Would you like to go the cinema?" I knew that he had been to the movies in Saint-Alban a couple of times with Victor and Linda.

The boy nodded, pointing at de Funès and making a comical grimace.

"But not that one," Lorca objected, shivering. "I don't want to see anything about the war, not even a comedy."

I was reminded of what Jeanette had told me about Lorca's background. Reaching into my pocket, I pulled out a couple of centimes and bought a copy of *Pariscope*, the weekly magazine that listed all of Paris's entertainments.

"Here's another de Funès film, *Le Gendarme de Saint-Tropez*."

So we passed the next two hours sitting in the darkness, watching the antics of de Funès as he cut a swath of confusion and chaos through the resort town. Glancing across at them, I saw Lorca smiling broadly and the boy's body shaking in silent laughter. Soon I forgot what lay ahead of us and began to enjoy the movie myself.

By the time we made our way back to the hospital after the film, Tobias seemed tired and a little withdrawn. He did not let go of my hand in the elevator on the way up.

In the hospital room, once the nurse had helped him into a gown and he climbed into bed, his Tintin book clutched in his hands, I sat down next to him and said, "Are you afraid?" He shook his head, but his eyes betrayed his nervousness. "You will fall asleep soon and Dr. Dault will look into your throat while you're sleeping."

Lorca sat on the other side of the bed and stroked his hair. "We will be here when you wake up," she reassured him.

He looked so helpless and alone and out of place. This wasn't his world; he seemed to belong in the woods of the island. Yet I knew that he could not remain in that paradise forever. I reminded myself that Tobias was just a little boy afflicted with a handicap, who, for all his apparent freedom, was living a deprived and isolated existence. It was my duty to help him, to give him a chance in the world, and to do so without harbouring any illusions about what that could mean for me. Père Caron's words came back to me: *Do this for Tobias.*

"When you wake up your throat will hurt a bit, but you can eat all the ice cream that you want," I said.

Tobias nodded vigorously.

Soon enough, the nurse came back. Tobias was given an injection, and in a moment his eyelids drooped, fluttered and he drifted off into unconsciousness. I gently eased the book from his fingers and placed it on the night table. We walked next to the gurney as he was transported to the operating theatre. Looking down at the slight frown that crinkled his smooth brow, I smoothed my thumb over the furrow, wanting to erase it, and felt a twitching response in the hand that I was grasping. I was afraid now, for this little boy, for all that might or might not happen. At the operating theatre, the nurse held up her hand, telling us that we could not enter. Then the door closed behind her and Tobias.

We took the stairs down one floor and sat in the waiting room. Lorca seemed strangely preoccupied. Time passed. I paced the floor. My mind was blank. Lorca went outside and smoked a cigarette, then came back and reclaimed her seat. It seemed like we had been sitting in silence for hours when, at last, Dr. Dault appeared.

"Success," he said. Seeing the hope on my face, he added, "As far as removing the scar tissue, that is."

"How is he?" I asked anxiously.

He told us that Tobias would fully recover from the anesthetic in a couple of hours and we should return then. I wanted to remain in the waiting room, but Lorca urged me to come outside. We strolled along the tree-lined walkway leading to the boulevard de l'Hôpital.

"He will be all right," Lorca said. "Don't worry. Why don't we go to a café and have some lunch?"

"I'd prefer to wait here at the hospital."

She looked at her watch. We stood awkwardly. Having acted in the role of parents, we now found ourselves unsure of the next step. We had not really talked about what would happen in Paris, other than in regards to Tobias. Of course I knew that she had a life here, but she hadn't brought it up. And neither had I. I wanted to pretend it didn't exist.

Nevertheless, I said, "If there's anything you need to do, since we're here, I mean anyone you need to go and see . . ."

"Well, there are some errands I want to take care of." She looked at her watch again. "But I'll be back before Tobias wakes up."

We kissed. Once on each cheek, like old friends. She moved away first.

"Will you be all right? What will you do?"

"I'll buy some newspapers," I said. "And I'll see if I can telephone the harbourmaster in Saint-Alban and ask him to relay a message to the hotel so that they can give Père Caron the news."

"Yes, he'll be anxious."

We agreed on a time to meet again. She hesitated, then touched me on the arm and said, "See you soon."

Watching her make her way to the boulevard, I wondered what her errands were. I wondered if she would let Daubigny know she was in Paris. And what would happen tonight? Would she go home? I wanted her to come with me to the apartment on rue du Figuier. But would she *want* to spend the night in another woman's apartment? Would she find the notion macabre?

I walked down the boulevard to Place Valhubert, where I waited for a break in the traffic before crossing onto Pont d'Austerlitz. Looking down the river towards Île Saint-Louis and the familiar shape of Notre-Dame, I thought how odd it was to be back in Paris under the present circumstances, half in and half out of my old life.

Below the parapet of the bridge the river flowed swiftly, echoing my restless thoughts. I looked in the direction of the hospital beyond Gare d'Austerlitz. A child slept there. That was why I was here. I could help him, I could share some of my talents with him. But could I ever fill the gap in my life? Was it fair to even want that?

On the river below, a long narrow river barge passed beneath the bridge. I glimpsed a woman sitting in the cabin at the far end. She was knitting. A small terrier appeared and went bounding across the deck. A man sat down next to the woman and put his hand on her shoulder in a familiar manner. She looked up from her knitting and smiled at him with a tenderness that opened her face. For a moment I wished I could be that man, could have someone look at me with that familiar look, and know that I was loved.

I remembered how the doctor had initially mistaken the three of us for a family. It had happened on the train too, when we were finding seats and there were only two adjacent, and a man sitting across said, "I can move so that you can sit with your wife and son." Lorca and I had exchanged glances. I had enjoyed the pretense.

After finding a post office and sending a telegram to the harbourmaster in Saint-Alban, which he would relay to Père Caron and Étienne at the hotel, I sat at a café and read the newspapers and drank two cups of coffee. Then I walked through Jardin des Plantes and watched some boys playing football on the grass. As I made my way back towards the hospital, I looked up to the sky and mouthed a prayer to a God I had not appealed to since those long-ago days in the chapel at the Guild. "Please God, give him a chance."

It was late in the afternoon now and lights were coming on in windows as the flow of pedestrians increased on the streets, people returning home from work, walking with brisk eager steps, going back to their apartments to meet children and loved ones, or looking forward to a drink with friends in a familiar café. I walked around the gardens and then sat outside the entrance on Square Marie Curie. A glance at my watch told me that Lorca was late. Would she even come back? I wondered. Maybe she had had a change of mind about the whole enterprise. I waited ten more minutes. There was still no sign of her.

I didn't linger, but went on into the hospital. In the waiting room I checked in with the receptionist. Just at that moment Lorca came dashing in through the double doors. She was out of breath and flushed as she hurried over to me. I took her in my arms and kissed her, almost fiercely, so that she stepped back and looked at me with alarm.

"Is everything all right?" she asked. "What's happened?"

"Everything is fine. I was just on my way up. I thought you weren't coming."

"Sorry." She made an apologetic face, shifting her heavy shoulder bag. "There were stoppages on the Métro."

Dr. Dault was waiting for us in his office on the third floor. "Can I see Tobias?" I asked. "Is he awake?"

"He was briefly, but he is very groggy from the anesthetic."

"I want to see him."

"Of course. I understand. He's still in the recovery room down the corridor."

The first thing we saw was a white bandage wrapped around the boy's throat. His face was pale. I brushed a lock of hair from his forehead, leaning over him, listening for his breath, just as I used to stand over Piero's bed in the dark hours when he was small.

"Why don't you let him rest and come back in the morning?" the doctor said.

"I don't want him to wake up alone. He's never been among strangers like this before."

"Monsieur Millar, I assure you he will be fine. Even if he did wake up in the next few hours I doubt very much whether he would be alert enough to recognize you. Come back tomorrow, as early as you like. I come on duty at seven. In fact, I don't see why he can't go home with you once I've checked him over tomorrow. The operation was less complicated than having one's tonsils removed."

I reluctantly agreed.

"We have to wait now. Until his throat heals. After that . . . well." Dr. Dault shrugged. "After that we wait and see."

Darkness had fallen. We walked through the hospital gardens, past the tall cedars, which had receded into the gloom that comes after dusk, back to the entrance onto the boulevard. The lights of the shops and cafés seemed to beckon and offer a promise.

"Are you hungry?" Lorca asked. "I didn't have lunch."

"I am, yes." I'd forgotten to eat too. I didn't ask her where she'd been during the afternoon. I didn't want to know.

"Let's go and find a restaurant. Do you know of a nice place nearby? I don't know this part of Paris. Somewhere bright and busy."

I considered. I too wanted to be somewhere with people around, with the noise of life, drinking a glass of wine while sitting across a table from a beautiful woman. I wanted that sense of possibility that Paris always seemed to offer.

"Les Belles Étoiles is nearby."

"Yes, I've been there. But it will be full of tourists at this time of year."

"There is a place near my apartment, where we used to go sometimes. On the quai de l'Hôtel-de-Ville. It's called Le Trumilou. The food is good and simple. And the place has a nice ambience. It's friendly and bright."

"Fine. I'd like to go somewhere that you know. I want to see something of your Paris. We can walk along the river."

As we made our way down to the Seine, I wondered if the choice of restaurants was wise. Would it have too many associations, too many reminders of the past?

Le Trumilou had a bar in front and a dining room at the back with one long table down the centre and smaller booths around the edge. The patron greeted us and we followed him to a booth at the rear. Lorca ordered a whiskey-soda and I asked for a Pelforth beer. She lit a Lucky Strike and studied the dishes listed on the blackboard.

"The plat du jour is usually good," I said. It was *blanquette de veau.*

"Steak frites and red wine," she replied. "My favourite."

"I wonder if Tobias is still sleeping now," I said.

"I'm sure he is. The doctor said he would."

The waiter brought a basket of bread and cleared away our

empty glasses. I ordered and he fetched the wine. I poured us each a half glass and buttered a piece of bread.

"Did we make the right decision? What if it is all for nothing?" I asked.

"This was the right thing to do. We had to at least try. Didn't Père Caron tell us this was the best thing? And he knows Tobias better than we do."

"What if something goes wrong in the night? Anesthetics can have serious side effects. He's just a small boy." I brushed together the bread crumbs and arranged them into a little pile on the tablecloth. "And what if he can't learn to talk anyway?"

"You must have faith, Leo. Everyone who knows Tobias thinks you are offering him a chance at a new life. Père Caron, Victor and Linda, everyone."

"Do you think so too?"

"Of course I do. Maybe more than anyone else. I know what Tobias means to you."

"You mean because of Piero?"

"Your reasons for helping don't matter. Your actions are what count."

I looked around the restaurant, at the familiar circus posters on the wall, then spoke quietly. "We used to come here. We all loved each other so much. I thought it would be forever."

"Oh, Leo." She put her hand over mine.

"You know, my childhood was really shitty. I grew up in an orphanage. People feel sorry for me when I tell them that, growing up without parents, not being loved and all the rest of it. But Claudine and Piero, they changed all that . . . and then . . ."

The waiter arrived with Lorca's steak and my veal stew in white sauce and slid the plates onto the table. He efficiently whisked away the bread crumbs into the palm of his hand, topped up the wineglasses and left us with a "Bon appétit."

I could not bear the look of pity on Lorca's face, so I changed the subject. "Did you manage to get all your errands done?" I asked.

"I didn't go and see Armand. I didn't see anyone. I went to Printemps to buy some cosmetics. Perfume." She extended her wrist so that I could smell it. "Something new from Guerlain."

I touched her wrist with my lips, then looked up guiltily as the waiter passed, but his face, in the manner of Parisian waiters, remained impassive.

Lorca said, "I also went to a music store on rue Saint-Jacques to get some manuscript paper and a metronome. It's something I don't have on La Mouche."

"So that you can continue with your composition. What did you call it, *Nocturne?*"

"*Nocturne for Lovers.*" A tiny smile touched the corner of her mouth.

We directed our attention to the food, our conversation casual, then I made a decision and plunged ahead. "Your friend Jeanette—I think she knows about us. I ran into her the day of the storm, and she told me a bit about . . . your past."

"It's not anything I want to talk about, Leo. At least, not now."

The waiter came and asked if we wanted dessert or coffee. Lorca said, "I think I need a brandy."

"Two," I told the waiter before he moved away.

"Do you still love your husband?" I asked.

"I don't think I've ever been in love, not properly." She gave me a frank look. "Maybe I only love my music."

I thought of my art. I thought of Claudine and Piero and the choices I'd made. "Does it have to be one or the other?"

"A teacher of mine, who was trying to dissuade me from a career in music, once said to me that the artist should not love, because next to love, art pales by comparison. He said that if I fell in love I would lose my music, that true art demanded sacrifice and suffering, and a devotion to the exclusion of everything else."

"Do you think that is true?"

"It's true that you have to be something of a selfish bastard to make art."

"Without love, without family, I don't see how an artist can have anything really worthwhile to say."

"I'm not sure. Sometimes it seems that unhappiness and suffering bring out the best in art. It's like a flower growing in a desert. In spite of the desert. Or because of the desert."

"I'm not one of those," I said. "I would rather love than make art."

Her smile was rueful in response. She lit another cigarette, saying no more.

I paid the bill and said good night to the patron. The waiter held the door open for us. "*Bonsoir*, monsieur, madame."

Outside, the usually busy *quai* had finally emptied of traffic. We crossed and stood on the embankment above the luminous river. The white facade of Notre-Dame rose above the rooftops, white as the moon. A tour boat chugged past below, snatches of laughter and music coming across the water. Lorca linked her arm in mine and leaned against me as we strolled, just like any of the other lovers around us in the warm summer night.

But as we turned onto rue du Figuier, and I said, "The

apartment is just along here," she let her arm fall and moved away slightly. I sensed the tension in her body. On the top floor I unlocked the door and turned on the lights, then ushered her inside. There was furniture in the living room but little else, no ornaments, no photographs, no pictures on the walls.

"I can't offer you a drink or anything," I said. "I emptied all the cupboards and the fridge the last time I was here."

"Have you lived in this apartment for a long time?"

"More than ten years."

She looked past me. "Which room is your studio?"

"Through here."

The studio was empty except for one large blank canvas on the easel. The paints and brushes were neatly arranged along the edge of the long table. The only pictures were the two on the corner of the table. Lorca leaned over without touching the drawings and studied them. The first was of a curly-headed boy sitting in three-quarter profile, his eyes in the act of turning to the viewer, his mouth just opening, as if he is about to say something.

"I can see why Tobias reminds you of him," she said, then, "He looks a lot like you too."

My voice started to tremble but I kept it steady. "I drew that picture in this same room, a couple of years ago."

"Is this your wife?" she asked, lightly touching the edge of the other drawing.

I nodded and shoved my hands into my pockets. The drawing was done in a reddish chalk. The woman's face was composed, serene. "I did that from a photograph," I said. "Claudine didn't like posing."

"Oh? Why not? She should have been flattered."

Lorca turned around and must have seen the bleak look on my face. "I'm sorry. I didn't mean to remind you."

"I'm going to sell the apartment," I said. "That's why it looks this way. Everything has been packed up or given away to charity. I can't stay here any more. The place is haunted. You can't love ghosts."

"Or live with them," she added.

"It's hard to forget. Wherever you are. I miss them both terribly. And for a long time I have blamed myself for what happened." I folded my arms and stood in front of the bare canvas. "But sometimes . . . sometimes there are moments when I do forget. And then I understand that their deaths are absolute. Nothing I feel or think or do will make the slightest difference to that fact."

I sat down heavily in the single chair, leaning forward with my hands dangling between my knees.

"Maybe it was a mistake for me to come here," she said.

I picked up the drawing of Claudine and studied it. "You said earlier you didn't think you'd ever truly loved your husband. Well, I don't know if I ever loved Claudine. Properly, I mean. I failed her in some way. I think, sometimes, that she could have been happier with someone else."

"What do you mean 'properly'?"

I sighed. "In the way that we all want to be loved. Utterly, completely, without reservation."

"Sometimes we can only love our art," she said in a barely audible voice.

I stood up. Neither of us spoke. Everything was in the look we exchanged, all the unspoken longing, the hope, the fear. We knew each other, and at the same time it was as if we had just met. I understood that I must go to her, I must take those few steps across the floor and kiss her. Unless I took those few steps, we would stand like this forever, like those two figures in "Love and the Pilgrim," an unbridgeable chasm between us.

A shadow seemed to flit through the room, just on the corner of my vision, and I turned, but of course there was nothing there. The drawing of Claudine was still in my hand. I put it back on the table.

"It's late," I said. "I'll make up a bed for you."

She came towards me, glanced into my eyes and lifted her hand to me, but I moved past her, close enough to touch, but not close enough.

In the hall she collected her bag and carried it to the bathroom. I made up her bed in the main bedroom and left the door ajar. "Good night," I called and went into Piero's room.

I lay there in the darkness, listening to the silence of the apartment and the faint sound of traffic from the direction of the quai along the river. Maybe Lorca was right. Art could not break your heart and fill you with loss the way love could. And my art was really all I had, all that I had ever had. It was the only thing real in this confusing life. Everything could be taken away from me except that. A part of me had always believed that, ever since I started drawing at the Guild.

I must have dozed off, for a sound brought me awake, as if a voice had called. I got up from the bed to stand at the window. The moon was still bright. I turned away from the window and crossed to the door and went into the hall, walking with that dreamlike motion that is almost a floating, not quite knowing what place I was in yet knowing my destination. The hall was in darkness, but a thin band of white showed at the bottom of the bedroom door. With that same floating motion I saw my hand reach out and rest on the door handle. I hesitated, feeling a presence watching me. Looking over my shoulder, I glimpsed that shadow again, the same one I had sensed in the studio earlier. I waited. A strange feeling came over me, like a warm breath of air, familiar, comforting. And then it was gone.

I turned the door handle.

The room was filled with a soft warm glow, like the honeyed light of a harvest moon. She was sitting propped against the pillows with the edge of the sheet resting across her waist. Her hair was black against the white linen and her eyes were black against the paleness of her skin.

"Lorca," I said, to hear my own voice and know that this was not a dream.

She had been waiting for me. I lay down on the bed and put my arms around her. This was what I wanted. Just this—the simple, essential fact of the two of us together. The wondrousness of it, me in her and she in me, and nothing else.

When I wept afterwards, her lips kissed the tears away.

CHAPTER 30

I HAD MADE THE DECISION. I WAS GOING TO ABAN-
don the restoration. "Love and the Pilgrim" would remain in
their landscape of shadows, the gap between them would never
be breached; they would always be reaching for each other.

After manoeuvring the picture back into its place above
the doorway, I removed my palette and paints and brushes and
all the other equipment from the makeshift table and moved
everything to the far side of the chapel. There was a broom in
the vestry, and I used it to sweep up any charcoal dust and bits
of paper, then filled a bucket with sea water and gave the floor
a good wipe-down.

I turned my attention now to the large blank canvas on
the opposite wall. Though I was forsaking those two figures
in Asmodeus's lost pastoral, whoever they were, that did not
mean I was going to abandon the chapel, or my commitment
and promise to Père Caron.

Reassembling the table, I set out my equipment in an orderly
arrangement. The palette had been wiped clean, the brushes had

been washed. I had enough colours, having filled a suitcase with painting gear in the studio on rue du Figuier. I was ready.

The morning was bright and clear, the blue air fresh with a breeze from the west, small puffy white clouds like bleached scallop shells hanging in the sky, the smells of beach and ocean and lavender coming in through the open door.

I wanted a fresh start. The surface had been prepared with a priming of my own recipe, powdered calcium carbonate and titanium white pigment, mixed into an emulsion with oil, glue and some dammar varnish. I began by brushing a wash of raw umber, thinned to a liquid consistency with turpentine, over the whole canvas, covering the charcoal sketch of the two figures and the building. This was my usual procedure, since I never liked painting on a white surface. Tones were impossible to judge accurately against the brightness of white, and this way, any little patches that remained unpainted while I worked on the picture would not stand out as white holes. The umber would unify the whole surface.

Because I was using so much turpentine the chapel filled with a powerful odour that made my eyes water. I opened both windows and the front door to let in a cross-breeze. An unusual sound came to my ears, an engine burping and chugging in fits and starts, as if being coaxed along reluctantly. The sound was coming from inland. I laid down my brush and stepped over to the doors. A green tractor lumbered across the narrows, smoke belching from the exhaust, a low cart pulled behind. At the wheel, his laughter audible now, was Père Caron. Perched behind him, hands on his shoulders, Tobias stood balanced, shirtless and wearing his straw hat, his face crinkled in silent mirth. The bandage around his throat was bright against his browned skin.

The tractor shuddered up to the door of the chapel, where the priest shut off the coughing engine. Tobias jumped down and ran over, taking my hand in his, beaming up at me, tugging me towards the tractor. I waved away a cloud of oily diesel smoke.

"You've picked an unusual way to arrive, Père Caron."

"It's a humble chariot, I admit," he said, dismounting and rubbing his knees. "And not the most comfortable either. Since the tide was out we thought it would be best to come along the sands instead of trying to navigate the paths. It did the job." He patted the tractor. "We've brought you a few things."

"Me?"

The priest walked round to the trailer. "For your work."

In the little cart were two squat metal containers with the word Fioul printed on them.

"Gasoline," Père Caron said. "I also have three flood lamps for you and a little generator which will run on the gasoline. Now you will be able to paint no matter what the light conditions. At night too. I've noticed you sometimes work late, and that little oil lamp you've got isn't much good."

Tobias was busy untying the rope holding the equipment and pulling down what looked like a battered but serviceable wicker rocking chair.

"This is very generous of you."

"Thank Victor and Linda. The generator is theirs. The lamps are from Martin Levérrier at l'épicerie. The chair is something I found in my attic."

"This is all marvellous." I lent a hand to Tobias, who was struggling to unload one of the fuel canisters.

"I have also decided to give you as much peace and quiet

as you need. Services will now be held in the hotel. The chapel is yours."

"Absolutely not. I can't drive you out of your own church."

He smiled. "With all these odours, you will probably drive out my parishioners anyway. But seriously, it is no bother to anyone, and a small gesture in return for the gift you are giving us."

"All right. But you can throw me out at any time." We began to carry the equipment into the chapel. I cast an eye in Tobias's direction. "How does he seem to you today?"

The priest shrugged. "The same boy that he always was. No better, no worse."

"He probably doesn't need that bandage any more. The incision from the operation is healing nicely."

"Yes, I looked at it," he said. "But a few more days, just to keep it clean."

In the past ten days, since our return from Paris, I had been to the clinic in Saint-Alban with Tobias three times, and once to Rennes on my own. Tobias was apparently suffering no ill effects from the surgery to his throat. On Tuesday the doctor had removed the three small stitches binding the incision in the boy's neck, leaving a thin vertical line of puckered skin about an inch long. Otherwise, he was given a clean bill of health. He was no longer on a liquid diet, broths prepared by Linda in the hotel, and had switched to mashed potatoes and soft stews and rice pudding.

During the last visit to the clinic, out of earshot of Tobias, I had asked the doctor, "Is there any hope? Should I arrange for a speech therapist to see him?"

"Too soon," the doctor replied. "Much too soon. Let the body heal itself first. If he is capable, the sounds will come naturally. Only then can you consider trying to form those sounds into words."

Nevertheless, I had been to Rennes to see a speech therapist. Her advice was to not force matters. Before the operation, Tobias had often made sounds, guttural utterances that were obviously an attempt to form words. He was familiar with language, the therapist said, and I should continue to talk to him. There would be no point in therapy until, and unless, he actually formed a sound with his vocal cords. She too advised me to wait.

After we returned to La Mouche from Paris, Père Caron had thought Tobias should stay in the presbytery while he was recuperating. In an aside he told me that since Étienne was fond of sampling his own Calvados, the boy might be better off under more watchful care. I realized I'd been hoping, somehow, that he could come and stay with me, but it didn't seem the time to suggest it. He did, however, move a few things to my place, some books and his precious Laguiole knife.

While he was still his usual cheerful and mischievous self, there seemed to be a new fragility about him, as if his experience in Paris had shaken him in some way. For the first days he attached himself to me like a shadow. I was glad of the company. For too long I'd lived in silence. Now I talked constantly to the boy, even though the conversation was one-sided, wanting him to hear language, to be comfortable with the flow of words.

I had seen Lorca only once, at the Hôtel des Îles, where I had taken Tobias for an ice cream. She too seemed more fragile than before, and withdrawn. She mostly talked to Tobias, and when I had a moment alone with her she said, "I must be on my own now, Leo. I'm working. Hard. And I have to think about things. It's all been a little overwhelming." She squeezed my hand and kissed me, warmly, but in the end I was somewhat relieved when she left us.

The new painting progressed. Although, it was still in a rudimentary stage because I changed my mind about the composition often, wiping out and repainting. The picture was a landscape made up of elements from the island. But no figures.

Yesterday, while out walking in the late afternoon in the misty air, I had come upon a cluster of dark yew trees silhouetted against the sky. The foliage was like black ink splashed against the mist and the whole mass of twisted curving branches seemed alive, bending in a wind, although the day was very still. It might have been made to order for me—a motif in dramatic isolation, imbued with mystery. I could feel it inside me, that smear of darkness against the ashy light, dense and contained and mysterious.

Plain lamp black pigment would not give the richness of that darkness. It was too flat, too opaque. I wanted a colour like the glow in a raven's eye. I mixed Payne's grey and viridian green and burnt umber into a rich luminous inky green, black as her eyes when they looked into mine. When I brushed it onto the canvas the effect was like a burst of music, like the first bars of a Beethoven symphony. I worked through the day; the trees took shape, the sky appeared, pale and silvery, the chapel began to form, Naples yellow the perfect colour for the stone walls.

I made the sky darker than the land, so that the light on the chapel walls seemed to come from an unknown source, an effect I'd seen often along the dunes before a storm. Dramatic and vaguely eerie. The whole landscape was tonally restricted, almost monochrome, but at the same time luminous and atmospheric. I was painting again, in my old style, with my usual colours, dove greys, slate and stone, muted greens. My Corot tones.

Père Caron dropped by a couple of days later.

"What do you think?" I asked, as he sat in the battered wicker rocker, a cigarette smouldering between his fingers.

He squinted at the picture, then scratched his chin. He cocked his head to the left, then to the right, half closed his eyes, opened them again. "You have captured something of the island. No doubt about that. Yes." He puffed at his cigarette. "Yes, very interesting."

I smiled. "When people say 'very interesting' they are being polite to the artist, usually when they don't like his painting."

The priest raised his shoulders and let them fall. "I don't know. You have painted our island as a very lonely place."

I said nothing.

"I'm only giving my personal opinion, and I really don't know anything about painting. You must do as you like, you are the artist." He opened his hands in a placatory gesture. "We are all grateful for your work."

I didn't resume until after he'd left. His words had planted a doubt in my mind. This was my kind of subject, my motif, I'd been doing it for years, creating the kind of landscapes that I yearned for, that I could inhabit. Did he mean that he'd like a figure in the painting? I never included figures. It was a signature of my style, I suppose.

Was there more to it? I wondered now.

Claudine had voiced something similar when we quarrelled once, at an exhibition of de Chirico's paintings. He too had favoured solitude in his pictures, deserted arcades, long shadows, statues in empty plazas. I had been quite taken with them, but Claudine described them as desolate and lonely. When I said that I preferred pictures without people, she responded, with an edge in her voice, that I seemed to prefer a life without people too. It had never occurred to me, until now, that she might be saying she was lonely.

Now my picture seemed dishonest, relying on old familiar forms and gestures, metaphors and themes. My usual bag of tricks, so to speak. I had resolved to make the truest painting I could. But was this it? And was it appropriate for the chapel? My painting was not as dark in tone as "Love and the Pilgrim," but it was certainly darker in spirit.

I was rescued by Tobias. He appeared in the chapel, as silently as he always did. Often when I turned and saw him nearby I wondered how long he'd been there. This time he'd brought with him an old mirror in a simple wood frame and a bag of seashells, mostly cockles and the little spiral-shaped ones called turitelles. He wanted my help gluing the shells to the frame. It was a passion of his lately, to decorate objects with shells. I wondered how long it would be before he hit on the idea of decorating his paintbox.

While we were in Paris, I'd gone out and bought him a fine rosewood box with brass fittings, just like the one I used, the one with Piero's name engraved on the lid. Now, as we sat in the sunshine on the leeward side of the chapel, an idea occurred to me. I went back inside to fetch my binoculars.

"We're going to try something, Tobias," I said as I unscrewed the smaller lens from one end of the binoculars and had him place the paintbox in the bright hot sunlight. Holding the lens, which concentrated the sunlight like a magnifying glass into a small bright spot, I waited until the wood began to smoulder, giving off an acrid smell of burnt lacquer, which was soon replaced by the more pleasant smell of wood smoke. Tobias sneezed.

Gradually moving my hand and blowing away the puffs of smoke, I slowly formed the letter T. "We're going to engrave your name on your box," I explained, "just like the other little boy's name on my paintbox. You want to do the rest?"

Tobias nodded.

"Let me mark out the letters for you." With a piece of chalk I outlined the rest of his name.

At first shakily on the letter O, but with gathering confidence, Tobias began to burn his name onto the lid. The tip of his tongue showed pink between his white teeth as he concentrated. The way the light fell on Tobias's profile caught my eye, like a golden line down the edge of his forehead, across the bridge of the nose, lost for a moment under the nostrils, then resumed over the curve where the two lips joined. A smaller patch of light touched his upper eyelid and was echoed on his chin. He glanced up at me as he worked, and smiled. And I wondered how I could ever have mistaken him for Piero. Tobias's smile was beautiful, and very much his own.

I fetched my own paintbox and a small prepared panel. I began to paint directly, without bothering to make a pencil drawing. I used broad strokes, forgoing detail, just aiming for the effects of the light. Once a rudimentary but accurate head was in place on the panel, I took more time to mix the exact colours of the light that delineated the boy's face—touches of cadmium yellow into the flesh tones on the eyelid, a little vermilion on the chin, more white in the mixture for the bridge of the nose.

Then the sun moved behind the clouds, the band of light

on his face disappeared, the colours dulled. But I had enough. I let my brush rest.

Sitting upright, Tobias blew on the letters burned on the box, then brushed his fingers over them and proudly displayed the results to me. "Nice work," I said. Tobias scampered back into the chapel and immediately began to arrange his brushes and paint tubes in the rosewood box. I didn't even notice when he left and crossed over to the main island, for by then I was busy at the big canvas. An idea had come to me. A way to proceed.

Beautiful as the black yew trees were, I nevertheless wiped them out. In their place I would put an apple tree, like the ones in Père Caron's orchard, with a scattering of fallen fruit on the grass. A glimpse of forest to the far left, a curve of shore and sea to the right side. The chapel would remain, but the sky would be brighter. Not grey but cerulean blue. And my little donkey, he too would have a place. And just off-centre in the mid-foreground, the two figures would stand. The woman and the boy.

I worked intensely for the next few hours with an absorption and concentration that I hadn't experienced since I was a student. I worked on as the light changed and it was necessary to start up the generator and switch on the lamps Père Caron had provided. I worked until I was weary, hungry and exhausted. But only in body.

When I finally left the chapel and headed for home my heart and my spirit were soaring.

CHAPTER 31

SOMETIMES IT SEEMED THAT THE ONLY RESULT OF the operation was a small scar on his neck, a little squiggle that sat above the ropy line encircling his throat. Be patient, I told myself, it will take time. But time had passed. Tobias almost seemed to have forgotten the trip to Paris. He was his old self again, he came and went, sometimes sleeping at La Minerve, sometimes at his grandfather's. He visited Père Caron, he helped me in the chapel, he tended to the goats. But no sound that could be called speech had passed his lips.

He probably visited Lorca too, but I had not spoken to her in a while now. In fact, I had not even glimpsed her. My walks took me all over the island, from the lighthouse to Les Hauts-Vents, from Le Bassin to the long empty beaches near LeBec. Inevitably, I contrived to pass La Maison du Paradis. I knew Lorca had not left the island. Smoke sometimes rose from the chimney, and Linda at the hotel mentioned that Lorca had been in for a drink. But I had not managed to cross her path.

Once, I heard music from her cottage, and I listened, but not for long. The sound of her clarinet pained me in a way that I could not explain and I left after a few minutes. I was resolved not to go to her. If there was to be anything between us, then the sign, the gesture, must come from her.

On my walks, I noticed a subtle change in the light, especially in the mornings, when the sun cast long shadows and the air seemed thick, almost palpable, no longer the white of full summer but with a crimson tinting the gold. Signs of a change in the season appeared, here and there, on the edges of summer, like the slight fraying on the edge of petals in a bouquet past its prime.

In the garden of La Minerve the figs were soft and pulpy, dropping in the slightest breeze. Starlings gathered in the branches twice a day, morning and evening, making a cacophony of whistles and chirps and sudden screeches. Bees hummed lazily on the fallen fruit.

Tobias was still engaged in his project of decorating objects with seashells. Lately he'd been gluing them to unusually shaped bits of driftwood. Perhaps he was going to be a sculptor and not a painter. His mania now was only for *troques*, the little spiral-shaped shells, like miniature escargots, that were coloured with delicate red stripes, as if a fine watercolourist had been at work on them.

One early morning I went out with him when the tide had just turned, the optimal time for beachcombing. The best place for them was on the sands at Le Colombier, below Lorca's cottage. There was dew underfoot and a fine morning mist on the dune grasses as we descended to the beach. The tide line was fifty metres away and receding, leaving an array of shells sparkling in the rising sun.

Tobias had a straw basket slung over his shoulder. He immediately rushed down to the beach, chasing a flock of oystercatchers that lifted off in a grand arabesque. I sat down and removed my canvas shoes and rolled up the cuffs of my trousers. The black and white birds returned, digging into the sand with their long red beaks. Tobias scattered them again, dashing among them with his arms flapping, sending them into the air with high indignant cries.

I wished one of those cries had come from the boy. Just a sound would be enough, not even a word, just a sound.

I strolled along in the opposite direction, leaving Tobias to his games, my footsteps taking me towards the headland near La Maison du Paradis. When I reached the dunes directly below her house, I paused and looked up, remembering the day of the dog fight and how angry I'd been with Lorca, thinking the dog was hers. What became of those dogs? I wondered. I'd never encountered them again. Perhaps they had belonged to someone visiting the island.

The beach here was dense with scallop shells that had been washed up on the tide, all of them picked clean already by birds. Among them were little clusters of the periwinkles I was collecting. I gathered the prettiest ones and stowed them in my pockets.

When I looked up I saw Lorca. She was facing away, looking in the opposite direction at a white ship heading out into the Atlantic on the distant horizon. The way she stood was so much like the classical contrapposto pose, with the upper torso slightly turned away from the hips, the shoulders and chest angled in a different position to the lower body, that I immediately regretted not bringing my sketchbook this morning. I tried to memorize her posture, imagining how the pose of the woman in my painting could be adjusted.

When she turned and saw me, she took a step backwards, as if to hide herself, but I was already waving and I shouted her name. She returned the wave and came down the dunes to meet me.

I took her hand, her fingers were cold, and kissed her. "How are you?" I asked. "Are you managing all right?"

"I'm fine." She blinked, smiled. She looked a little worn, I thought.

"I've missed you," I told her.

"Is that Tobias down there?"

"It is. Why don't you come and say hello. I'm sure he misses you too."

"Oh, he was here yesterday."

"I'm jealous that he gets to see you and I don't."

"He invites himself. Not that I mind. He wants to play the clarinet."

"You mustn't let him!"

"Don't worry, Leo, I know better than that. In fact, I was a bit harsh with him last time."

"Harsh, how?"

"He walked in, as he will, and just picked up the clarinet and started to blow on it. I grabbed it out of his hands and shouted at him. He's so odd sometimes, like an animal. He put the clarinet down and stepped away, sort of in slow motion, like a deer, you know the way he lifts his feet sometimes, as if he is walking on glass. I said to him that he mustn't strain his throat, that it was for his own good, but he just gave me a reproachful look and disappeared."

"I wouldn't worry too much. He never stays upset for long. Père Caron and I took him into Saint-Alban again the other day."

"Yes?"

"He's healing well. His throat is a bit raw inside still, but otherwise fine. He'll be ready to go and see a speech therapist soon. Maybe even start the clarinet again."

She paused and put a hand on my arm. "Leo, I know he needs someone to mother him, and my heart breaks over it, but it can't be me. The closer I get to him the harder it will be to leave him. And I have to, eventually. A little boy like that will fall in love so easily."

"You are something quite glamorous in his life," I said, wondering if her words had been meant for me too. She fell silent, scuffing one sandalled foot in the beach sand.

"How is your music coming along?" I asked. "Are you composing much?"

Lorca shook her head. "I've done neither playing nor composing these last couple of days."

"Oh. That doesn't sound good."

"No, it is good. I'm listening."

"To the radio? Records?"

Another shake of the head. "Neither."

"What then?"

"Everything."

"Everything?"

She smiled. "Come sit down a minute with me."

We moved to the bottom edge of the dunes, where the tide had not reached and the sand was dry. Lorca was wearing white shorts and a black and white striped St. Tropez–style jersey. She kicked her sandals off and stretched her long legs out, then bent and scraped at the worn crimson nail polish on her toenails. She dug her toes into the sand, hiding them, and took her cigarettes from the pocket of her shorts. Bending her head against the slight sea breeze she cupped the flame from her Zippo and inhaled.

"My father was a musician," she said. "Not a professional. He was the choirmaster at the school in our town. I remember once when we were on our summer holidays in the Pyrenees, the two of us were walking in the forest, looking at birds. He knew the names of every single species we encountered. It was phenomenal."

She tapped the ash from her cigarette and watched it fragment on the breeze. "We'd sat down to listen to a Dendrocopos major, what you call a woodpecker. A black and white bird with spots and a red patch on its head. Anyway, we weren't listening to its call, but the drumming noise it made on tree trunks. My father suddenly put his hands over my eyes and said, 'What do you hear?' He had large hands, they practically covered my face. I can remember the smell of soap and his pipe tobacco.

"'I hear the woodpecker,' I said.

"'Nothing else?' he asked. 'Listen harder.'

"I could hear my own breathing, and I told him that.

"'Listen to what else is out there,' he said. I tried to imagine the forest, any other birds, or sounds from nearby farms. I mentioned these things, but he said, 'You are not really listening. You are thinking. Stop thinking. Just listen.'

"His hands were on my eyes the whole time. At first I heard nothing, not even the tapping woodpecker, which had stopped. Then, as if it had just sprung up, I heard the breeze, like a distant breath in the trees, a rustling exhalation. A bird called, two quick peeps. An answer came from another direction. Then a faint drone sounded, far off, a tractor climbing the slope. I heard another drone, much closer. A bumblebee. I listed each one of these sounds for my father.

"'What else can you hear?' he pressed.

"He removed his hands but told me to keep my eyes closed. The light behind my eyes changed, became brighter, and it was as if sound flooded in with the light. Suddenly I could hear everything. A car on the main road, its tires hissing on the macadam; the flapping splash of a duck landing on the lake behind the trees; distant church bells across the valley; the sound of children's voice from the town; the rustle and creak of my father's leather jacket as he shifted slightly; the liquid sound of him swallowing. I seemed to hear even the beating of his heart. I thought to myself that if I listened carefully enough I would be able to hear faraway oceans breaking on beaches, and the whispering of light as it travelled from the sun to the earth. I even imagined I would hear the turning of the earth on its orbit."

Lorca had closed her eyes while she spoke and she opened them now and looked at me. Her eyes were shining. "I think that was the real beginning of my musical education. Just listening. For the first time. My head and my ears have filled up since then, with all the sounds of life. I don't hear the world in the same way any more."

"And that's what you've been doing all this time in your cottage. Listening."

"Trying to. Does that make sense to you?"

"Absolutely. If I substitute the sense of sight for that of hearing, I know exactly what you mean."

"But it's not the world I'm listening for. I want to hear myself. You understand, don't you? I want there to be a perfect silence, and in that silence I want to try and hear myself. If I can. I don't know if I have ever done that. But until I try, I don't feel I can call myself a musician, much less a composer."

I nodded. I wanted to tell her of my own breakthrough, of my renewed creativity, my excitement over the picture I was painting.

As if divining my thoughts, she said, "I talk too much about myself. How is your own work progressing?"

"Why don't you come and see it? Tell me what you think. I can always use a fresh opinion."

She got to her feet and brushed the sand from her hands. "I will. Soon. Not just yet, though. You understand?" She touched my arm.

"Promise?" I said, though I felt an emptiness in my chest.

"I promise. Soon." She peered down the beach to where the small figure of the boy was hunched over something on the sand. "I don't think I'll talk to Tobias today. I want to get home." She leaned forward and kissed me quickly on the mouth, then turned and walked back over the dunes, head down, not looking back.

CHAPTER 32

THE BOY STANDS IN THE FOREGROUND, JUST TO right of centre. Part memory, part reality, part something else entirely. He wears only a pair of faded blue shorts, his skin young and brown and smooth, his thick dark curls unruly. There is no bandage around his throat, neither is the scar visible, although a faint shadow beneath his chin hints at it. He is half turned away, looking back towards a white stone chapel.

The apple tree that I had originally placed in the centre of the canvas had been erased, but at the boy's feet, among the grasses and flowers, are scattered apples, green with a red blush. On the far left is a line of black yew trees. The light is diffused, but it is not that silvery misty grey light I used to paint and love so much, the Corot light. This light is rosy, the rising light of morning, the light that will not fail.

I had begun by using sketches and memory for the figure of the boy, but then I had asked Tobias to pose, placing him near the door with the daylight on his skin. Later, I made a trip to the orchards on the east side of the presbytery and gathered up a basket of apples, which I brought back to the studio, and I had Tobias stand beside them in the same pose while I painted the fruits. I paid careful attention to the faint hints of green reflected light on the boy's legs, on the side where the apples were scattered. I wanted naturalism, and to that end I tried to paint what my eyes saw.

From the shore I made numerous oil sketches of the chapel at different angles, and then I rowed out in the skiff and sat at anchor, painting the chapel from the seaward side.

I worked on every aspect of the painting, except for one blank section of unpainted canvas. An absence. Tobias, who had helped me with bits of filling in here and there, once tapped the bare section and raised his hands palms-up in a querying gesture. I shook my head. I knew what was needed. I knew what I wanted to place in that void, to fill that absence. But I could not paint it from memory, and I couldn't paint it from sketches. I would have to wait.

For long stretches of time I sat staring at the canvas. Sometimes I got up and crossed the floor and studied a particular section. Sometimes I reached for a brush and made an adjustment. When my eyes blurred and I couldn't think straight any more, I scraped the dried paint from my palette and wiped it clean. I soaked my brushes in turpentine, then lathered them in soap and water and shaped the bristles and set the brushes in a jar on the windowsill.

One day I trimmed my hair with a pair of scissors and put on a white shirt, which was clean but wrinkled because I had no iron and had dried it on the clothesline in the garden. At first I put on shorts, but then changed my mind and dressed in my khaki chinos.

In the little garden, standing on a kitchen chair and reaching up into the branches, I picked a basket of figs, my hand seeking out those that were deepest green. The starlings had been at most of them, but there were enough hidden where the branches grew thick towards the trunk. I wanted figs that could be eaten within a few hours. Too soft and they would break at the slightest pressure, too firm and they would not yet have developed their full flavour. From La Minerve I followed the familiar route des Matelots and turned west along the chemin des Sirènes, pausing along the way to gather a small bouquet of pale violet malva that were growing by the wayside. They were very pretty next to the green figs.

The blue wooden shutters on the ground floor were fastened shut. The curtains were closed in the upper windows. I raised the iron knocker on the front door and let it fall. I waited a minute and knocked with my knuckles. No response.

"Lorca? Hello! Lorca?"

I went around to the walled garden at the back. A rap of knuckles on the garden door brought no answer. I walked down to the beach and surveyed the shoreline in both directions. Nothing but a solitary black-backed gull drifting back and forth above the sand. She wouldn't leave without telling me. Would she?

I set the basket down on the sill and tore a page from my sketchbook. I need your help, I wrote. With my painting. I'm in the chapel every day. Low tide is roughly between 8 and 3. Leo. I wedged the note between two figs and nudged the basket closer to the door. She would come, or she would not come.

SHE CROSSED THE NARROWS with the rising sun behind her. Aurora, bringer of the morning. She looked like the vision that I had encountered on that far off day when I'd climbed the cliff after my fall. How long ago it seemed now. As if it had happened to a different person.

I was standing in the doorway when she arrived, and her greeting was brief, a clasping of hands, a kiss. She wore a thin white dress that reached to her knees, the cloth almost transparent, and she was unadorned, no makeup, rings or bracelets. She stepped into the chapel and stood in front of the painting, looking at it a long while.

"You once said to me that the island had a strange beauty." I said. "A hush. As if something strange and beautiful were about to happen."

Raising a hand she touched the section I had left unpainted, echoing the inquiring gesture Tobias had made. "You're waiting to put something here," she said.

I had missed the sound of her voice, that smoky, slightly hoarse way she had of speaking. "Yes."

"What?"

"Who, you mean."

She nodded slowly. "Me."

"Yes. I want you to step into that landscape and complete it."

She nodded again. "Tell me how. Tell me what to do, Leo."

"Just like that, like you are, but move back into the light." I took up a stick of charcoal. "The pose I want is called 'contrapposto,' where the upper torso is turned off-axis from the hips. So that tension and graceful relaxation are contained in the same posture. It's a classic stance. Artists have been using it since the time of the ancient Greeks."

"Like the *Venus de Milo*," she said. "Should I be nude?"

Bending to grasp the hem of her dress, she began to draw it up her thighs. I shook my head.

"Not nude. Much as I want to see you naked again."

She graced me with a tiny smile. "Nothing sacrilegious, then?"

"This is a church, after all. But I like you in that white dress. It has a sort of timeless feeling." I tilted my head and squinted. "Put your left foot forward slightly. And turn this way a little, your upper body, as if you have just heard something. A voice calling, from a distance."

"Or music?"

"Or music."

I worked quickly, charcoal giving way to brush, monochrome to colour, white and crimson and ochre mixing to create flesh tones. Then I reached for a tube of pure cadmium yellow. A touch of white and crimson gave it a hint of peach. Coming to stand just a foot or two away from her, I peered at her bare arms, then crouched and studied her calf, comparing the tones with the mixture on my palette.

"Perfect," I said. My fingers grazed the top of her foot. "Exactly right."

Returning to the painting I brushed in the new colour. Now came black, ultramarine blue, a smidgen of green, and I painted her hair, black as a raven's feather.

Gradually, I stopped looking at Lorca, all my attention on the canvas. At a certain point it is the painting that is real, not the model. When she relaxed her pose and went to sit on one of the pews, lighting a cigarette, I barely took notice.

I don't know how much time passed before I set down palette and brushes. Finally I stretched my arms above my head and flexed my fingers. Lorca was stubbing out a cigarette in the bleached oyster shell on the table. I looked around the chapel like a man waking from a dream.

"Is it finished?" she asked, coming to stand next to me.

"For now. The idea is there, the feeling. The rest I can do without you here. Thank you for posing."

"And now you can pour me a drink," Lorca said, her voice lighter, forcing a change of mood. "I did see a bottle of wine here somewhere."

"You are correct, m'lady. Stocked especially for your pleasure, and in the hope of your return."

I brought out two glasses and uncorked the wine. We carried the glasses outside and settled ourselves against the warm stone of the chapel wall on the seaward side. I touched my glass to hers.

"Thank you again. I wish I could help you with your music in some way. But musicians don't exactly need models."

"Has Tobias seen the painting?"

"Oh yes. In fact, he's helped me so much that I'm going to have to credit him as the co-artist."

Lorca laughed. "Père Caron will be happy, I'm sure. It's a wonderful addition to the church."

"I hope so. It's not really a religious painting, well not overtly. But I feel it is spiritual. He told me I should take Love as my subject."

"What will you call it?"

"Mmm. I haven't thought of a title."

"Why not use your original title?" she suggested. "'Love and the Pilgrim'?"

"But then I would have to paint myself into the picture."

"You don't need to. Leo. You are there already. Whatever those figures are waiting for has arrived."

"Do you think so?" I took her hand and ran my fingers back and forth across her wrist.

"Things are changed," she said. "The landscape has changed, you have changed. Tobias too has changed."

"And you?"

"I . . . I think I've completed my work. Would you come and listen, Leo?"

"But that is wonderful! Of course I want to hear it. When?"

"Come tomorrow. But not too early. I want to practise a bit. Come in the evening. At dusk. It is a nocturne, after all."

THAT NIGHT I DREAMED OF HER, and in the morning I realized I couldn't recall ever dreaming about a woman before. Not Claudine, not Hollis, not the few other women I'd known during those years before I married. Except for long ago, during the long nights at the Guild, when I used to dream about a woman who came and went, and sometimes called my name, and never quite showed me her face.

CHAPTER 33

IN THE TWILIGHT, IN THE BLUE HOUR, AS THE brightness of day softened towards dusk, I made my way to her house. The stacked hay bales were orange in the evening sun, with long purple shadows stretching across the fields. In the fading light the swallows darted overhead with high distant cries. In my hand I carried a bouquet, stalks of rye and red nasturtium flowers with bright green leaves.

The air was very still and warm, the sea flat, dark and blue. Candlelight showed in the windows of the house, yellow against the western sky, a sky that was a deep velvety tone, neither ultramarine nor sapphire nor indigo, but all of them—the blue hour.

I knocked on the door and she answered immediately, a little shy, a little serious. Her face lit up with pleasure when I gave her the flowers. She touched my lips with her fingertips and put the flowers and rye stalks in a tall white jug on the table next to a bowl of apples.

A music stand on the table held the sheet music, the same

pages I had seen earlier, handwritten, with the words Contra Mortem et Tempus at the top. Her clarinet lay next to it, golden in the candlelight. There was a book there too, *De l'obscurité à la lumière. Poèmes de C.P. Cavafy.*

Lorca pointed to a chair. I sat down facing her. Neither of us spoke. She was wearing a simple black dress that buttoned down the front and fell to her calves. Her feet were bare. She moved over to the table and took up her clarinet.

It began with a jarring sound, high-pitched and slightly atonal, like shimmering violins, but not sweet, a sound that induced tension, like shards of glittering sunlight on water. Just as it reached an agitating constancy, a wasp now, there came three bass notes, a harbinger, then repeated higher, suggesting the arrival of something but not revealing it. I found the music disturbing, almost sinister. I shifted in my chair and directed my gaze away from Lorca, to the evening sky framed in the window, to the soft blue sea and the first white stars.

The music crescendoed suddenly, like a crack in the sky, revealing only a vast emptiness beyond. A long silence followed. When it began again it was plaintive, regretful, full of mourning and remorse. A lament. The music frightened me. It was like a wound, a heart ripped bare. The suffering, the long, long suffering was unbearable. It wasn't even personal, but some grief of the ages, a music that came out of smoke and ruins. I knew that sound and I wanted it to stop. I shut my eyes.

And it did stop.

I could hardly bring myself to look at Lorca. When I did, she was pale, breathing deeply, her face drawn. She stared past me, through me, to some distant place where the smoke still burned.

"That's the first part only. But I didn't write it. Betsie did." She spoke in a whisper.

"Who is Betsie?" I asked, whispering too, the way one does when pronouncing the names of the dead.

Lorca looked down at the clarinet in her hands. "This is hers." The candlelight threw her face into gaunt shadows.

"On a Wednesday afternoon in June 1943 the Gestapo came to the music school where I was studying and took us away to a prison camp. Myself and two other women, Brigitte Delpeche and Michelle Lyotier."

"To Rosshalde," I said, remembering what Jeanette DuPlessis had told me.

"Yes, to the concentration camp at Rosshalde. When they came for us we had just been playing some Beethoven. The adagio from his String Quartet number 15. Ironic, that, since the piece is titled *Heiliger Dankgesang*, which sort of translates as 'Holy Song of Thanks.' There are some references to it in what you just heard."

She carefully placed the clarinet on the table and fetched her cigarettes from the kitchen counter, lighting one before going across the room and lifting a photograph from the wall. "Winter of 1944. A bitter winter." She placed the picture in front of me. "France had been liberated by then—we'd heard that through the grapevine—and we were full of hope, knowing that the Allies were striking towards Germany. At night you could hear the bombers overhead, hundreds of them, invisible in the blackness, just that drone that seemed to go on forever, like the sound of some great beast in anger. We listened for it every night, wanting to hear it. Hoping. But then the Germans launched a big offensive in the Ardennes and it seemed like they were going to be successful and we would never be freed. Young people today look back and it seems to them that the end of the war was inevitable. But not to us, not then."

I looked down at the photograph. It was faded, but I could make out a hall full of women, all dressed in the same drab uniform. A few looked at the camera, but most had their attention directed towards the front of the room, faces rapt, concentrated, some with eyes closed.

"They are listening," Lorca said. "Not to the bombers. To music. You can't see the musicians. We are just off-camera. Our little quintet: Jeanette, Betsie, Michelle, Brigitte and myself. They were all better musicians than I was. Especially sweet Betsie. I don't even have a photograph of her." She shook her head. "More is the pity." She took a deep inhalation from her cigarette and let the smoke out in a slow trickle.

"It was shortly after I had arrived in the camp that I heard the sound of a clarinet in the barracks. Like a nightingale in a place where no birds sang. It was Betsie's music. The Nazis considered themselves cultured, you know, so they had allowed her to keep her instrument when they rounded her up. After hearing the music I sought her out. She introduced me to Jeanette. The five of us formed a little chamber music group. I remember that we used to practise in the latrines. The acoustics were good in there. I suppose you could say that our music was created in the stench of shit."

She leaned over and stroked her fingers across the photograph. "The commandant of the camp gave permission for us to entertain the other inmates on Sunday evenings. That is what the people in the photograph are listening to: a quintet of starving and cold women playing music for a few hundred

other cold and hungry women. The day we gave the concert—
you see it in the photo—it was bitterly cold. Many of us had
pulled the straw from our mattresses and stuffed it into our
shoes so that the blood would keep circulating. I remember
that the hall smelled of damp wool, smoke from the stoves,
unwashed women and despair. But they listened! We could not
comfort those poor women, or feed them or warm them, but
we gave them beauty. And maybe hope too."

She took the photograph from my hands and studied it.
"We were lovers. Betsie and I. As much as you can be in a barracks with a hundred other women. Does that shock you?"
Without waiting for a reply, she crossed the room and replaced
the photograph on its nail, taking a moment to straighten it.

"Betsie was a great talent. She would have become a great
musician."

"She didn't survive the war, did she," I said.

She shook her head. "In February I became very ill. I didn't
want to go to the infirmary because sick people had a habit of
not coming back. The SS arrived in the camp one day, like dogs
from Hell in their black uniforms and the death's head badges.
They came round to the barracks with a list, culling out all the
Jewish women. I was in my bunk with a high fever, barely conscious. When my name was called, Betsie stepped forward and
raised her hand. I never saw her again."

Thrusting her hands into her pockets, Lorca went to the
door and opened it, letting in the night smells and the soft
breath of the ocean. An owl called. "The thing is, Betsie wasn't
even Jewish. If it were possible to will yourself dead, I would
have died. I wanted to die. I carried her name until we were
liberated. But I gave up music. I was dead inside." She sighed

and shut the door. "And when we came back to Paris, I tried to kill myself."

She turned and held up her hands towards me, wrists outward, showing the scars I'd noticed earlier.

"Jeanette DuPlessis brought me here. To heal. Eventually I met Betsie's older brother, Armand. We mourned together. And we healed together."

It took a moment for what she'd said to sink in. "Armand is Betsie's brother?"

She nodded. "It's possible to love in many different ways, and to love many people. But sometimes in love all you end up with is a heart broken into pieces."

It was said gently, but it seemed a warning.

She came back to the table and stretched out her hand, caressing the clarinet. "So you see, Leo, I have some debts, some obligations. I promised myself, and I promised the spirit of Betsie, that I would make something of her music. Out of that place of darkness and suffering and death I promised that I would make something beautiful."

She rearranged the sheet music and raised the clarinet to her lips. She began with a little two-note trill, like a bird calling, like a name, repeated and held until it seemed she would have no more breath. The waves came next, a soft rhythm, like the breaths a child takes when it sleeps. Not a lament now, but a lullaby. She played simply, without gestures or embellishments or flourishes. It was the sound of the island I heard. But so much more. There was no hesitation, no falsehood, just *de l'obscurité à la lumière*, from darkness to light.

Her music spoke all that words could not express, of the past and the future, her heart and my heart and all the beating hearts that make up the world. My eyes welled as I listened, as I looked at her, but my tears were not bitter.

When it was finished there should have been silence, but the notes seemed to linger, to permeate the room, and only gradually to fade, until just a memory remained, contained in the other sounds that now flowed back: the sea below the house, the soft whisper of a breeze, the sputtering of the candle, my own breath.

She stood holding the clarinet lightly, a faraway expression on her face, her gaze on the window, and beyond. "There you have it," she said, as if speaking to someone else. "A nocturne, for lovers."

We sat on in silence. I watched her face. She was smiling slightly.

I thought, not for the first time, about the title of the piece, *Nocturne for Lovers.* I had wondered if those lovers could be Lorca and myself. At other times I thought of the two figures in Asmodeus's painting, the lover and the pilgrim. But it was more than that. There was Armand Daubigny, and there was Betsie, and there was Claudine and Piero and Tobias. This music was for all of us. All the promises kept. For the lovers, for beauty, against time and against death.

At last, she spoke. "You know that I must leave you."

"No." I pushed up from my chair and was at her side. "No, Lorca. I know that you love me. I feel it."

"Yes," she said, placing the clarinet on the table, "but we are two wounded hearts. We love each other out of pain."

"It doesn't have to be that way." I took both her hands in mine and turned them over, pressing my lips to her wrists, kissing the scars.

"My whole life as a musician has been leading to something, Leo, and I need to know if this is it. It's different for you."

I understood what she meant. I had found something. I had begun to paint again. And there was Tobias. And this island. I realized that I could not imagine leaving La Mouche, at least not now.

"My music needs other people for it to be real. It needs to be played and to be heard for it to be alive." She looked up at me. "I owe it to Betsie."

I nodded. There was no other answer. She owed it to herself, too, and in time, I thought, she would realize this.

She touched my lips with her fingers, and then kissed me for the last time.

CHAPTER 34

SHE LEFT ON THE MORNING TIDE, ON A DAY WHEN the flat sea glittered with shards of blue light and the *Stella Tilda* drifted away from the pier, hardly seeming to move, just becoming smaller and smaller as it slipped out of the harbour. She stood in the stern leaning one hip on the rail, wearing a leather jacket and her black hair blowing loose, pale-faced, beautiful and grave, looking back to the small group of people on the quay—Père Caron, the storekeeper Martin Levérrier, Victor and Linda from the hotel, all waving. I had not seen Tobias all day, but I knew that she would have made her farewells with him.

I stood a little apart from the others, my eyes fixed on her face as the vessel glided away from the island. When she raised her hand in a final adieu, I lifted mine too, holding it in the air. As the boat passed the last headland her arm dropped and she faced away.

I remembered the day she had first come to the chapel and seen "Love and the Pilgrim." The day she had suggested

I make a new painting, the day I first drew her portrait. The day I first kissed her. She had quoted Keats to me as we stood looking at those two lovers reaching for each other: " . . . *do not grieve; | She cannot fade, though thou has not thy bliss, | For ever wilt thou love . . .*"

I remained there with my hand held out, continuing to watch until I could no longer make her out, until the boat was just a fleck of colour on the wide blue sea. The pulse of the engine came faintly across the expanse for a time, and then that too disappeared, leaving only the slap of the waves against the stone quay.

I remembered her parting words on that faraway day. *Don't have any illusions about who I am, Leo. Or what I can be.* As I lowered my arm, two sharp notes from a whistle broke the stillness. Two notes marking a departure, calling a name that was already in the past. Then two more notes, a different name, a summons. I looked up.

On the ridge above the harbour stood a small figure. He lifted his arms and stretched them out—echoing that gesture from another place and time, before our lives would intertwine. I turned away from the wide empty sea and walked up to meet him.

I had no illusions. But I had love. And hope had been restored. This was not the end of the world, not the last place, after all.

Acknowledgements

A BOOK IS NEVER THE WORK OF JUST ONE PERSON. Many talented and dedicated people at HarperCollins Canada have made invaluable contributions, and I thank them for that.

I am extremely grateful to my editor, Phyllis Bruce, for her wisdom and her patience on the long journey. Her contribution is immeasurable.

Thank you to Allyson Latta, who brought in a new broom at the end and wielded it with a perceptive touch.

Thanks to my agent, Hilary McMahon, always a fan and supporter.

The Canada Council for the Arts helped along the way with a grant.

Till min livskamrat, Gunilla Josephson.